POWDER & POISON

JULIA JACKSON

PRAISE FOR *POWDER & POISON*

"POWDER & POISON serves up the cake and it's rich, delicious and oh so satisfying. Julia Jackson delivers a fresh and haunting take on the infamous queen known for her opulence while showing us she was never truly known at all."
DANIELLE PAIGE, author of the Dorothy Must Die series, Stealing Snow, and Wish of the Wicked series

"With a mesmerizing blend of body horror, femme history, and a bittersweet dash of romance, POWDER & POISON dazzles brighter than all the riches in Versailles."
AMANDA HAVILL ADGATE, author of One for Sorrow

"POWDER & POISON takes the shine of Versailles and grinds it into something jagged. Julia Jackson drops us into Marie Antoinette's first weeks at court, where perfume can't mask rot and whispers curdle into threats. Ghosts linger in mirrors, blood stains the gardens, and the crown itself feels like a trap tightening around her throat. This isn't just historical horror—it's a reminder of the cages women have been forced into for centuries, dressed up in silk and ceremony. Dark, decadent, and unflinching, this debut is one to remember."
@ISHAUNTED

"Gripping, gritty, and ghostly, POWDER & POISON expertly blends history with horror for an emotional ghost story unlike anything you've read. Absolutely captivating."
BRIANA MORGAN, author of The Reyes Incident

"A suspenseful, gothic take on royal politics, friendship, betrayal, and the consequences of unchecked power. Think of HOUSE OF HOLLOW or a darker, more chilling BRIDGERTON."
@SPOOKY_BOOKWORM

PRAISE FOR *POWDER & POISON*

"POWDER & POISON is Versailles reimagined as a haunted house, a palace dripping in silk and shadows, where every gilded mirror hides a ghost and every whisper threatens doom. Julia Jackson's haunting debut doesn't just retell Marie Antoinette's story; she resurrects it in blood, bone, and dread. This is horror at its most intoxicating: lush, lyrical, and unflinching in its portrayal of female rage and survival. I couldn't look away, even when the palace itself seemed to reach out from the page to claim me."
RACHELLE GONZALES, author of dark and twisty speculative fiction full of complicated, morally grey women

"Haunting, visceral and filled to the brim with desire and deception, Jackson's POWDER & POISON is a gothic-psychological thriller that had me on the edge of my seat!"
STEVE STRED, author of Mastodon and Churn the Soil

"I loved every second of this book. The story of Marie Anntoinette in itself is a huge piece of important and interesting history. This takes that story and amplifies it. The way Julia Jackson writes is perfection. The detail and the twists! The horror and history blend is rich and bloody. It was a psychological horror that still tells an important story about and for women and the pain they have endured and continue to endure."
@CRYSTALLREADS

"POWDER & POISON is like biting into a decadent slice of cake and realizing that cake is filled with blood. Every page drips with an opulence and hunger that left me guessing right up until the very end. Jackson's debut not only gives voice to a woman whose voice was stolen from her, but also to the experiences and pain women around the world have faced since the beginning of time. Gorgeously creepy and laced with teeth."
TEAGAN OLIVIA KING, author of Spit Back the Bones and Bitterbloom

"Your happiness can vanish all too fast, and you may be plunged, by your own doing, into the greatest calamities."

-Empress Maria Theresa of Austria in a letter to her daughter, Marie Antoinette

ONE

The voice in the mirror taunts me. I should be used to it by now, the childlike tone that replaced my sister, strangling my sanity and staining every happiness in black.

"They'll cut you apart, rip through your skin, make you a girl, who's fit for a king."

If only it *was* the voice of my dear sister. Josepha was more often than not the only person to lean on and to make me laugh in the palace.

It never gets easier. Her disappearance. A wound that scabs, but scratches open easily.

She left and the voice showed up, speaking the most annoying riddles. I've tried to understand *why* it appears, what it is chanting about. At first, my neck would snap back and forth, searching for the source. Even when others were around, it made no difference—no one could hear it but me.

Anything that reflects the light brings it to life.

The words slip close to curl around my shoulder before I can glance away from the mirror, the silver platter, the glimmer in a puddle. Each time the voice fills my ears, needles prickle across my flesh, a knowing that it is trying to tell me something.

No matter the strain I place to understand, the words only sing impossible riddles.

Perfectly good drinking glasses often fall from my trembling fingers and smash to bits. Bowls of soup thrown to quiet the sounds.

But *mirrors*.

Mirrors are the worst.

"Look at you, Marie, Marie, so sad she's gone, and all that's left is me."

It seems to be louder than ever as I stare at my naked reflection.

As *everyone* stares at my exposed body in the clouded glass set before me. Strangers from the French court, judging every move I make. Over a dozen gazing eyes from men with powdered wigs and women with rouged cheeks. They lean in closer, whispering under their foul breath.

"Please! Don't!" I cry as fingers press into my arms, pulling them apart, while a girl attempts to steal my yelping dog away from me.

"Anne, hurry up!" Comtesse snaps, but the girl looks at me with wide saucer eyes. Like she is apologizing for what she must do. I release my hold, and Anne hesitates before taking my best friend from me. Her wide eyes turned red from burning tears.

There is a girl with red hair by my side, who whispers in my ear, "all will be well. Do as you must for now."

I don't bother turning to her, too focused on straining my eyes to catch the final glimpse of Mops, my sweet puppy, leaving the tent. I deflate when I'm unable to see him and pinch my eyes shut as hot tears run down my cheeks.

The girl with the red hair was right. I have no choice but to quell my feelings.

They have stripped me of everything but my skin for the handing over ceremony, though I think they'd take that too if they could. Every inch of my ivory flesh trembles as I cross my arms over my bare breasts. The wind weaving through the tent freezes the bundle of anxiety climbing up my throat, threatening to turn to tears. The heavily perfumed scent of alcohol and rose singes my nose and chokes me further.

"Stand tall, dauphine," Comtesse de Noailles's voice is as cold as my tiny shivering frame. It matches her dress, all blue ice and shine like the surface of a frozen lake. The woman who ordered my dog be ripped away from me—my beloved Mops, with his wet pug nose and cuddles, the very same pup who helped me get through the dark nights after Josepha vanished. "I know, I seem harsh. But I am trying to help you. The king charged me with taking care of you, and preparing you for court is the best way I know how."

"It does not feel as though you are helping me," I mutter under my breath.

"The women of France do not mumble, especially those of your soon-to-be standing," Comtesse says with an arch of her brow, shaking her head in contempt.

"My apologies, Comtesse. I was just saying that—" I stumble, in search of an excuse, "that I am cold." The words are bitter on my tongue. If only I could scream at her. For dismissing Mops like he was garbage, shooing off my loved ones, tearing off my clothes, and leaving me exposed for all to see.

"Patience is a virtue, young dauphine. You will be warm and married soon."

I nod, sifting through my memories of all Mother told me in the months before I was to leave. My mind can barely grasp all the instructions and reminders, but I do remember her swearing I would have someone to provide me with comfort, and support me in my new role as dauphine. It was but a lie, for this woman's calculating eyes and thinly pressed lips make me want to run back to Mother and remain a princess of Austria forever. I am but a doll, small and alone, articulated to suit Mother's needs...and now Comtesse's expectations.

The only thing I'm allowed to keep now is the voice, always lingering, forever faithful in those damned reflections. I don't know what it is. Who it is.

I stare at the last hint of my blonde hair hidden beneath layers of white powder. The mirror's glass is encased by a thick, gold frame etched with hundreds of fleurs-de-lis. A delicate mirror which spawns the voice that fills my ears.

"You wear their mask and play their play. But underneath you slowly decay."

The girl with hair as red as strawberries raises her eyebrows as the comtesse continues to speak, then shakes her head while undergarments finally find their way on my body. "The threads that tie you to Austria must be severed. The future king's bride must embody all that is France."

Comtesse studies me in this tent made of the finest hand-woven navy fabrics, complete with sparkling chandeliers casting a dance of light in the otherwise dark tomb in the middle of Forest Compiègne. The place where all that I am has come to die.

In each corner stands gold statues of mythological figures, holding lanterns high in their carved hands. All four illuminate the dark reality of my future, riddled with dutiful royalty. Medusa stands out compared to the other three. Snakes protrude from her scalp, weaving knots explaining the pain in her face. A beautiful girl, cursed. An innocent, turned monster.

Above the mirror is a glistening sculpted face of the softest measure, surrounded by the striking rays of the sun—the symbol of the Sun King. Louis XIV was my future husband's grandfather, the visionary who built Versailles, which I shall now call home.

My eyes trace down from the carved sun, back to my own reflection, my eyes pale blue, giving way to the numbness I feel in my heart.

"It 'tis but flesh, all that is left, we'll shed it off, until the snake is fed."

The disembodied voice calls to me again and again and again. A haunting high pitch I swear could be that of my sister—vanished from Austria a month after my twelfth birthday, leaving *me* the duty of marrying Dauphin Louis XVI.

I am unable to hang on to a single emotion for longer than a few breaths, each a thread being pulled from a poorly woven tapestry in my mind. The thread of my wedding day falls to the forefront. The thought of being a bride *today* sticks to me, a thick sweat of overwhelm and dread.

I can't blame my sister for disappearing—running off before they dragged her away from her home like all girls are. For the past year I've felt the crushing weight of expectation from our mother and our country to become someone who would please a foreign prince.

To run is not a choice I have. And would I if I could?

I would give anything to find Josepha, but my dreams tell me it may be fate—her escape to find happiness is exactly what will now provide mine. Sudden excitement pulses through my veins. A lavish life awaits me on the other side of this tent because of her absence. The conflicting feelings tear me in two, like fabric abruptly ripped, leaving frayed threads in its wake.

Maybe she's in Paris. Maybe I'll find her waiting for me at the Palace of Versailles. Maybe she married for love, like I dream will happen for me when I meet Louis.

Some nights, I imagine his face being smooth as silk, with a kind smile and powerful arms that sweep me across the dance floor and whisk me away to the gardens for stolen kisses. That the people of France adore us, that we one day stand together with our crowns and gowns and fancy feasts, that our love runs pure and deep for all the days of my life.

"Fingers grab, begin to bind, crushing your heart, no love you shall find."

Stop it.

Stop it.

I fight the clench of my fingers, the need to claw their way up to my ears—a familiar and pathetic attempt to silence this cursed voice, lingering like suffocating fog, wrapping its melody around me since that morning Josepha was suddenly nowhere to be found. The absence of my sister, my best friend, festers like an aching, open wound upon my heart. A beating, bleeding heart that must be silenced—*tighten the tourniquet, Maria.*

It's not my Josepha, though. This voice from reflections is that of something—*someone*—else.

We'd sneak from our bedchambers each night, my sister and me, tiptoeing down the palace halls to huddle by the roaring fire in the salon. Josepha's dimples became hollowed shadows as the light of the flames glowed upon her porcelain skin. I'd study each dainty feature, so much prettier than me, as she recited tales of hauntings long ago in our very own home, and of the omens that followed our family. Ice coursed through my veins whenever she reminded me that those dark shadows cling to *me*, forever unshakeable.

Yet, it was my happy place—with Josepha, knees curled to our chests, warmed by the fire. Sisters. Best friends. I'd give anything to hear another of her chilling stories just one last time.

"The blood will pool wherever you go, will drip and drown all those you know."

The voice from the mirror pulls me back to the hustle and bustle of the courtiers. Shaking my head to eliminate the thoughts of ghosts and ghouls calling out to me through reflections in the glass, a strand of hair comes loose from my coiffure. For a moment Comtesse de Noailles' eyes meet my own in the reflection. My heart thrashes against my ribs, hoping she hears the voice too. That I'm not alone.

Comtesse's thick gray brows knit together over her dark eyes as she pulls tighter on the corset ribbons. She doesn't hear the taunting that vibrates in my ears. She sees nothing but her own disappointment in me. It's a look I'm quite accustomed to. Without trying, I always let Mother down and come secondary to my siblings.

Comtesse de Noailles's frown accentuates the many wrinkles in her face and speaks louder than anything else in the room.

I take a deep breath, letting it steady me. All will be well. I'm sure of it. She will grow to love me.

I stand taller. My hands lift to the sky, and the soft linen sends needed warmth to my bones. I look down and run my palms over the fabric, a distraction from being the soul on display in front of so many courtiers.

"Stand still, child. Many young women would commit the most atrocious acts to be in your place," she says as a group of chambermaids swarm around me, efficient as bees embellishing my body with the fashions of France—pulling up stockings and tugging the corset even more, so tight I lose my breath and have to gulp for air.

More whirring and buzzing, and powders and perfumes. I catch small words whispered from their judgmental lips.

"Undeveloped."

"Underwhelming."

"Unusual."

Nothing I haven't heard before. Still, nausea slithers up my chest from all these strangers talking about me, touching me, adorning me. They dress me, but their bony fingers linger on my skin too long. Their eyes judge each inch, yet they press closer. Wanting.

I bite my lip and shut my lids over my eyes, focusing on my breath again.

This is all for the best.

It is my duty.

My destiny with my true love.

Suddenly, the chaos stops, and I dare to open my eyes, finding the redhead moving toward me, causing the grimace the comtesse wears to deepen further.

"I think you've prodded and primped this girl enough. Her poor neck couldn't take the weight of another necklace without falling plum off," the girl says, followed by a cackle. A forceful yank at my finger sends me into a twirl, and I can't help the giggle that sneaks through my lips.

"Geneviève," Comtesse de Noailles scolds the girl with strawberry curls, spinning me like a top, but I catch the corner of her mouth tugging into a slight smile—though it could be a sneer.

Geneviève releases me and steps back into a low bow, hand in front of her chest, folding the yellow linen of her gorgeous, flowing dress. "Yes, yes. No way to treat a future queen and all." Her body dips lower, but her hazel eyes sparkle before giving me a quick wink. "Your Royal Highness, I do beg your pardon."

The single note of a laugh escapes my lips, and Comtesse de Noailles latches onto my upper arm like talons on prey. "Let us see."

I exhale when she loosens her grip. Then she walks ever so slowly around me. Judging every part of me. The rest of the vultures join her, and I find myself searching for Geneviève.

The girl, a few years older than I, rolls her eyes when I finally spot her. It's exactly what Josepha would have done in the middle of such a production. Warmth expands in my ribcage, the tension in my body slowly releases.

"I believe you are ready to meet your husband, Dauphine," Comtesse de Noailles announces proudly.

To the courtiers, this has been a grand metamorphosis from pupa to butterfly. A glittering persona of who I am to be in this new life of mine. No longer Maria Antonia of Austria, haunted by omens. Once I walk out the other side of the tent, I will be Dauphine of France…

Marie Antoinette.

"Marie, Marie, the name a sliver, but under your skin, we'll shift and slither."

I catch a last glimpse of my powdered face in the mirror as I'm spun around by too many hands. A departing reminder that the voice is eternally with me despite my new name and home; it's buried deep within. And it must always have the final word.

Comtesse de Noailles ushers me out of the tent, into the forest of lush greens. The sun blinds as it refracts off the many gilded carriages scattered among the trees. Their glittering presence is as opulent as the tent and its statues and chandeliers.

Now, *I* am their newest sparkling ornament. A role I was meant to play. Above anyone else. Joy builds in my heart with each pressing moment.

"And now, you are French," Comtesse announces. Simple as that.

Shielding my eyes with a delicate hand, I see him. The face from the painting I've studied in the weeks it has taken to travel to the borders of France. Even from a distance, his red coat shines amongst the greens and browns of the forest. The way he is in the center of everyone confirms it is him.

My husband.

Geneviève links arms with me. "Just breathe and stick with me. Try not to tremble so. They will love you."

"Geneviève!" Comtesse points her finger toward the ground, and Geneviève responds by letting me go to return to Comtesse's side.

This is it. My moment to ensure they do indeed love me as Geneviève promised. Yet it is impossible to stop the tremble of my bones.

Here lay my only opportunity to rid myself of the omens that shadowed the entirety of my life.

Sixty thousand souls died the day I came into the world, earthquakes demolishing so many of the people of Lisbon.

Throughout the years of my short life, I've watched family and friends die at my feet, plagued by illness. Smallpox has killed many, young and old, rich and poor. I hope it has not spread in Paris as it has in Austria.

I prayed that the fire in the tiny village we passed on the journey here was not another nightmare to add to my ever-growing collection.

I have been on my best behavior. Done everything they've told me to. My family reputation is on the line—I've been a disappointment to Mother so many times before, always wanting to play and dance, ignoring my school lessons, and muddying my dress on a rainy day.

But somehow, I now have an opportunity to change everything for my family. For my people. Mother made me swear to honor her, make her proud, and make France believe she gave them an angel. I wasn't the first choice to be sent to Versailles, but here—as the sun breaks through the trees to shine light upon me and my Louis—I feel the fates smiling, ready to change my luck forever.

Damn the omens.

I refrain from flinching each time a twig snaps under my pointed powder blue shoes. Each step I take toward Louis is calculated. Poised. I must fight the doubts manifesting in my stomach, slicing through me like a sharp blade.

If I can be rid of the voices and omens, fit in at the Palace of Versailles, survive the corsets and expectations, then one day… *one day*, I will be the Queen of France. It may not be my name given at birth, but I have a new name for my new life now.

Marie Antoinette.

TWO

The king takes my hand gingerly, kissing the top of it to signal my welcome. His small mouth purses then smiles, framed by thick jowls. When he steps back, I bow again while I take in his outfit—a gorgeous array of satins and sashes and furs. He stands between me and my Louis, the anticipation a pounding clock in my temple. I'm so close to the moment I've been waiting for.

Guards stand at attention, their tall halberds with sharp ends seemingly keeping them all upright. Their serious look and identical uniforms creates a little cocoon around those who don't belong in this beautiful and peaceful place within nature. I don't understand why such a presence is required for our gathering of overdressed royals and their servants.

The king catches my wandering eye, and smiles at me. "Fret not of the guard. Though we are close to God, the royals are often targeted by dangerous folk. Stepping out of the palace requires some extra…precautions. These are my very best men, here to keep my soon-to-be granddaughter safe from anyone that may cause harm."

I swallow. Suddenly feeling safe in this cocoon, aware that trouble may lay behind the guard within the woods cast in shadow.

"Thank you," I say, bowing my head slightly.

The king's furrowed eyes now graze the rest of me. The weight of his contemplation is crushing—I'm never good enough. Not bright enough, not pretty enough, not mannered enough. Mother was forced to turn me into something else completely to fit royal standards. "Remind me, how old are you, Marie?"

Marie. Not Maria. Not anymore.

Omens followed Maria. They won't follow Marie. My chest expands until my corset digs into my ribs, then deflates with relief.

The brush beneath our feet crunches as Comtesse de Noailles moves in closer. "My king, Marie is but fourteen. I assure you; she is bound to develop. She has already received her menarche, and has regular courses."

Heat burns in my cheeks. My head turns slightly to find Geneviève, instinct telling me to seek her for comfort. She's behind Comtesse, and provides a warm smile and a wink—enough to give me a sliver of strength.

I stand taller, pressing my shoulders back awkwardly so what little chest I have appears a bit larger. Grand bosoms are adored, and I want them one day to impress the king and the court, but especially my Louis.

"They seem quite nice to me. Much more than simple bee stings, Louis." The voice of a young man with an unsightly mole on his cheek pierces the crisp air. No regard for how his words may slice through me and no care for the formality of this meeting. I'm sure they'll grow bigger than your head in time. Especially once she is with child." With an impish grin, he rams a shoulder into Louis. The dauphin smothers his own smile from the jest and braces himself from losing his footing. With a cough to silence his friend, he finally steps forward to greet me.

My heart flutters to life. Months of changing myself, weeks of travel, and days of staring at his portrait have all culminated to this single moment. Meeting the one that will cherish me, love me, and make me queen. I have never wanted anything so deeply in all my life.

I begin walking to him, but am stopped dead in my tracks by two guards. They tower over me, creating a wall between me and my Louis.

"This is my future bride, there is no need to guard her from me," Louis' voice says behind the royal blue uniforms. They each step aside and he walks through them. "Marie is the future queen. I will not have her blocked from doing anything she pleases. You are to tell all the palace guards." They nod in agreement.

I stand my ground, though all I want is to run into Louis' arms. His command over the guards is grand, yet in contrast to his appearance. The black velvet hat covering his dark hair is far too big for his head. The medallions pinned to his stiff, red jacket glint in the sun, so large, I see my nervous features staring back at me in them.

"We coil up your legs, round and round, squeezing all life, 'til the truth is found."

Cursed voice. I inhale, focusing on the boy in front of me instead of the whisperings in my ear.

"Welcome, Madame." Louis bows slowly, then stares into my eyes.

My future husband. Here in the flesh, more than the mere painted portrait that fits in my palm. He's different from the brush strokes. So much younger, with cherry-stained plump cheeks and a bulbous nose. Who am I to judge, with my small breasts and tiny frame?

I curtsy as deep as my dress will allow, the cool air nipping along the back of my exposed neck as I lean over. I crave the warmth of the palace, to heat my bones by the fires in Versailles. To learn to love every feature upon Louis' face.

"Merci." My voice is soft, calm.

"Your accent is lovely." His four words bloom in my chest, a thrill spreading through my blood at the thought of him liking me. Loving me.

Of everyone loving me.

"Your Highness will be pleased to know that Marie has worked with a coach for several years to truly embody the French dialect." Comtesse de Noailles addresses Louis, then smiles at the king. As if *she* were the one to go through the torture I've endured. "She is one of the first to have metal wires used to straighten teeth, so that her smile may light up all of France." The mention of braces awakens a phantom pain in my gums, the metal sharp and piercing. "Her scalp has undergone full transformations so that she may have a petite forehead and be the embodiment of beauty for our country."

"I'm surprised she can even breathe in that corset you've tied her up in," the annoying boy pipes in. His hair is the color of mud, sticking out of his hat and bouncing in front of hazel eyes.

"Alexandre," she scolds, her voice enough to make him take a semi-step back in line with Louis, "that is no way for one of the court, the best friend of the dauphin, to speak of the dauphine."

"We are all quite impressed by Marie Antoinette." The king turns to me. Though his eyes are a dark brown, they seem to brighten when he looks from me to Louis. "And we are all happy to welcome you, especially my grandson."

Louis' mouth presses into a thin smile, still staring into my eyes, seemingly unsure of what to say.

I break the stare, looking over his shoulder to a boy beside Alexandre. His dimples light up his smile, and his eyes are a blue more crystalline than any water I've seen. I feel my cheeks heat, sure they will turn a violent shade of red. He is familiar, as though he has lived in my dreams. My fingernails press into my palms, and I scold myself for thinking of anything but my duty of making my future husband happy.

Comtesse de Noailles clears her throat, and I'm thankful. It snaps my attention back to Louis, still standing awkwardly silent before me.

"She is lucky indeed to have the favor of the dauphin," Comtesse says, dropping her head slightly, her voice more serious than ever.

"Comtesse, enough with the formalities!" The king's laugh bellows and his arm falls on her shoulder. Color drains from her face.

"Yes. Well. Shall—shall we proceed to Versailles? This is, after all, the biggest day of their lives."

The king chuckles. There's a warmth to him that eases my tension, yet makes Comtesse de Noailles look ill. I wonder why she needs to remain so rigid next to the king's informality. He claps his hands together, a smile spreading across his face to match his jolly laugh. "Let's go have a wedding!"

A wedding.

My wedding.

Today.

I try to swallow, but my mouth has gone dry. Am I good enough? Will he love me?

It takes all my power to smile at the king, all the while ignoring the way the world seems to spin around me—trees and carriages and royals and guards whirring in my vision. Perhaps Alexandre was correct, and my corset is too tight.

"Fingers grab, begin to bind, crushing your heart, no love you shall find."

Or perhaps the voice is right and more omens await me at Versailles.

Geneviève is beautiful. Her cheeks are flush with excitement as she bounces into the carriage, swinging the teal velvet door closed behind her. It's a relief to be alone with her on this last leg of the long trip to Versailles. She seems so carefree, full of life, yet kind beyond measure, offering her winks and words of advice in the tent.

She flutters down beside me, snuggling in close as though we have known each other our whole lives. I hesitate at first, then lean into it, a grin spreading across my face that I can't control.

"So, what do we think?" Her red hair is disheveled, a frizz that matches her wild demeanor—she's the only one that seems to have lost their filter for refinery, and I adore her for it.

"Think of what?"

"Louis, of course. Is he all you ever dreamed of?" The back of her arm falls to her forehead, swooning with a giggle.

A lump appears in my throat, not used to being asked my opinion. And truly, I don't know what to say. My mind flickers to the other boy, the one with blue eyes. "Louis seems sweet. I just hope to make him happy."

She bolts up, taking my hands in hers. "What about him making *you* happy?"

"He will make me happy if I can give him a son. Do my duty."

"No, no, no, Marie. Your happiness has to be more than an obligation decided by a bunch of old, stuffy monarchs. I hate that we are only born in order to breed, and if we birth a girl, we are a disappointment."

The flight of butterflies in my stomach begins to fade, losing their momentum. Should I not be honored? If it weren't for me, Austria and France would be enemies. I distract myself by looking at the glass cylinder in front of me that holds a candle for late night travels.

"To bear, to bleed, to dance, to please. This, Marie, is destiny."

I should know better than to stare into glass. I rub my temple, desperate to make the voice stop. My destiny is good. Bright. No more omens. *No. More. Omens.*

A headache vibrates through my skull. Geneviève must notice the way my fingertips press to the spots of pain because she places a hand on my leg, over the many layers of fabric that make up my glittery new outfit. "Breathe, Marie. All shall be well. I have a good feeling about your life here at Versailles."

An exhale empties from my lungs, replaced with hope as I inhale again.

We both fall into silence, staring out the tiny windows, watching the forest turn to fields, the sky shining brilliant blue upon the procession of carriages behind us.

Our chariot rumbles gently as the wheels roll over unsteady ground. I enjoy the melodic sound of the horses' hooves taking us to my new home. My life *is* going to be good. My shoulders lift while I inhale the hopefulness that swims in my mind again.

"Are there many fun things to do in Versailles?" I ask.

"Well," her sly smile returns, "there are many boys to play with. Though, I suppose you can't take advantage of that, marrying the future king and all."

My fingers find my hair, but the loose strands I wish to curl are concealed within the tight, powdered wig.

Geneviève senses my unease. "I know. I shouldn't be so...free with my heart. But I love the excitement of someone caring for me, if only for a moment in time. The Gods know my father sure didn't."

"Oh, Geneviève, I'm sorry."

"No bother." She waves a hand dismissively. "If it weren't for him, I wouldn't be riding in this carriage with you. I wouldn't be favored in the Comtesse's eye. I would be a chambermaid like my mother."

It all clicks into place now. The way Comtesse danced around Geneviève's sharp tongue and playful ways. Geneviève balances along a fine line between the royal and the help. An illegitimate child with certain allowances and privileges, but often without love. Cast away from the inner circles because, though they didn't choose it, they were born out of the marriage bed, destined to live on the fray of high society.

"Was your mother in the tent with us this morning?"

"No. Mother died when I was little. Father practically left me in Comtesse's care, claiming he was too busy with court to raise me. Or love me." Her eyes sparkle with rising tears, lines of red raging around the hazel.

"Oh, Geneviève," I repeat, looking to her as she stares out the window at another forest rushing by.

"I was glad to see her suffering end. Smallpox. It's ended so many lives. Those it's taken and those who have been left behind." Geneviève's lips have turned to a deep frown. I place my hand on her lap, encouraging her to face me.

"It's so many more women than men that die." Geneviève still doesn't turn to look at me, the words falling faintly from her lips. The first time she's shown any hesitation in speaking. "Many of us are sure it isn't just from illness. There are stories of little blue bottles. Little blue bottles carrying poison."

I find my dress bunching in my fingers, grip tightening. A temptation to jump from the carriage beginning to overtake me. "Poison? Who is poisoned? By whom?"

Geneviève brushes hair from in front of her eye. "Well, I guess somebody is going to eventually tell you. May as well be me." She tilts her head, studying me. "In this glittering palace of ours, women tend to have an expiration. We look good, we breed, we die. Poison flows through these walls, waiting to drip down our throats."

I stare into my lap and shake my head. Mother would never allow such tragedy into our home. Suddenly fearful of what kind of world I am entering without the ever-watchful eyes of Mother, my teeth pierce my lower lip.

"How horrible," I say, mustering the will to ask about my sister, fear twining around my heart at the thought of Josepha being caught up in all this. "Do—do you know of a girl named Josepha? She is like me, only prettier, and always wore a violet ribbon in her blonde hair. She is my sister who ran away from Austria without me."

"I've not met anyone who looks near to you, Marie. I hope that if she did find her way here, she stayed clear from blue bottles, unlike those poor souls long gone." Geneviève stares blankly while my stomach ties in unbreakable knots.

The carriage bumps off the ground, jostling us to the side, and Geneviève lets loose a loud laugh. The jump from silence to laughing grates along my nerves. "My, my… look at me getting all serious. That is simply no fun at all. But promise me, Marie. Promise me we'll be best friends, that you'll stick by my side. I am going to be here for you, through thick and thin."

A smile spreads from ear to ear so sharp my cheeks hurt. *A friend.*

"I promise. And I'll be here for you, too."

Her hands find her chest, hazel eyes sparkling with amusement. "Me? A lowly chambermaid with royal blood?"

"I don't care what your status is, Geneviève. Royal, chambermaid, or the best of both."

"Well then you're unlike any other royal I've ever met."

"Good." And it is. I want to be loved by everyone, whether they are best friends with the king or spend their days milking cows.

I tumble forward as the carriage comes to a stop, heart racing in my chest when I notice dozens of faces filling the glass window. The seat below me vibrates, the entire carriage shaken by the hands and voices surrounding it. An empty feeling in the pit of my stomach consumes me.

"What are all these people doing?" I ask.

"They've been waiting for *you*, Marie," Geneviève says.

"*Me*?" My voice trembles and my heart gallops faster than all my horses back home. There are so many people, the volume of their joined voices rises higher and higher. More throw themselves from the crowd and push their faces to the window, staring at me. A little boy with wide eyes. A woman with a dirty face bangs a fist against the carriage. I fear the protection of the glass may break. That they hate me already and are prepared to do something about it.

Guards open the door and briskly take my hand, clearing a space for me to leave the carriage. My eyes focus on the ground as I fear facing the peoples' hatred.

"Marie!" Geneviève's voice breaks through the crowd. "Look!"

I brave it, tilting my head up slowly, coming face-to-face with a sea of smiles.

The people aren't yelling. They aren't angry.

They're *cheering*.

Hundreds of people fill the palace square, clamoring to get a glimpse of me.

Me.

Any clutch I had upon Austria fades quickly at this realization. Heat spreads through my chest and I feel weightless—like I could take flight with the birds that soar happily through the crystalline sky. I look back to the line of carriages, hoping Louis is nearby so we can relish in this moment together. But he must not have arrived yet, or perhaps he has already been escorted in.

"See?" Geneviève says. "This is where you belong. Your destiny at Versailles."

I smile, wanting to hug each and every person that has gathered in welcome. A laugh bursts from deep within my heart when I see a little girl waving with all her might, looking at me like I'm the most important person in the world.

Surrounded by guards, I walk through the massive front gates, golden bars with carvings of the Sun King. My shoes slip on the polished tiles, the alternating black and white squares barely visible beneath the feet of so many people.

"Marie!" they cry. "Dauphine!"

I wave, first timidly, then with as much fervor as they show me. Their excitement is palpable, rattling in my ribs. Women, men, children, fanciest wears and torn rags…all here to see me. Excitement pulses through the crowd and through me—connected as one. I ignore the memory of my sister telling me that omens follow me. Damn the omens. Damn the omens.

My eyes follow the edges of the crowd and catch the bold edges of my new home. I laugh again. I was so busy basking in all this adoration, I failed to notice the magnificent palace sprawling far and wide.

Versailles.

Its grandeur is more than I've read or heard about from visitors to my home in Austria. The columns shine the brightest white, rising high to meet the roof that is as blue as the lapis the queens of Egypt once wore. My mouth falls open at the sight of the grand clock, adorned with the symbol of the Sun King—that cherub face with rays of the sun emanating from it, illuminating the whole spectacle.

Scanning the many faces of the court and commoners mingling together, my eyes are carried up, up, up to the side of the palace, where the great columns meet the roof. Stone carvings of angels and cherubs sit, looking down upon me. Blank eyes and hollow faces cast an eerie shadow in my gut.

My stomach rolls with dread. The statues looking down on this place feel like a warning, like their faces are frozen in terror because they know what is to come.

I look back at the people around me, focus on their love, their cheers growing more intense, building like one of Mozart's symphonies, the crescendo pressing on my chest with overwhelm.

A man grabs hold of my collar, pulling my face to his. I rise to tiptoe and begin screaming as I strain to stand back on the ground.

"You can't fool me. You're just like the rest of them. Letting us rot," he says, and I wince when his foul breath hits my face.

"Let me go!" I shout, wriggling and writhing in his grip. Straining my neck to see Geneviève. Louis.

His face is caked with dirt, his eyes wild. Until suddenly they are not, and as his face falls, so do I. The bloodied tip of a sword pokes out through his stomach, before the guard behind the man pulls it back to him.

A shrill cry pierces through it all. My hands clap to my ears as chaos erupts around me. Voices and arms, screams and shouts. I am yanked toward a guard, and tears sting behind my eyes from the strength of his grip on my arm. Everyone attempts to run, but the space is so small, so cramped, so full.

We are almost to the front doors when I see the bodies sprawled lifeless before us. Pools of blood gather on the sparkling marble tiles around each of the trampled souls, and the voice I know so well returns its warning from earlier today, as if the riddles were prophecy.

"The blood will pool wherever you go, will drip and drown all those you know."

Every inch of my skin turns to ice. These poor people died because of me. Trampled to death, crushed by feet, drowned in their own blood while reaching to touch me, screaming my name and crying out for a moment of my attention. Because this man hated me.

My stomach lurches as my eyes widen.

Life is such a strange and fickle thing. Fleeting, unplanned, impermanent. I want to help them all, drop to my knees and attempt to shake them back from the dead. But it won't work. They are gone.

I'm drawn to a young woman only a few paces from my feet, her heart barely beating. A small child cries over her, tugging at her shoulder to encourage a full breath to return to her lungs. Her chest rises only a bit, followed by a cough of blood that sprays from her lips. The boy seems completely unaware that his mother's blood has soaked his clothes through as he kneels, each movement he makes causing the deep red liquid to ripple.

"How can we help her?" I break from one of the guards and take the boy into my arms, holding him close to my chest.

"We can't. We must get to safety."

The boy wails, slicing through my heart. This is all my fault.

The guard grabs at my arm, and I yank back, determined to hold this orphan with all my might.

The guard exhales, then walks to the woman's head. He leans down and places his hands at her temples. Instinctively, I pull the boy in closer, averting his eyes while his mother coughs her last shaky breath.

With a twist of the wrist, the guard has killed her. I look at him angrily while chaos continues to stir all around us, and more guards circle around me.

"Kindness sometimes appears to be cruelty," he says, and before I can fight him or anyone else, the boy is ripped from me, just like Mops. Guards grab at me harder and harder, beckoning me away from the horror filling the square. I finally see Louis, just a glimpse of him between guards, being pulled in the same direction they take me in now. My legs don't dare stand their ground anymore. I am ready to flee.

The omens are not my fault.

My cold hand claps over my eyes, unable to bear the sight of what is underfoot. I do not want to see the reflection that stirs in all the blood or hear the voice that will accompany it. A voice that will surely blame me.

THREE

All that blood. Gone. Just on the other side of the palace door.

Everything is hazy. I feel sick to my stomach.

The cheers-turned-screams outside are now muffled to those of us in the palace. The *swish* of thick dress fabrics and *click, click* of crimson-stained heels fill the hall as everyone scurries away. Small dots of red leaving evidence behind of where they have walked.

"Aren't we to help all those people?" I call out to the back of heads moving farther and farther away from me. "We can't just leave them. What if more people are hurt? Where did the guard take the boy?" Words fall from my mouth, leaving me near breathless, but are met with silence.

My feet, unsure of where to go or who to follow, remain planted firmly on the wooden floor. I scan for someone to help—a doctor to save souls or a mother for the boy who is now orphaned. But all I'm met with are glittering chandeliers and floor to ceiling arched windows that burn away reality with bright sunlight. The quiet somehow deafening, the chaos from outside still ringing in my ears.

The guards stand at attention at the door, emotionless. Statues. They won't help me.

Nobody answers me, and my Louis is nowhere to be seen. My pounding heart now flutters hollowly.

Warmth greets my trembling hand.

Geneviève.

Suddenly able to breathe again, I squeeze her hand, thankful for the touch of another in my moment of abandonment.

The hem of her skirt is lined in blood. My chin dips to my chest, guilt washing over me for not thinking of her while we were amongst the chaos and death.

"I'm so cold," I stutter, noticing my shaking knees. "How could they—"

"Welcome to Versailles." Her half smile is full of sadness, and I can see that spark within her extinguished. "I hate to say, but I feel no much safer in here than out there."

"We aren't safe?" My arms cross, snaking around each other while I look to Geneviève for answers.

"Geneviève," a commanding voice echoes through the opulent hall. Comtesse de Noailles steps in front of us, rubbing the space between her eyes with her fingers, "can I trust you to show Marie the palace? There are so many things to do for the wedding still, I—"

"You go. Marie and I will be just fine." Geneviève winks my way, her mask of sadness and ominous warnings quickly replaced. She steps closer to me and I lean ever so slightly toward her. A magnet drawing me to the only comforting thing between the dozens of plinths holding whispering ceramic busts. My fingers curl into my palm.

"Very well. Stay inside and—" Comtesse begins.

Geneviève places her fingertips to her heart. "I solemnly swear that we will stay indoors, away from mud, and will meet you in her chambers in an hour."

Comtesse de Noailles studies Geneviève, lips pressed so tightly together I fear her teeth may puncture straight through. I recognize the unsteadiness in her gray eyes, the same way Mother looked at me when she was unsure if she could believe me.

Her gaze darts to me for a second and I quickly force my knees to stiffen. To be strong. To stand tall. Then she turns back to Geneviève. "Her dress and attendants will be there in an hour. Don't be late," she says, spinning on her heel to hurry down the hall.

Geneviève saunters to the nearest plinth, leaning an elbow on the pristine white that holds a bronze sculpture of a man with a beard yet no eyes. She wags a finger and scrunches her nose once Comtesse is out of sight. "Don't be late," she says in a whiny voice, a laughable imitation of Comtesse, yet funny nonetheless. I catch a laugh before it escapes my mouth, suddenly aware of the poor taste it leaves while so many people lay dead just outside the door behind us. I turn toward it, swallowing the guilt of not running through it to help someone. Anyone.

"Why are we not safe on this side of the door?" I try again.

"I told you, Marie. Poisons. Blue bottles…" She hangs on to that last word like a song, as if what she says doesn't hold the weight of the world.

I take a timid step forward, but her words echo in my ears. I stop and look at my feet. The ground is solid, but I feel like I'm falling.

"Forget them." A close whisper sends my soul to leave my skin for a moment.

I feel foolish when I realize it is Geneviève, grabbing onto my hand, helping me feel steady once more. She's like a cat—moving about silently when she needs to, and making her presence known when it suits her.

"We can't possibly proceed with the wedding today. Not with all that death," I protest.

"If you allow the death to creep in, it shall swallow you whole, Marie."

"But—"

"There is no other way." Her voice remains low and she leans in closer still as we stare at the door surrounded with a blue sea of guards. "I have spent so much time aching for the lost. For those I loved dearly and those I didn't know at all. At first, the fear of having my throat slit for demanding more care and compassion drove me to silence. Then, one day it all became clear. I must relish the life still within me, not live for the dead."

I struggle to find the right words, desperate to sit and sort through what she has said, but Geneviève is already dragging me forward. My hand moves back and forth across my chest as I think. The mere *thought* of death makes my heart swim with unease, let alone the sight of it.

The crystal teardrop dangling from a chandelier reflects the sun pouring in from the windows, casting the light into a beautiful rainbow. But the voice returns from the crystal, eliminating the beauty of the colors.

"Push it down, push it down. That's what you'll do. Laugh it away, they'll all die soon."

I clench my eyes shut as tight as I'm able. The absurdity of this all is becoming too much to bear. How is one to process the stripping away of all they've known, taunting voices coming from reflections, and witnessing such excitement turned to blood all on their wedding day?

I must laugh. Must laugh before the tears fall and drown me. And so I do. I turn to Geneviève and laugh from deep within my belly.

"She is quite serious. Comtesse de Noailles. Her name should be Madame Etiquette!" My voice rises in pitch as I mockingly wag my pointer finger. "'Do this. Don't do that. You must be fit for France.'"

"That's it. We must laugh and live. Especially at Etiquette's expense! The name that shall be our inside secret." She swiftly takes me by the hand. "Now let's go have some fun."

I squeeze onto her tightly, trusting her to guide me through the labyrinth. The first room we whir past is stuffed with furniture adorned with the lushest fabric the color of saturated rubies and emeralds. Through a doorway we whirl past the boy with the dimples and blue eyes. He smiles brightly as I look back at him, trying to keep pace with Geneviève. "Who is he?" I call to her, though I should bite my tongue for even asking.

She stops abruptly and I nearly topple over her, panting. "Who?" She asks, surveying the space we just left.

"He was the boy in the forest, by Alexandre."

"Oh, do not go near anyone who keeps company with Alexandre," her voice is foreboding.

My eyes squint, "isn't that Louis' best friend? The best friend of my fiancé?"

"Yes, well…. I do not see any boy over there."

I look back through the doorway, but he has left. I am jealous of whomever he left with.

"He is no longer there," I say, trying not to let the deflation of excitement show in the slump of my shoulders.

"Good. Marie, you should keep your eyes away from anyone but Louis. You just got here and I would hate for you to be killed," she laughs, but I shudder at the hint of truth I catch in her tone.

"Of course. Now, let us get to my chambers."

Geneveive says no more, only breaks back into a run. So quickly the hallways change from being covered by a stifling amount of gold, to stark whites and grays within seconds. Warmth followed by cold. The faster we run, the more of a blur they become and though I laugh, something twists in my stomach, afraid of being lost here. Trapped.

I shake my head. There's no time for such thoughts.

Another room is covered in paintings from floor to ceiling that must have been commissioned by the most talented artists in the world—the people in them look so real.

Gasps and turned heads are left in our wake, and I consider slowing. I should stop. Behave as a royal. Yet…

"Where are you taking me?" I call to Geneviève, her long flowing curls bouncing with each quickened step. A carousel of rooms, the palace feels never-ending.

"Everywhere!" she yells playfully.

I giggle, and the urge to behave is slowly shadowed as I notice the same people gasping are also curtsying quickly. Watching me with wide eyes. Adoring eyes. A pain in my cheeks throbs from smiling.

My heart glows at the realization that this place of decadence is where I will live. Where I will rule.

Like the palace of Schönbrunn where I've spent all my summers, each inch of Versailles drips with honey gold and whispers. The talk behind thin fans and hand-covered mouths in my new home is only of excitement, fortunately.

The whispers in Vienna only carried doubt toward me. A disbelief that I was the daughter being sent to repair our country's relations with France.

But to hell with them all.

I'll prove them wrong.

I am royalty. A one-day queen in a place that is ever more grand than Schönbrunn.

Keeping pace with Geneviève proves difficult. Each gulp of air I suck in makes the boning of my corset pierce into my ribs. But each time she turns her head to check that I'm close is all I need to endure the pain.

Her dress is simple yet beautiful, linen an off-white, with the softest hint of yellow like the inner flesh of a lemon. Everything about Geneviève is free. The loose fit of her dress, the words that roll from her tongue, the wildness of her spirit. But the hem of her skirts brushing along the perfectly laid floors is still saturated with blood. My friend wears the evidence of death outside the palace doors, just as I do.

A friend. My friend.

We run faster. I catch glimpses out the windows—so many windows—all revealing the grand gardens I've heard so much about. A bead of sweat gathers on my upper lip when I think of how easy it might be to lose one's self in the tall hedges grown into a maze. I turn away only to find that though we keep running there is no end in sight for the wall of mirrors beside us. The hall is beautiful, the sun filtering in from the windows only to reflect off the mirrors, yet a space like this is like a living nightmare to me. I must be careful to avoid this room from now on. Avoid the—

The voice starts, singing its warnings and whispering its horrors.

"Run and weave, but don't get lost. In the hedges we'll skin her alive with our claws."

We crash into something. Hard. I fall to the marble floor, my palms bearing most of my weight from behind me. Sneering above are two girls, huddled together, looming over me with pure disgust in their gaze. One is tall and slender with pasty white skin. I barely see the pearl necklace around her neck, the same color as her flesh.

The other is short with bosoms so large I find myself a bit jealous. A gigantic mint bow on her chest accentuates them even more, not that she needs anything more to stand out from the crowd. Of course she's the one I bumped into; her face nearly as purple as her dress.

"Apologies," I beg. "I'm M—"

Geneviève steps close to my side, protectively, and I drink in the moment. She reminds me so much of my sister. I'm thankful to have Geneviève until I find Josepha.

"Marie," she says, "you don't need to apologize. We didn't mean to—"

"Marie? As in Marie Antoinette?" The tall girl with an awfully pointy nose leans in closer to get a good look at me.

"Your future family, Victoire. Might want to fix that sour pout on your lips." Geneviève finishes.

"And *you* should remember your place, Geneviève." The purple of the other girl's cheeks begins to soften below what must be forty layers of powder makeup. She shoots an arm out to help me up. I take it, reluctantly.

Their faces transform in a flash, bright smiles as they take me in. They fall into deep curtsies. "Allow us to introduce ourselves. I'm Adélaïde. This is my sister Victoire. We are the king's daughters and we are delighted that you will be joining our family."

Victoire steps in front of her sister seamlessly, as though it is a move she often makes. "Yes, we have been awaiting your arrival for weeks. We need someone of class around this place—and you are absolutely stunning."

"Thank you." Heat flushes across the entirety of my face. I could bask in their compliments for an eternity.

"Excuse me—I have class," Geneviève chimes, clearly ignoring Adélaïde's warning of minding social standing. But instead of further scolding, there's a moment of silence, then all three of them laugh. I'm taken aback, but can't help but join in.

"Ah, Geneviève. Always on the pulse." Victoire's face turns from joyous to a sneer, as though smelling something grotesque. "Speaking of those without class…"

I follow her seedy eyes to a woman in a gorgeous ruby dress. The sun streams on her from the light outside, and though older than I, she has a glow about her. Diamonds the size of grapes dangle from her lobes, nearly reaching her sharp shoulders wrapped in a sheer black shawl.

"I heard another soul died of that treacherous disease last night. Too bad it wasn't her," Adélaïde says, taking me aback. How could anyone want another to die from such a painful illness?

"You two really hate her, don't you?" Geneviève turns to Victoire and Adélaïde.

"Hate who?" My stomach aches the second the words leave my mouth, anxious to ensure it isn't me they despise.

Adélaïde moves close to my ear. She smells of cinnamon, cloaked in a pungent layer of lilies. "Our want-to be step-mother. Madame DuBarry. She's horrible, but our father is blinded by her ability to open her legs with such ease."

Victoire tugs at Adélaïde's elbow, pulling her away from me, but it doesn't stop Adélaïde from talking. "You *must* be on our side, dear Marie. You have power in this palace. More so than us. You must ignore that whore."

I feel my eyes bulge from my skull. Victoire notices and quickly pulls a blue fan out from the folds of her dress and swats Adélaïde with it. "Oh, I'm sorry for my sister. We'll tell you all about her—"

If it weren't for the *swish* of that ruby dress, I would not have noticed her at all. I stumble on my own ankles, but not enough to fall. Enough to lean upon the mirrored wall with an elbow, careful not to look into it. Madame DuBarry approaches without a word, and the moment our eyes meet, she falls into such a deep curtsy it appears she is sitting on the ground.

Something in my stomach slithers darkly. Intuition screams to not speak to this woman, though I know I should. I know Mother would have my head if she received word of my rudeness. Yet, my lips remain sealed. She smiles at me, her own lips painted near the same color as the thick fabric adorning her small frame.

A dry cough breaks the silence. It's a woman as close to Madame DuBarry as Geneviève is to me. Protective.

Her barking cough continues, causing her tall white wig to tremble. She rounds her shoulders, and the top of her pink dress stretches with each struggle her lungs make. I rub my own collarbone. It sounds incredibly painful, so much so I feel it in my own throat. I search the folds of my dress to give her a handkerchief but find none. I should offer to find her help, but Victoire moves in front of me just as easily as she did with her sister.

"You are dismissed, Chloé. DuBarry," Victoire says with a chill in her voice.

Madame DuBarry looks at me with wide eyes, but I am at a loss at what to say, and who I need to impress. Who matters most in this new world of mine.

At my silence, she walks away.

Chloé's fits continue as they walk down the way they came. She finally pulls a square of fabric from her pink dress, coughing deeply. I watch, ignoring the girls beside me who continue to talk about the two women, as the handkerchief comes away from her lips covered in scarlet. The blood from her mouth slowly creeps across the pristine white fabric and stains the pink lace of her cuff.

Madame DuBarry hands her friend a square blue bottle, the shade of sapphire, and Chloé pulls a cork from its top before swallowing down its contents. My eyes strain as they move farther into the distance, remembering Geneviève's mention of blue bottles. Blue bottles carrying the poison that kills unwanted women.

"You just ignored the king's mistress." Geneviève snorts as soon as DuBarry is out of earshot. Her, Adélaïde, and Victoire roll with laughter. I snap myself back into the conversation with the girls, the goosebumps tickling the back of my neck not something I want to draw focus to on the day of my wedding. But the blue of the glass sticks to me, worry that this coughing girl has little time left.

"She didn't even address me," I point out, attempting to rid myself of guilt.

Adélaïde places a soft hand on my shoulder. "She can't. You are the dauphine. Nobody can speak to you until you say something first. So keep that tongue hidden when you're around her. She truly is something most vile. 'Tis a shame it was not her who was attacked today instead of you, Marie."

My stomach drops, remembering the man's dirty face, how hard he held onto me while my feet dangled like a worthless doll.

Victoire replaces her sister's hand with her own upon my shoulder, pushing ever so slightly to turn me around in place. "Pay no mind to my sister. We are glad you are safe."

"How did you learn of what happened?" I ask.

She shrugs. "This is Versailles. Word travels at lightning speed. Though we hoped no attacks took place upon your arrival, Father did increase the guard. There have been threats made upon us all."

Adélaïde claps her hands, shutting her sister up while I sense all color has drained from my face. I am at the center of all this now. What was Mother thinking, sending me here? "That's quite enough, sister. Marie has our wiley Geneviève assigned to her, and she will be quite safe. Besides, Marie, you need not worry of such things today. It is your wedding day. Speaking of, shouldn't you…" she looks around, the halls suddenly empty. "…be getting ready?"

Where have all the people disappeared to?

A groan sounds from behind me. "Etiquette is going to kill me!" Geneviève tugs at me again, flinging me to a swift sprint. Victoire and Adélaïde wave behind us. I can't wait to hear more about Madame DuBarry, the king's mistress, and all these rules of court I had no idea about. But each step I take is one closer to marrying my Louis, and that's more important than all else in this shiny, new world of mine. A world where everyone has welcomed me.

They adore me.

We come upon a closed door the color of fresh cream, outlined with more gold. I wonder how this entire palace can be adorned with so much gold—it makes my eyes strain. There is beauty in that which is carved into the metal though. My face stares back at me through the rose above the knob of the door. Each petal kissing upon the next, the flower frozen in gold just as it is about to bloom.

"You're all alone, don't forget. They all will die; our omens are set."

The abandonment I felt when I first stared at my reflection within the Forest of Compiègne, and when I first stepped foot in Versailles after walking over the dead in the square, surfaces again. Thick and heavy in my chest.

But Geneviève is here. I am not alone. Her fiery hair and spirit are with me. I watch her, waiting to know what is behind this door, swallowing down the worries so I may enjoy my luck. Not omens. *Luck.*

Geneviève scratches on the door. What *is* she doing?

The fingernail she scratches with is longer than the rest, dirt wedged below. She must notice my dismay. "Ah, I forgot you don't know the ins and outs. How different Versailles is from, well, everywhere else. I grow this hideous nail out so I can scratch on doors."

"Why would you scratch on a door? Just turn the knob and go in."

"That would make sense, wouldn't it? But there are two rules I must follow. The first, to enter a bedchamber, I must scratch on the door. Not knock, in case I might interrupt slumber, or… other things." She winks at me again, and it's beginning to be a secret language just between us.

I let out a yelp when the door abruptly swings open in front of us by a man dressed in a more subdued blue than the guards, with thin white linen protruding from the collar and sleeves. He bows and holds the door open with his back.

Geneviève enjoys my scare with a grin from ear to ear. "And the second rule is that fine gentlemen such as Jean here, are the ushers I must wait for to open a door. Going in *or* coming out of a formal room."

"That seems silly," I say in amazement. At the same time, I admire how Geneviève knows Jean's name, that she respects everyone equally.

"Shhhh. Madame Etiquette might hear you." We muffle our laughs as we cross the threshold.

The door closes, but Jean remains in the room. I want the space alone with my friend without being under watch. "Is it possible for us to be alone?" I whisper to Geneviève.

"You are the dauphine. You may dismiss the guards, the help…anyone for that matter."

"Jean," a whimper narrowly escapes my throat as I wring my hands together.

"Madame?" He bows.

I cough, trying to rid myself of the doubts coiling in my chest. "You may be excused. I wish for this space to be only my own. I do not need assistance."

He bows again and leaves without a word, the heavy door sliding against the floor behind him. I bite my lower lip with a smile.

Finally turning to the new space, I immediately fall in love.

"Your apartments, Dauphine." Geneviève curtsies to encourage my laughter.

My apartments. It seems surreal that I should be the one to sleep here. I hurry over to the closest wall and pet my hand down the beautiful image of blue, pink, and yellow flowers bundled over and over again in a pattern of bouquets bursting from one down into the next.

I take a run at my bed and flop onto my back, allowing the pillowy blankets to catch my fall. The whites and pinks threaded in gold are stuffed with so many feathers I shudder to think how many birds had to die for my bed.

My bed. I wave my arms up and down, finding the pillows with my fingertips. After such long travels to get here, it's nice to have a place solely mine.

"Quick, Marie. I have a little something for us before Etiquette gets here with your wedding dress," Geneviève hisses from across the room.

I turn, and on my way to join her, she runs a finger along the wall. I think she is quite a strange girl, until a gap appears and the wallpaper parts perfectly, revealing a secret compartment. A hidden cupboard in the wall—how wonderful! Geneviève holds the door open with one hand, and with the other pulls a shiny green glass bottle out.

Champagne.

"I hid it here just for us. For a few sips. Since they won't let you partake until the reception. And Etiquette would murder me if I made you drunk before walking down the aisle." She takes a drink for herself, and holds the bottle out to me. I take it, gazing into the bubbling liquid within the green glass.

"Swallow it down, drink in your lies. Taste the poison, hear the dead's cries."

I take a swig.

FOUR

The room is in a tizzy. I'm not sure if it is the flurry of women running all about or the champagne I may have had too many sips of, but my stomach lurches to and fro.

I focus on Etiquette to steady myself. She wants my attention anyway, to make sure I am good enough for the royal ceremony.

The ceremony.

My marriage.

I'm already adorned by the beautiful wedding dress. It's heavy. So heavy I question how I will ever walk down the aisle in it. But I will. Toward my Louis. Nothing could keep me from him.

"Walk into darkness, no hope, no love that's true. You're blinded and binded, but the truth is always with you."

I shouldn't have looked in the gigantic mirror hanging perfectly on my chamber wall. Of course the voices don't want me to marry. To realize my happy ending. I want to throw the very pointed heel of my shoe at the glass and end the hissing. But I won't cause a scene. I won't let any further doubts slither into the minds of those around me.

I will have my happy ending.

"I hope Louis changes for your sake." Geneviève's face falls grim. I don't like the way it warps her expression, usually so full with a lust for life.

Not her too.

"The future king need not change, Geneviève. You may have noble blood in your veins, but you are not to speak of the dauphin in such a way." Etiquette pushes in front of her, adjusting the skirts of the white fabric weighing me down with thousands of opalescent beads.

I seal my lips, pressing them together. I don't want to hear anything bad about Louis. He is royalty, chosen by God to be the King of France. There can't be anything wrong about him. There can't.

Geneviève weaves through the chambermaids, finding an overstuffed chair in the corner of the room before sighing so loudly the groan bounces off the floral covered walls, commanding attention. "All I'm saying is that sometimes he scares me a little bit. Always creeping. Lurking around in the shadows observing us all."

"Geneviève, that is what he is meant to do. The dauphin is the ruler of the kingdom. He must observe." Etiquette speaks as if it is just her and Geneviève in the room, like she is her daughter and must be taught a lesson.

"I don't know…those science experiments, working alongside doctors, that rude little friend of his, Alexandre. And have you seen those haunting eyes of Louis'?"

"I quite like his eyes," I interrupt, ignoring everything else she said. "I stared at them for hours through the painted portrait. It is what I hung onto. Those eyes gave—"

"And it's not the strangeness of living in the shadows alone. He's so quiet."

"I'm quiet too. I am most excited to walk through the halls at night. Perhaps he and I shall walk together hand in hand." My heart beats at the thought of holding my husband's hand, exploring Versailles once everyone else has gone to bed. My fingers twitch imagining it.

"And there are those rumors," she says.

"Shush, Geneviève. There are no such things." Etiquette's patience is being tested, as is mine. My face tightens, like I've just eaten a lemon.

"He hunts all day. He must have a thirst for blood. You should run now, Marie." Geneviève leans deeper into the chair and I laugh. Surely, she must be joking.

"That's actually wonderful," I say as Etiquette has a final look at me and shoos the ladies out of my chambers. She must be impressed with the way I look, and this fuels my confidence. "I had many horses in Austria. He and I will ride together. I'll join his long hunting trips."

I spin in the middle of the room and stare down at my dress, admiring the way it moves like waves of the ocean. In the blur of pinks and blues, I notice the far off look crossing Geneviève's face. I plop onto the side of the bed and attempt to catch my breath.

If Mops were here, he'd already be on my lap. If I sat, there he was. My sweet puppy. I miss his curly hair and wet kisses already. Before I cry, I look to Geneviève. Her hands folded on her knees, and shoulders slumped like they carry the weight of the world on them.

"I hope it works out for you, Marie," she says. "I could be wrong, but I'll always tell you what I think. It is what the best of friends do. Like the poison."

Honest to a fault.

My blood heats to a slight simmer. I don't like that she is saying these things. My Louis is perfect. I know it. *I know it.*

"Hush, child! Don't you mind her, Marie." Etiquette taps on my back, urging me to stand. "Just look in the mirror, my dear. I believe you are ready for the biggest day of your life. I think the dauphin and the king will be quite pleased." Etiquette's hands find my shoulders and she guides me toward the mirror.

I don't want to look. Afraid of the voices. The warnings.

"Mold you, shape you, sculpt you out of clay. Becoming someone else until your dying day."

My eyes meet Geneviève's in the mirror, and the voices from the reflections cease. I let loose a sigh, only to be strangled by my corset.

"Don't worry, Marie. If your Louis isn't all you deserve, I'll be here for you. He can have his shadows, and we will have the light."

"That is quite enough, Geneviève. You're going to get yourself killed." Etiquette's mouth playfully turns up into a slight smile and Geneviève shrugs. They must be closer than I realized. "Now Marie, let's go get you married."

The floor is full of suns and the sky is full of angels.

That's what I focus on as I take each slow step down the aisle of Chapel Royale.

To the sides of the aisle, there is no floor. Too many people gathered, stacked one on top of another with their yellowed teeth smiling at me. A balcony circles around the chapel with people pushed up against marble railings so intensely to peer at the scene below, I fear they may topple over and land at my feet.

The organ is loud as thunder, and I feel like it and my heartbeat have become one. But I don't like the song. It's somber and reminds me more of a funeral than the happiest day of my life.

Yet between the haunting notes being played, I hear that painful cough again. Chloé leans over the balcony with the rest of the most finely dressed, attempting to muffle her coughs while Madame DuBarry whispers something into her ear.

I recall Geneviève's words during our carriage ride.

Poison flows through these walls, waiting to drip down our throats.

I finally see my only friend as I near the altar and my jaw, which I now notice was tightly clenched, releases. Geneviève forces a smile, her mouth pinching together even though her eyes droop with sorrow. Madame Etiquette is shoulder to shoulder with her, and in the single second we share a glance, she flips her head to the side, directing me to keep moving down the aisle. I hadn't realized I'd slowed.

I quicken my pace despite the weight of my wedding dress. I just need to get to the altar. A few more steps. Then I'll be with *him*.

Instead of the hundreds of faces of those I have never seen in my life staring at me, I look at the inlay design of the Sun King's emblem in the stone floors. I ignore the hammering within my chest by looking up at the dome ceiling, painted with the image of angels flying between clouds, God's light shining down upon them.

But once I get close enough, the light shines only upon him. Louis. A sign from God, the heavens open and shine upon my one true love. This is meant to be. A sign of no more omens, only luck and fortune and love.

My Louis. Waiting for me at the altar with the archbishop. My smile hurts my cheeks.

This is all real. All of the pain I endured to get here. The braces, the lessons, the discipline. The long hours in the carriages. Stripping me bare in the handing over ceremony. I see now that it was all leading to this moment.

But when I look up, I notice the organ pipes towering over us. Long silver teeth with pointy ends—a wild beast ready to chomp down and gobble us for its dinner.

Thankful for the champagne Geneviève encouraged me to drink whenever Etiquette was not looking, my nerves don't run away from me as I ascend the stairs to Louis. I focus on the stone steps below, instead of the organ bellowing through gleaming pipes above.

Louis nods his head as I join him. I am sure he likes my dress, and I try to fix my eyes on his, to catch the stars that must lay there as he looks upon me.

The Archbishop's words and chants are a blur as he bellows and balances the impossibly tall, ivory biretta atop his head. I imagine him falling backwards and catching fire on all the candles lining the altar behind him—he just might, were it not for the large, gold staff he clings to with his wrinkled hand.

The ceremony runs smoothly and quickly as I admire my now husband. He always seems to be looking off to the heavens. He must be nervous, too. I remind myself that Louis will grow into his features and become handsome with age. He is but a boy, only a year older than I. He will grow into his nose. Surely. He must, because I've dreamt of us together years from now, waving to our adoring masses while we adorn our crowns.

Focusing on the wings of the bronze angels standing tall on the altar, I attempt to push the warnings Geneviève gave about Louis out of my mind. She must have drank too much.

Besides, I am blessed by the angels. I stand here, in the grandest palace, wearing the most beautiful dress with skirts that spread wider than my outstretched arms and a line of perfectly tied bows down the front bodice.

Blessed by angels. *Me*. This is what Mother has always said.

When it is time to sign the wedding certificate my hand shakes uncontrollably. I try my best to steady it as I dip the quill into the inkwell. The tip of the white feather is stained black by the liquid before bringing it to the parchment. I find my new name within the scrolling font on the parchment—Marie Antoinette.

Drip.

A black dot forms on the paper, and I scurry to my name to sign before I ruin this paper that shouldn't mean so much, but does.

The quill meets the parchment and in pressing too hard in my hurry, a large blot of ink expands across the page. I use my best cursive, but the name is new to me and I slant the letters. A smile creeps across my face. Despite how a simple feather with ink weighs so heavy on my shoulders, I have exceeded every expectation people have had about me.

I return the quill to its pot and burst into laughter. I laugh so loudly and so inappropriately I'm sure Madame Etiquette will come up here and scold me any moment now. But I'm too happy to conceal it.

I am married. Mother must be proud.

Louis gapes at me, shocked. I swallow hard—perhaps I shouldn't have drank the alcohol from the green glass. But then, by some miracle, he joins my laughter. "I have never met anyone quite like you before, Marie Antoinette."

"I hope that is a good thing," I reply, sheepishly. All I had hoped for coming true.

His hand moves across the signing table, fingers closing in on mine, an inch apart, yet close enough I can feel his body heat. He wants to be near me. He wants to feel my touch. "It is," he says.

And then his hand fully embraces my own. On display, in front of the entire court as we sit before them at the front of the chapel. Something inside me bursts to life as my fingers intertwine with his and he raises me from the chair at the signing table. He leads me back down the aisle and the entire court claps and bows as we pass.

It feels as though a dream has been ignited. All the endless hours I spent as a child staring into the clouds under the Vienna sky weren't all for naught as mother told me they were. I had been concocting the image of just this, here in the chapel, fulfilling my role and finding love.

If only Josepha were here.

As always, I search for her amongst the people piled into the marbled church. For the violet ribbon that never left her hair. Oh, how mother hated that ribbon. Josepha refused to take it off, regardless of the occasion or the color of her dress.

"Purple is meant for mourning the lost," Mother would say. Always so many words of wisdom, it's difficult to keep them all straight.

"Aren't we all a little lost? Aren't we always losing someone?" Answers like this would immediately quiet Mother and impress me. How I would love to speak to her that way, to be as brave and unapologetic as Josepha. My sister teetered on the tightrope of life and death with her obsession of remembering the dead and reminding me of the dark omens nipping at my heels.

"Are you a good dancer?" Louis' voice snaps me from the daydream and disappointment floods my veins when I don't see Josepha in the crowd. Had she been in Paris at all, she surely would have been here today to witness my wedding. How wonderful it would have been to have one single person here that I knew.

His sweaty palm releases from mine and I soak in the moment of being alone with him in the hallway.

"I adore dancing, Your Highness." I curtsy, but his arm quickly links into the crook of my elbow, pulling me up.

"There's no need for that. You are my wife now." He snaps his arm away and looks down toward the floor. There is a meekness to him, something so unexpected for the future King of France. "I like to dance. It is quite mathematical, you know? Counting, distance, measurements, predictions."

"I like the music. And the spinning."

"Yes," is all he mutters before turning his back to me, walking away. My heart falls to my stomach, setting my mind into a spiral. Have I read everything wrong? Or maybe I said something wrong; I can do that. I always do that.

Stupid girl.

"Shall we?" he calls after a few paces. I pick up my skirts and hurry towards him. Happy again. This marriage will be wonderful. We will have joy and rule all of France together. Together.

The sun settling upon the gardens of Versailles has transformed to a magnificent red. The sunset casts a glow on the sculptures rising from their fountains.

I follow Louis through the palace in utter silence. Our footsteps echo through each new hallway, bouncing between pillars and high ceilings, against panes of stained glass I avoid looking directly at. The halls look different than they did this morning as sunlight filtered through them. Now, the faces in portraits are shadowed, shrouded with dark brushstrokes that make them look mysterious. Like they hold secrets of the past.

I'm not quite sure what to say to Louis, and so I say nothing at all. Nor does he. The silence is a ribbon tying around my nerves. When we finally come to the threshold of the grand ballroom, he takes my hand again and smiles.

The awkwardness of our silence is quickly erased by the soft melody of violins and the beauty of the ballroom. Were it not for the stage at the far end, I would never have guessed this was the new theatre turned ballroom.

No light left in the sky, the windows are full of only twinkling stars. Hundreds of golden candelabras hold tight to white candlesticks, their flames creating a glittering effect filling the room.

Ushers meet us within seconds, offering glasses of champagne. The liquid warms my throat as I empty the crystal glass in four gulps. Another usher appears to replace the drink. Back home was never like this. I wasn't allowed alcohol. Let alone have someone there at the ready to provide more.

I attempt to steady myself, not swallow too quickly, but the stem in my hand begs to be lifted. I face the honey-colored drink, waving within the crystal.

"Marie, Marie. Don't forget about me. The bubbles upon your lips, you'll lose your wits."

A warning?

Damn the voice. Damn the omens. Damn being proper.

I have done all they wanted today. All mother dreamed I would pull off. Now, I deserve to celebrate.

I drink the champagne down, and hand it to an usher.

"Let's dance," I say to Louis. He nods, ever so proper.

How quickly the ballroom has filled. Strangers watch me like a bird in a gilded cage. But what a beautiful cage, with rows of tables covered with pastries in every color of the rainbow, some I have never even seen before. Crystallized fruits fill plates, gleaming with their sugary syrup so beautifully I can taste them on my tongue without taking a bite. Scattered between the plates are incredible arrangements of soft pink roses. I move to one, grazing over it with my thumb and forefinger. Softer than velvet. And it's all for me. I can barely believe it.

The glaring court is also dazzling in their finest wear. The men's wigs of white have tight curls resting over their ears, the women's hair stuck with long, wispy white feathers.

The fabrics. *Oh, the fabrics.* Mother would be so impressed with the velvets and satins and embroidered details of each body in the room. An ache blooms in my ribs at the thought of my mother missing my wedding day.

Mine and Louis' movement to the center of the floor sends a signal to our guests. A formation of two lines appears, shoulders close together with me in the middle, facing Louis in the line opposite. He may not be the most handsome in the room, but I am sure he is kind, not at all as Geneviève painted him to be.

I know the dances, the moves. Etiquette would be proud of my knowledge in this. I only wish more of my lessons in Austria could have been about dancing and piano.

The music grows from soft violins to an entire orchestra—booming cellos and horns and piano from the corner. I could get used to this. I make eye contact with Louis and smile as brightly as I can. He smiles back as he spins, the night quickly becoming the best of my life.

We all move in unison, and it feels like pure magic. I could spend each and every day of my life drinking alcohol and dancing and die a happy girl. The lines become entwined as we hold hands up to partners and rotate round one another, before moving on to the next partner.

I meet up with Louis again, and trip on my dress ever so slightly. His arms find my waist, saving me from meeting the shiny marble floor. His hands remain there to steady me and his dark eyes look into mine, a smirk forming on his lips. My head falls back and I laugh. Louis joins me and we both laugh so fiercely it hurts my stomach in the best way, finally joined as one beyond a piece of paper.

His hands slip away from me as we begin dancing again. I twirl in delight, continuing to laugh. Until I see *her*.

From deep within the sea of people she appears. Blonde, natural hair bouncing within the powdered wigs worn by all the other women here. I become weightless as my heart races faster than the notes of the music we dance to.

Someone blocks my vision, their hand out to me, ready to take our dance steps. I raise my hand and turn with him so that I may find the blonde again. The blonde with the violet ribbon.

My neck cranes, moving back and forth, searching through the symphony of dancers. It must be her. It *must* be.

There!

I knew it. I knew she would not miss today.

My feet carry me towards her. I push aside the bodies standing in my way.

Her face. I see her face. The pale porcelain and perfect dimples are unmistakable. But why doesn't she look at me? Why does she not run to me?

Louis grabs tight to my hand, pulling me back to the dancefloor. He twirls me in close to him, face to face. "Are you well? What is wrong?" He asks kindly, his brows furrowed with concern.

"I must go," I rake his fingers from my own.

"Who did you see?" He says, trying to grab my hand back.

"I will miss her!" Is all I manage to say over my shoulder, my feet carrying me to my sister. My heart drums with excitement to see Josepha, and the fear of the consequences I may face for leaving Louis alone on the dance floor on our own wedding night.

"Marie!" Louis calls out, the volume soft from the distance I've already created.

"Josepha!" I call out desperately. "Josepha!" My hands cup around my mouth to amplify the sound. She doesn't respond. Doesn't acknowledge my existence. I follow her, falling over people, careful not to let her loose from my sight.

The sway of her hair is burned into my memory after so many afternoons chasing butterflies and fleeing from our governess. The way the violet of the thin satin ribbon curled through the air then is exactly as it does in front of me now.

"Stop! Josepha!" The plea burns my throat. "Josepha!"

Warm air surprises me and I nearly topple down stairs and into a fountain. She has led me all the way outside, and still has not acknowledged my existence. Tears prickle and sting my eyes.

As my feet hit the compacted dirt below them, I realize I've lost my shoes along this chase. The drink that tasted so delicious upon my lips now influences my mind.

"Feeeee, faaaaw fummm. I smell the blood of an earthly man." The melody carries from the garden hedges my sister has disappeared into. "Let him be alive or dead, off goes his head."

Not the voice from reflections. It's her. I would know that voice anywhere. The nursery rhyme she would sing while we played hide and seek in the winter palace. Calling to me through song to come find her.

"I'm coming, Josepha! I'm coming!"

My fingers clench into my skirts, lifting my dress higher so I can run faster.

I turn around a corner and close in on her. She has stopped, just staring at the hedges.

"Josepha," I say breathlessly, pulling at her shoulder to turn her around. "It's really you!"

We hold each other close, relishing in the hug I've prayed would be mine once more.

"Marie," she whispers as we part.

My lips pull into a wide smile simply hearing her voice. I have so many questions for her. The mixed emotions urge tears to cascade. "Why are you at Versailles? Why did you leave me?"

She presses a finger to my lips. Then her own, shushing us both. I blink, perplexed, when she suddenly turns like a top and takes off behind a wall of greenery.

"Stop playing games!" I shout, running after her yet again.

My vision turns to a blur of green within the labyrinth. My chest heaves as I grow lightheaded from loss of breath.

I can't lose her. Not again.

The minutes melt into an eternity of my nose running, throat swelling, and vision blurring. The perfectly manicured hedges close in on me as the uneven earth plays tricks on my feet. My world turns as dark as the night sky above me.

I've slowed, but I won't give up. She's here. After all this time.

Josepha.

Josepha.

My fingers find the hedges, sharp enough to ground me. To make my head stop spinning. I turn another corner in the maze when my stomach hits the dirt. My hands dig in and I immediately feel layers of skin on my palms have been torn from catching my fall.

I crane my neck, twisting my torso to look behind me and catch a glimpse of what knocked me down.

A pile of white linen rests just beyond my feet. White with the softest tint of yellow. I push myself up to sit, noticing pale skin covered in freckles illuminated by moonlight sticking out from the heap of fabric.

A body.

I slowly crawl over, my elbows shaking from the sight before me and the weight of my body.

Red is everywhere. A mess of fiery hair. A thick gash of crimson along her throat. Scarlet staining the neckline of her dress.

Not Josepha.

Geneviève.

Geneviève and so much blood.

FIVE

At first the screams are silent.

My mouth hangs open, but nothing comes out.

Light hits the pool of blood around her. The voices hissing from it.

"One of many, gone too soon. She's dead and broken, beneath the moon."

Small pebbles imprint themselves into my palms as I scramble to Geneviève on all fours. My fingers finally reach her shoulders, and latch on tight to shake her.

"Please," I cry to her unmoving face, "please, Geneviève. Wake up. Wake up."

She's alive. She *must* be alive.

Of course she is. Because she and I are going to be like sisters. I lost Josepha. I can't lose her. I need Geneviève.

"What happened?" I ask, trying to shake her when I notice a sprig of violet on her chest, caked to her by blood, the purple flower barely poking through the crimson. "Geneviève, what happened? Help! Someone, please, help! I'm getting help now, Geneviève. You're going to be laughing and running with me in no time."

I caress her lovely face, unintentionally smearing her own blood down her cheek. She is so beautiful. But her face is pale, white as porcelain with a hint of blue tinging her skin and lips.

"Help!" I try again, sure I hear footsteps, but still no one comes.

My heart turns to stone with the truth—she won't wake up. My skirts drenched with blood tell me she's not sleeping.

Screams fill the night sky. So loud God Himself must hear. No words form, only a piercing note of horror that flies from my throat.

She promised she'd be with me. That we would be best friends forever. Stick by my side.

Fear hammers in my heart, waking me from the reverie. Who could have done this? Hot tears spill down my cheeks as I look around. But I can't see anything but green walls of branches and the black sky above.

"Help!" I scream it again, and stare back down at Geneviève. There is no helping her. Not anymore. Not with the thick slice gouged into her throat, from ear to ear, revealing her insides. It breaks me. It is Geneviève's voice that made her so strong, so sure. Yet here she lay now; the source of her cunning words left a gaping hole slick with blood.

"Help!"

It is me who needs saving now. A knot in my belly loops and tightens. My eyes dart from one direction of this wretched maze to another, realizing how isolated I am. *Exposed.* Whoever killed my friend may well be just around the corner of this devil's maze.

I should not have yelled for help, announcing where I am.

Sounds of the party linger faintly in the distance, but someone is drawing nearer.

Footfalls echo with each step in the dirt. Moving closer.

I attempt to quiet the beating of my heart raging within my ears to decipher which direction I will need to flee from the killer. He has come back to finish me off too.

I'm too late.

My body curls into itself, folded over Geneviève's body. I can not stop the quivering of my body, preparing for its end. My chest rises and falls quickly, while I look beyond her slashed throat to make my friend's face the last thing I see. She looks so peaceful. No more suffering at the hand of men, the neglect that hurt her heart so.

Someone is behind me now. But they are gasping. More than one person. I turn, met with more gasps. Not from a killer, from the guards and ladies of the court. The many who just witnessed my wedding now find me kneeling beside Geneviève, covered in blood, still in my wedding gown of white silk and sparkling crystals.

I will live.

But Geneviève will not.

A cry rips through me. The court watching in silence as I fill the air with my screams.

Mother would kill me if she were here. A spectacle of the worst measure—one that fuels sour words on lips and disapproval of the crown on my head.

"Hush, now. Hush, Marie." A coo in my ear. Hands pulling me up from the crooks of my arms.

My Louis.

Come to save me. A hero in the midst of chaos.

Louis adjusts his hold on me as we hobble through the maze, taking me in the opposite direction that my sister fled. And away from my new friend.

I don't feel my feet walking, nor do I see my husband's face. Only the cold stone I'm eventually seated down on.

"Fetch her a drink, damn it." He demands of someone off in the distance and within a moment his small hands press my own to the stem of a glass. The tickle of bubbles on my tongue wakes me from the haze.

"Louis?"

"Yes, I am here. You are safe." I gaze at his mouth as he says the words. Wishing they were true. Because I don't feel safe. I feel cold, and the goosebumps across my flesh won't dissipate since finding Geneviève like…that.

"What happened?" he asks. "You ran so quickly from the dance. The guards had quite the time finding you— what in heavens were you after? How did you come across the girl?"

"Geneviève," I say, wanting the whole world to know she is much more than *the girl*.

"Yes. How did you come to find Geneviève?"

"My sister—she—she was here," I sniffle.

Louis' head swivels, looking behind him for a girl who looks like me. "Which sister? Where has she gone? Where was she?"

"Josepha. She ran into the maze, but I lost her. Again." Mucus runs from my nose, and I don't bother to wipe it, not when it will meld with the salty river of tears.

And then I found Geneviève.

She's dead. She's dead.

"You saw Josepha? What does she have to do with finding poor Geneviève in such a way?" His questions are too fast. Too many. They hurt my head. I have no answers. Only more questions that come with each new tear streaming down my face. Where did my sister go? What happened to my sister? And my friend? How can Louis be so cold, demanding so many answers from me I cannot possibly possess in this moment?

I try to soothe the pain in my head, rubbing at my temples.

"Hush. No worries of such matters," he says, beginning to stroke my hair. "I will deal with all matters and examine the body. You just rest your pretty head."

I am not comforted by his words. A film of fright still sticks to me. Afraid I'll meet an end like Geneviève.

"Thank you, Louis," I say, forcing myself to look at him and feign a small smile. The thought of the fingers in my hair poking and prodding at the corpse of my friend makes me feel more hollow than I already do. He claps a hand on my back twice before breaking contact and focuses back on the party. I'm thankful.

The opening to the labyrinth of hedges is barely visible beyond the sea of people who have gathered. As though all of Versailles has come together to witness the spectacle of death. I fear it will end in more trampling as it did upon my arrival, as the savages with pockets full of gold pull and pry at one another to get a better look at the victim. Of Geneviève. The hum of so many voices is indistinguishable but the volume continues to rise. And then the sea of glittering fabrics parts.

Alexandre appears, holding Geneviève's dead body in his arms. A fresh stream of tears bursts from my eyes again, uncontrollably. *She is really dead.*

His left arm is wedged below her knees, and her back is arched across his right arm, leaving her head to lull and bounce. My nails dig into my palms, wanting to run to my friend and cradle her in my arms. To scream at Alexandre for not taking care. Why is *he* holding on to her? Why is a doctor or even the guard not taking care of her?

My lids close—I can't bear to watch, and I can't do anything to help her. So I shut it out. Perhaps if I close my eyes this will all go away and I can go back to my happy wedding night.

The trickling of the fountain at my back assists my breath to slow.

"Look at me, Marie. Do not focus on all of that." I wait for Louis to reassure me with his touch, but it never comes. So I turn toward him and open my eyes, chewing the inside of my cheek raw. He is my husband after all, and if he asks me to look at him, that I shall do.

There is no emotion in his face, no comforting smile, no kind eyes. But of course there wouldn't be. He didn't know Geneviève like I did. She hadn't been there for him through the chaos of today. She was *my* friend. I can barely control my trembling lips as I bring the champagne glass to them. The only person who genuinely cared about me in this new world is gone. Carried away without a care in the arms of my husband's best friend.

"It is a shame. Geneviève had such a—" he inhales through his crooked nose, "fire about her. And I am sorry it was her you connected with today just to be killed."

"You knew her well?"

He waves a hand dismissively. "Barely. Enough to know she enjoyed the company of boys, and boys do talk. She was the subject of several mornings in the forest while we hunted."

My stomach tightens, growing heavy as the stone ledge I'm perched on. Does he have no idea how special she was? How her red hair floated as she ran? How her smile made me giggle? How that little side grin of hers would set my nerves at ease if only for a moment?

No, he mustn't. Otherwise, he wouldn't say such things.

"Were you given a tour of the grounds today?" he asks.

Why would he ask such trivial questions? "No. We—we stayed in the palace."

"Ah, then you did not see this magnificent beauty." His torso twists toward the statue in the fountain behind us, and I follow his lead. "Just look at it. Apollo, the God of the Sun, just as my grandfather was the Sun King."

The metal sculpture is large and domineering, yet the way the water shoots from it—raining down into the pool below—is entrancing. But why in God's name does he focus on a bloody sculpture right now?

"Look at his strength," my Louis continues, "he grabs onto the reins of his horses, steady in his chariot. He struggles though. Because look below. Look at all the horses. They are said to be set afire, as to light up the world."

Apollo's chariot is pulled by four horses, all galloping from the depths of the water, their hind legs immersed completely. Each face is pained and I imagine in place of the splashing water flames licking up their bodies instead. The muscles in their muzzles are strained, bulging up through metallic skin. But it's the eyes that will haunt my dreams tonight. The artist captured that of tortured souls. For wouldn't any living creature be tortured to endure the burning heat of fire to serve others?

Moonlight dances amongst the waves of the splashing water, but not loud enough to drown out the voice that makes me shiver uncontrollably.

"You'll pull, you'll scrape, but from this place there's no escape. You cry in vain, for all will happen once again."

"They seem to be treading with all their might," Louis says, as if pulling the thoughts straight from my mind, "like they are trying to survive being drowned within the waters. And that's what they do. Day after day they keep treading, keep moving along."

"They look so scared," I say, and he grabs my hand and squeezes tight. I almost fall into the fountain, his touch so unexpected. But I ease into it. Relishing his skin upon mine.

"Death is normal, Marie. Especially in these times. Especially as my bride. Just listen to the news of our streets being lined with piles of the dead, ravaged by diseases. It is everywhere. But Apollo, he survives. He must. And so must we. But not everyone can, and you must learn to accept that." His hand releases mine as quickly as it had found it a second ago.

"We must keep treading." My words are a whisper.

"Ah, my grandson, you fail to remind sweet Marie that we of course will survive. You. Me. Her." I leap out of my skin when the king's firm grip meets my shoulder. He appeared out of nowhere, but seems to have heard every word my Louis has said.

"Why then didn't my friend survive?" I ask, but it comes out more like a plea of desperation to understand how this happened.

"My dear Marie. You have been chosen by the gods. All the kings and queens are. Divine intervention birthed you into royalty, and even better, brought you to France to stand beside the most noble of blood. Your friend, and all of the people around us," his arm sweeps into the darkness, gesturing to the hundreds of people dancing and laughing in the gardens like a dead girl wasn't just carried past them, "are not of our status. We will die, to reunite with God in heaven, but we will not die like the rest of them. We die with dignity. They die from a place of petulance. Of lower class, and amongst their filth and disease."

My fingers curl around the champagne glass with force. Geneviève was not filth. I imagine Mother's hushed voice, demanding me to bite my tongue until it bleeds. I can't. "But I—"

"No need to worry. You are safe. Correct, Louis?" The king's unruly gray brows lift to get Louis' attention, who is sitting on the other side of me still lost in thought looking at Apollo.

"Yes. Safe." His eyes don't move from the strained and horrified faces of the horses.

"There you have it, Marie. She was no one of importance. Now, we need to refill that glass of yours and celebrate this night. Don't allow some silly little illegitimate's end to soil the beginning of something so grand. You are officially my granddaughter now, and so we shall celebrate." He moves to his feet and pins his shoulders back to puff out his chest, then crosses in front of me and stands by Louis. His elbow nudges him in the arm. "And then the real fun part comes, when you make a man of Louis."

Louis' face flushes and he stays silent. As do I. The world around us is the exact opposite. It's cheering and laughter, violins and footfalls, conversation and shouting. It's everything that my heart is not.

Eying a girl my age, holding tight to her belly while she giggles and a man whispers into her ear, I ponder how she does it. How she pushes her surroundings down, pretends that reality is only gossip, and not a truth to be faced.

Another glass of champagne appears before me, and I swallow it down along with the pain. They don't care. Maybe I don't have to either. I stand, but my knees do not agree. I fumble, nearly falling to the ground before the talons of Etiquette pierce my arm and pull me in close to her.

"Keep your wits about you, girl," she scolds. Always scolding me. But then her hand moves to a strand of hair pressed to my cheek, moving it to behind my ear. She holds her hand there for a moment, inhaling deeply. "I do not wish anything to happen to you too," she whispers.

"I'm trying to do as the king wishes. I'm supposed to—to celebrate." I scrunch my nose, hoping it stops the tears from creeping out.

"What happened?" Etiquette pulls her hand back quickly, a fake smile broadening as a pair of courtiers pass by.

"I do not know. I was searching for my—" I look around, stalling to find an excuse for being in the maze without telling her my sister is here. I'm supposed to be rid of all that is Austria. I cringe to think of how Etiquette would react to the mention of Josepha, the sister who shirked her duty, "—I was out for fresh air and to explore the gardens, when I found her. I tripped…" The vile taste rising to my tongue stops me from saying the words aloud. I look down at my hands, stained in crimson, matching the color of my once white wedding dress.

"Who could have…why…?" The slump of Etiquette's shoulders and her loud exhale surprise me. Her eyes become glazed but she quickly shakes her head and waves a hand in front of her face, wiping herself clear from emotions. "No matter. You must smile. Be presentable. You are the one everyone is looking to now and you must carry on with celebrating. The king is right. Of course, of course, the king is right."

She touches her lips to the back of her hand and walks away.

My feet freeze in place, watching the scene unfold before me. I see DuBarry in the distance, watching me, and

Victoire and Adélaïde watch her. It all seems so trite, their petty games. Yet, I'm the most important chess piece on the board now.

Alexandre's hand grazes the curve at the base of my back, petting me gently. I turn to him abruptly, pulling my skirt with me. "What is a pretty little thing like you doing just standing aside?" His voice is thick as sap. Like he is lapping up his prey, his next conquest before he leads them to the bedchamber.

"How dare—"

"I was merely complimenting you, Princess." He grabs my hand and kisses the tips of my fingers. "Louis surely was blessed when the deals were signed to have you be his wife. And don't worry, you'll grow those bosoms eventually."

A skitter runs down my spine. He should be in the stables with the pigs, not the best friend of the dauphin. "My Louis would not like you speaking to me in such a manner."

"Just between us then." A statement with a wink. Not a question. It makes my skin crawl.

Alexandre rubs his jaw, judging every inch of my body. The staining on his cuff brings me right back to the maze. Geneviève's insides stained on the white fabric. My eyes fall to the dry blood all over my hands, my arms. Nobody has rushed me to get cleaned up. This is just…normal. And Alexandre is too focused on my lack of breasts to care about the blood from the girl he carried from the labyrinth.

"Where did you put her body?"

"Do not worry your beautiful face about that. The girl's death is of no consequence." The nonchalance on his lips grates my nerves.

"I want to know. Tell me. And why is it *you* who carried her out?" I command, but he ignores me.

"We should not speak of the dead, Marie. I wouldn't want her ghost to haunt me," he laughs.

I need to get away from him.

Pushing past Alexandre, doubled over with his smugness, I head toward Victoire and Adélaïde.

I will dance.

I will shake the muck within me off. Listen to the king and my husband. They know what is best.

Grabbing a drink from a man's hand, I pour the alcohol down my throat as I continue to walk.

My sister is well and good, and *here*!

My life is good. I am blessed. I am royalty. This is my fairytale.

There are no omens. My duty has led to a happy marriage. My heart blossoms, knowing I will find my sister in these palace walls and we will once again cuddle by fires, telling stories.

If only I could bring Geneviève back.

"My friends!" The king calls for everyone's attention. "Please, come powder your wigs and noses. It is time to watch your future king and queen take to their wedding bed."

This is my fairytale. I'll repeat it until I believe it.

This is my fairytale.

SIX

There's not enough water in all of France to wash away the blood, and the death, and the guilt.

Not that anyone cared to see Geneviève's blood all over me. I had to insist a bath be prepared. It is no wonder Versailles singes the hairs in my nose—to bathe is a rarity. They don't believe cleaning is important, leaving their skin and stench raw until not even perfumes can mask it. But it would have been impossible for me to scrub through the layers of dried crimson and mud using the basin at my bedside with all those people standing around.

It all floats around me now though. My face distorted by the murky water, looking back up at me.

"Unclean, unclean, forever you'll be. Thousands of eyes, you'll never be free. Don't try to hide, they will soon see."

I swat at the reflection, disrupting the water covered with rose petals, frustrated at the reminder I don't care to hear. But the voice is right. It is as though I am in a cell, destined to experience the world on my own, yet I'm the least lonely girl in the world. There is always, *always* someone around. I am constantly surrounded, yet nobody pays me any mind. All show and lip service and I'm their doll on display.

Even now, a chambermaid stands against the gilded wall, arms clasped around a white towel, looking down at her toes. She is the same quiet girl with the saucer eyes who pulled my Mops from me. A part of me wants to dismiss her, like I dismissed Jean. Like Geneviève told me I had the power to do.

But I don't want to be alone with the voice right now.

The sounds of the court outside the door grows louder. Impatience slithers amongst them, angry for my request to have a few moments to wash before going to bed on display. Not a single soul asked how I was, nor if I was hurt.

Just drink more.

Swallow, swallow, swallow.

My palm runs along my upper arm, down to my elbow. Droplets of water graze my skin, leaving gooseflesh in its wake.

"Skin is slick, so was the mud, you slipped on her, bathed in her blood."

"Stop it. I need to get clean. I need to," I beg while rubbing my hands up and down my bare knees, pulled to my chest, glistening from the flickering candlelight bouncing off the water.

"Pardon, your Highness, I did not hear that. How may I assist you?" The chambermaid moves forward, eyes careful to only look above my neck.

"Oh, I'm sorry. Just talking to myself." Maybe I shouldn't have said that. Maybe she will think I am not of sound mind. "What is your name?"

"My name is Anne, your Highness." She curtsies, a strand of black hair falling from the ribbon holding the rest up. Her features are soft—rounded nose, pouty lips, and impossibly tiny waist without a corset. "And I—I do apologize about your dog. I did not want—"

"I know. We have all been made to do things we wish not to do. And you may call me Marie," I say, pulling my knees closer to my chest. Thinking of my darling Mops makes me miss him more, but I must be kind with Anne; her mouth hangs in sadness. "I didn't see you at the wedding or reception today, Anne."

"Comtesse de Noailles had me helping her with the wedding preparations today." I notice she doesn't say Your Highness or my name. "And after… well, I was trying to help her out in any way I could."

"Etiquette was upset about Geneviève?" I thought I sensed something by the fountain, but she made me smile so quickly I thought perhaps her heart was as hard as the stone of Apollo.

"Etiquette?" Her head tilts to her shoulder.

"A name for the Comtesse that Geneviève and I devised today." *Today*. It was only this morning that I met Geneviève in the tent. That she spun me around and made me laugh through the darkness. It was only this afternoon that we ran through the halls of the palace and her lungs breathed more life than anyone I've ever known.

"Oh, yes. She was close with Geneviève. But life must go on and we must fulfill our duties." Anne gulps and stares back down to her feet.

Every part of my body is screaming on the inside, desperate to be alone, but now here is an opportunity to uncover more about Etiquette and Geneviève, and maybe even my Louis. Geneviève's insinuation as I dressed for the wedding ceremony has itched at my skin since she uttered them—that Louis was always lurking and that he scared her.

What is he always watching for? Maybe he was trying to keep them all safe. Yes. Perhaps he should have been lurking more and Geneviève would be with me now. I should have pried while my wedding dress was being tied.

I scrub my face with my wet fingers. The powder quickly turns to a white liquid in my hands.

I must rely on the chambermaids now. They are all around the palace, waiting in silence with open ears. Surely, if anyone had information, it would be them. It would be Anne.

"Did you know Geneviève?" I ask.

"For a few years now." Anne takes a step back.

"I'm sorry."

"I'm sorry for you too, Marie." She finally says my name, but it's so quiet I barely hear her. As if there is more to follow but she is afraid to speak out of turn.

The water turns colder by the moment, but I try not to let it show.

"Thank you. Anne, I hope you can help me. There are so many whispers in this place, and I don't know what is fable and what is truth. Do you know anything about the rumors of Geneviève?"

"Just that she was well loved. Popular with the boys. I hope that had nothing to do with tonight." She squeezes the towel tighter.

Much like my sister, Geneviève longed for love. From men who think a woman is only good for one thing. Embers set flame in the pit of my stomach.

"I hear Madame DuBarry is also popular?"

"Oh, I can't say about the king's lady." Her voice lowers, "but I do know that the king's daughters truly dislike her. It's not a secret, but I believe it does well to follow Adélaïde and Victoire's lead in social standards. And so, I think many dislike Madame DuBarry."

I attempt to think of my home in Austria, and how Mother would never stand for us pushing out another of such high standing. My fingernail grazes my eyebrow. How can everything be *so* different here?

Shifting to the edge of the tub, I prop my arms on the edge, criss-crossing them and laying my chin upon them, thinking of the blue bottle Madame DuBarry slipped Chloé. "What about the poisoned women? Geneviève told me a bit about them. Is that really true?"

"There are many women who wind up dead here." Her face turns white, and she inhales deeply into her nose. "You must be getting cold, Marie. Can I help you out of the bath?" I do not press her change of subject when I notice the tears welling in the corners of her eyes.

"No, no. This is nice, talking with you. There's a lot waiting for me out there, and I'm not quite ready." We both look at the door, the clamoring getting louder as my bath gets chillier. Gooseflesh rises along my arms.

"Did you happen to see a girl with long blonde hair with a violet ribbon tonight? I saw her right before I went into the hedges." I bite my lip, hoping Anne knows who I'm talking about, and that she somehow knows Josepha.

"I did not. Everyone I saw was wearing their white wigs."

"Have you met someone here named Josepha? She would have been among the royal, I'm sure." I swallow, doubting myself. Perhaps Josepha tried to stay hidden, not shiny and glittering in gold, so Mother would not find out she was in Versailles. It was our little secret, her adoration of Paris. As children she would whisper how much grander life was at Versailles compared to our home.

Anne looks up to the ceiling, searching her mind. "No," she finally says, "I know not of a girl named Josepha."

My teeth release my lip and I can't help my disappointment. I need to change the subject. Change it before I break down, naked in this tub. "Do you have a boy in your life, Anne?"

Her eyes make little jumps back and forth as she studies my face for the first time. Trying to read me like a book, see if she can trust me through my blue eyes. I smile to set her at ease.

I need friends. I need to be loved.

"I ask because I may be a bit nervous about tonight, but I'm excited too. To connect with Louis in this way. There is nothing that sets my stomach aflutter more than talking about love."

Anne finally smiles back at me. "I was in love once. He made me have that same flutter you speak of. Where hundreds of butterflies flap their wings in your belly and your chest at the sound of his voice or the mention of his name."

"What *is* his name?"

"I shouldn't say. He no longer looks at me the way he used to. I thought he loved me. I gave everything to him. But there were too many other chambermaids for him to play with, and I became a discarded toy."

"That is horrible. You must tell me his name."

She bites her lower lip. I must know him, otherwise she would not be so afraid to share the name. I pray it is not Louis. Not my Louis. Please, please, not the boy I am about to lay with. The boy I have married and will spend an eternity with. It would kill me right here in this bathtub to know that he sleeps with women, uses them as Anne describes just to spit them back out.

"Alexandre," she finally says.

Blood rushes back to my head to know it is not Louis, but the lump in my throat does not dissipate, sorry that Alexandre's smooth talking had worked on such a sweet girl like Anne.

"He is despicable. I shall speak to my husband about him."

"No, Marie. Please." She runs to the tub and drops to her knees. Our noses almost touch as she leans in close. "He would have me—"

"Anne!" Etiquette appears from nowhere. We had been so enthralled in our conversation, we hadn't heard the door open. "What are you doing?" Her voice is shrill and horrified.

"Comtesse, Anne has done nothing wrong. She was just about to help me out of the tub. The water has become ice and I'm afraid I might freeze and not be able to carry out my duties. And I know how much you would hate that."

Etiquette shoves Anne out of the way, yanking the towel from her hands. She unfolds the fabric and gives a flick of it in the air before pulling me up and out of the water. She doesn't give a single care that I am naked and exposed, barely letting the towel touch my body before I am standing shivering at the side of the tub.

"You have held everyone up long enough, Marie. I do not want people to speak ill of you. So please, let's get you dried and dressed." She pats my arms down with the towel, her speed resulting in aggressiveness. Though I don't love her rough exterior, it warms me to think she cares enough about me to be concerned about the perceptions of the court.

"My life has always revolved around what others think," I tell Etiquette, sucking in a breath and wondering why I open to her so freely. All of my decisions are weighed heavily, each bearing the burden of responsibility and entire countries. "Mother would want me to keep up with court— that much I'll always keep in the back of my mind. And so I shall impress them. I will make new friends."

"You *are* impressive, Marie," she says, and my heart flutters at the compliment though my body shivers while she dries my legs. "But they always long for more. Your mother is right. And you shall make plenty of friends."

"I made a friend," I breathe the words while my eyes draw down to the shiny floor.

Etiquette pauses, then wraps the towel around me. She turns to fetch the nightgown hanging on the back of a chair.

"I am sorry your time with Geneviève was cut so short," her voice cracks before facing me again. "She truly adored you, Marie. And she was a wonderful girl, despite being the target of ridicule. I put her in your charge as I thought it was what would keep you safe, and now—now Geneviève is gone." Etiquette's mouth draws a thin line, commanding herself to not cry, but I see it in her eyes.

My nose begins to run and I sniffle it back quickly, hoping to hold the threatening tears. "I adored her too, and how now am I to make new friends?" My chest aches, especially since Geneviève reminded me of my sister…both lost in a single night. How can I ever possibly give myself to others when they eventually leave me?

My own sister left me in the maze after hushing me. She was always more careful than I and she must have wanted me to remain quiet to keep me safe. My jaw clenches tight, thinking of what she had been so scared of, what she was warning me of and running from. My poor Josepha.

"We shall both try our best," Etiquette says.

My head emerges from the creamy linen nightgown Etiquette pulls over me, and I gaze at the bath. The filth stands still, blades of grass and perfect pink roses along with bits of Geneviève's flesh floating on the surface of the brown, muddied water.

"Pretend all you might, but you can not hide. We will keep eating you from the inside."

I shake off the voice's words rising from the reflection. Instead, I focus on my feet bouncing in place, ready to make their way to my bedchamber. Forcing excitement that I am to seal my destiny by consummating my marriage. To take the next step towards the happy life I have dreamed about since I was a child.

I can't wait for my Louis to look into my eyes, cherish me, and love me. Just as Mother said he would.

For all the days of my life.

SEVEN

"A happy day turns to a happy night, and my boy becomes a man," the king proudly announces with a tug of his ivory jacket adorned with swirls of gold before silence falls over the room and the priest steps forward.

I'm not sure what to do with my hands. My back pushes against the bed frame, legs stretched toward the priest, and my hands fold over the blanket pulled up to our hips, the threads of the embroidered flowers tickling my fingertips. The scent of whatever incense the priest is burning is overwhelming, and the smoke is making people cough in turns. But nothing like Chloé's cough. I shiver at the thought.

He is saying something in Latin, arms waving in the air, blessing us from the foot of the bed. I rub my hands together and focus on my breath. In. Out.

The priest, dressed in all red, begins walking around the bed, slow and steady, still talking. I don't make out the words—it sounds like he is under water. My stomach turns as his words settle with the weight of expectation and duty.

My hands trace outside my thighs, and I tuck them under my legs. Maybe I should reach one to my side and hold Louis' hand? No. No. It's not time for touching yet. Besides, he is as still as I am. His fingers interlaced at his chest.

The floor is barely visible in this large room, full with sweaty people of the court. A particularly sweaty man is practically panting like a dog, glaring at me. I grasp at the sheets below me, wishing I could cover myself completely, away from his eyes. From all the eyes.

This all feels so…dirty. Like the filth in the tub I left behind in the next room. Even the garments of the onlookers are worse from the wear of the celebrations. Frills and jewels laced with salt and dirt. The smell of their sweat mixed with the incense is just as foul, and I wish I could cut off my nose on the night of my own wedding.

My wedding. I'm married.

In. Out. Breathe.

The priest stops talking, but I can still taste the incense smoke. I realize that everyone is in prayer position. My hands leave the warmth of my legs to meet at my chest. I tilt my chin down toward my clasped fingertips and mumble, "amen."

King's turn again. He leaves Madame DuBarry's side, and Chloé breaks into a fit of coughing. She wheezes, her throat closing as a fine mist of blood releases from her mouth in front of everyone. Madame DuBarry catches her friend just in time as she grows weak, falling to the floor. Seamlessly, several men move to her, pick Chloé up by her feet, arms, and head, and sweep her out of the room. My heart twinges with worry for the coughing girl in the pink dress, then gallops harder than ever remembering the image of Madame DuBarry handing her the blue bottle.

Why did Madame DuBarry have a bottle of poison? Why would she give it to her friend?

Worst of all, why does Madame DuBarry stay here at the foot of my bed while her dutiful friend fights for her life?

And there's nothing I can do. No way to stop the ceremony around me to see if Chloé is safe, nor end the raging of my heartbeat as the king saunters to the foot of the bed, his voice bellowing over us all.

He proceeds as though nothing has happened. Like Geneviève wasn't found butchered. That his mistress' friend isn't spewing blood. I scan the rest of the room with horrified eyes and a caught breath in my lungs—but everyone just looks to the king, smiling.

I don't hear the king's words. I follow Louis' lead and transition from the frozen prayer position I've been holding and move my palms flat on my knees. It arches my back, shoulders pulling forward slightly. The small shift is uncomfortable, but if I move more, it will take attention from the king.

Stay still.

In. Out.

Pretend there is no killer within the walls of Versailles. Ignore it as the rest of them do.

Laughing. They're all laughing. My teeth clench. Are they laughing at me? They become muffled by the sound of blood rushing through my veins. It allows me a moment to focus. To remember that this is all happening *for* me. That

I should feel happy to not only be fulfilling my duty, but to be the most useful woman in the entire court.

The king's face glows red from the heat in the room and his insistent chuckling. His arm pats down on someone with a crooked wig beside him. I realize they weren't laughing at me. He's just putting on a performance.

He makes his way around to Louis' side of the bed and whispers something in his ear. Louis' face remains emotionless, staring straight ahead, unfazed. The king straightens back up and claps his hands, beckoning the procession surrounding our bed to leave the room.

An usher sees them out and bows deeply as he begins to shut the door. The sudden realization that he will be there, just on the other side of some wood and paint, sets my nerves on edge. I don't want anyone to hear what happens within my marital bed.

The ears can be just as watchful as eyes, and I will not have his on me.

"Sir," I call to him. He holds the door open, waiting. Louis stares at me, his head tilted. I fear the need to explain myself, so I inhale courage instead.

Geneviève told me I could dismiss anyone I please.

I can do this. I can *do* this.

"Do not stand waiting at the door. And please, have guards stay clear from this room," I say.

"Are you quite positive, Your Majesty?" he asks, hand trembling on the doorknob, eyes darting between myself and Louis. Louis remains quiet.

"I demand some privacy," I shrink into myself, hating to command another. "Please," I beg.

"Very well. I shall alert the guards and attendants of your instructions," he states and closes the door. The final *click* a welcome sound.

And then it is just me and my Louis. The silence between us grows bigger, expanding to a suffocating size as he continues to stare ahead blankly.

Mother instructed me on all I am to do. How I must make my husband feel good with my hands and my lips. The way to fill myself with him. And she told me something else…what was it?

The time has come. The tremble of my hands reminds me of this.

I inch toward him, shimmying my hips to get closer.

I bat my eyelashes and attempt a coy smile, but it doesn't come naturally. "Hello, husband."

He leans away ever so slightly, but enough for a brick to drop in my stomach. His black eyebrows are bushes that shadow his eyes. Eyes that have no spark within them, no matter how hard I try to find it. "It was a busy day."

"Yes," I say, sliding my hand across the silky, smooth bed sheets, my voice sweeter than icing on cake. I must have misread his shrug. Surely, he wouldn't recoil from me. "But a wonderful one to be married to you."

He cranes his thin neck to acknowledge my presence, but his fingers don't touch mine. Louis clears his throat. Two coughs followed by a grimace. "I am tired."

"Me too. With all that travel, and the wedding celebrations—"

"Good night, then." He slinks down into the sheets, turning on his side facing away from me. The knotted black hair on the back of his head and the thin white cloth covering his back is all I'm left with to see.

"But we—"

"I am happy you are here. You will make a good wife."

That's it? I should be happy with the words themselves. He sees potential in me. He is pleased with my presence. But his words are cold. As cold as the shards of ice piercing into my belly. A belly that is meant to be full with a growing child. "We must—"

"I have to wake early to check on an experiment before I go hunting. I must sleep."

I watch his back move from his breathing, bewildered. "Good—good night," I stammer as I lay my head down on the pillow.

We are supposed to be joining as one right now. Creating new life through our love. He must know our marriage is not bound without consummation. He *must*.

Is it me? Did he not want me as his wife? Did he not stare into the painted portrait of me sent to him from Austria as I have stared at his? I spent hours wondering what it would be like to kiss his lips.

The room is so dark now, save the bit of starlight streaming in from large windows facing the bed. Counting the tassels hanging from the canopy of the bed, doubts swirl like an unwelcome storm in my head.

Does he not want me?

If he finds me unattractive, he will never want to do what we must to have a baby. And that's my duty. I am to birth an heir to the throne. I want to please Louis. Please him, and he will love me. I can not be as one of the useless women slipped poison, as Geneviève had warned.

He snores beside me already. The tension in my bones releases. That's it then. He was just tired.

I smile. Of course he is just tired.

It is difficult to believe my day started in a carriage, arriving at the border of France. That I am married, and the dauphine of a new country. And I have a new name and identity completely—Marie Antoinette.

I also made a friend, and lost her just as swiftly. Pulling air into my lungs through my nose, I remind myself of what I've been told—smile and move on. I must clear my mind, wash it from the flashes of Geneviève in the mud. Her unmoving face.

Smile and move on.

Smile and move on.

The pillow is soft and my eyes have no issues fluttering closed.

I will have my kisses tomorrow.

I wake to my lungs being squeezed, air escaping me and heart pounding. There is nothing in the room that I can see. It is so, so dark. As I raise the heavy blankets up to my nose I continue to look into every corner.

Something is—*gurgling*.

Gurgling between Louis' loud snores, but it's not him. The urge to wake him tickles at the back of my throat. But I wait. He does not need to be disturbed for my being silly.

The sound must be from water, perhaps a malfunctioning fountain outside.

It's too close though. Just on the other side of our door. Something is there.

A menace intent on ending another life. Like they ended Geneviève.

No. No.

An *usher*. It must be an usher making some strange sounds. The one I dismissed come back.

The gurgling persists, and I feel a pull toward it. A cold sensation rising up my spine and tugging me to the wooden door.

I sit up in the bed, peering at Louis one last time before standing on my bare feet. Ignoring my rising pulse, I cross the room on tiptoe.

There is no need to be afraid. There is no need to be afraid.

Versailles is full of guards and watchful eyes. I am never truly alone. If I made a peep, there would be many who flocked to me in an instant.

And perhaps it is my sister, finally come to find *me*. If she heard news that I found Geneviève, then she is here to console me.

The doorknob is slick and freezing, like it is covered in frost. How peculiar. I lose myself in it for a moment, seeing a tiny version of my face in the gold looking back up at me.

"Accept the cold, it's part of you now. Death, decay, straight from our soul."

There is no need to be afraid.

Turning the knob with ease, I am careful to open the door gingerly, slowly peeking my head around to see what is on the other side, hoping to be greeted by Josepha's playful smile.

There is nothing. Even the sound that brought me here ceases once the door is open. No guard, or usher, or chambermaid is waiting on the other side.

A few steps forward lead me into the hallway.

Moonlight highlights the opulence of the palace. A dark cavern holding the greatest treasures, I venture past what feels like a hundred windows, each one curved at the top, nearly kissing the high ceilings. The enormous chandelier crystals look even prettier holding the pale blue of the moon than the soft yellow glow of candlelight. I put my arms out and spin under one in the middle of a great hall, smiling. It is too dark to see the painted faces of the murals adorning the ceiling, so I turn and turn, enjoying the cool floor on my bare soles and the absence of eyes watching me—painted *or* human.

My lips part in awe at how a place so full of life during the day becomes quiet as death at night. I like the quiet. It feels like warming your toes by a fire with no distractions.

A guard passes, and I nearly fall over from the fright. He cocks his head. "Couldn't sleep," I say, "just out for a stroll." I feel entirely silly. No strange sounds. No killer.

He bows slightly before moving on. I'm lucky Louis instructed the guards to allow me where I please. Relieved Geneviève provided the support in wanting to have my own space and using my voice to get it. With eased nerves, I want to explore. And be alone.

I stumble through a few steps, the smell of champagne rising from my breath. The bit of sleep I caught before the sounds awoke me was not enough to end the dizzy haze of too much drink and a day full of chaos.

A tightness takes hold in my chest as I recall the events. I had my sister in my sights. After all this time. That lilac ribbon there one moment, gone the next. Like magic, playing a horrible trick of the eye on me. But she was there. Where did she go? And why?

Sweat builds upon my brow, recalling what—*who*—I found instead of Josepha. Geneviève's body was so broken, laying there in the mud. The fire in her eyes snuffed out, her freckles bright in the sunshine lost their life when she lost hers. My only friend, left murdered for me to find. I can't contain the tremble of my hands, sweat building thicker and thicker despite the chill in my bones.

So much pain within these gilded walls. Young girls being tricked into giving their heart away, only to have it pulverized and tossed aside by boys like Alexandre. Being killed in such brutal manners. How can life just go on normally?

We are more than they give us credit for. I feel it. A strength simmering inside me, ready to boil over. Yet we all play the perfect little dance they expect us to, afraid of the consequences. We give boys our bodies and hearts, left with only a crumbling soul to cling on to.

My head whirs while I enter yet another hallway. Do these halls ever end? I step on a white square tile, then black, the checkered floor growing smaller in the distance while frustration takes root in my belly. Damning Josepha for leaving me after I finally found her again.

I stop at a portrait and gaze into it, forcing my eyes to see past the darkness.

The king's face. Wrinkles frame his eyes. His cheeks stained a cherry pink the artist captured quite accurately. I shake my head, walking from the painted face of the man I spent years trying to impress before even meeting him. The monarch whose grandson would not lay with me tonight. The same soul who insisted that Geneviève was nobody.

To make a difference in Versailles will be an unimaginable feat. To try could impact my standing as dauphine and ruin everything I—my *country*—has worked for.

I must listen to the king. I must play my role. I must do as the rest of them do, and push it all down and move forward towards parties and laughter.

Everything is going to turn out wonderfully. My Louis was there in the moment I needed him the most, as I knelt next to Geneviève. I wish he had been able to provide more comfort, but it was an overwhelming day for us all.

My feet become anchors as I suddenly sense something. Intuition beating like a drum, banging my insides to run back to my chamber, to seek safety in Louis. A shadow fills a doorway in the hall ahead.

"Hello," I croak, so quiet that if it is a guard, they'd never hear me. The shadow disappears, and the tension in my shoulders releases before I continue on.

The hedges loom beyond the window frames. The last place I saw my sister. Hope never beat so hard in my ribs as it did when I saw that ribbon in the ballroom. Josepha was in the hedges, and then gone—is it possible she ran from the murderer? That she's hiding, scared and alone?

If she's hiding, she's safe. I cling to that thought. I shall find her again.

Somehow all my walking takes me far from my room, and I'm in the hall of mirrors. I shudder, afraid of what the voices are readying themselves to say to me. The grotesque lyrics to be burrowed into my skull.

The beauty of the space helps me face it. The hall is so different at night, without the sun gleaming in from the wall made of windows against the wall made of mirrors. Instead of bright white light, the reflective glass glitters with a sea of stars, illuminating the line of golden statues of women and intricately laid wooden flooring.

Mesmerized, there is no avoiding reflections in this expansive hall.

"Open your ears, listen to me. A bird in a cage, who'd kill to be free."

My breath hitches. The voice has never *instructed* before. I have turned away from seeing my pale skin, white-blonde hair, and blue eyes to avoid the voice so many times from fear. But now—now it has my attention.

"I hear you," I whisper, feeling utterly silly once more as I search the dark space around me through the reflection of the mirror before looking back at myself. My tiny mouth. My hollowed collarbone rising and falling with my breath.

"Death to two, then three to four, we'll save you all, but speak no more."

I inch closer to the mirror, my nose nearly touching its reflection. "Tell me what you mean, please. *Please*," I whine.

"Ghosts are here, they all come back. A killer is loose, but you knew that."

"So it's true. All Geneviève said, what she warned me about. A killer is in Versailles. I don't want this… I never wanted any of this." Softly my forehead presses to the mirror, resting there. Imagine what Mother would say if she caught me talking to my own reflection.

The side of my fist thumps softly against the reflective glass. Why do I listen to this voice? It has caused me nothing but pain. Providing only useless riddles I am unable to decipher.

A cough carries through the hall, snapping me from my misery and fear. I stand up straight, wiping my face dry.

Someone is choking. The same sound that woke me and pulled me from bed. An echo of gurgling water encircles me. I spin around, searching. Someone is gasping for air.

"Hello?" I cry. "Where are you? I can help you!"

Nobody is there. But it *feels* like they are right beside me.

I pace. Up and down the hallway, over and over again. The sound of my footsteps joins the disembodied choking and gurgling.

"Are you hurt?" What if they are? What if this is just like the maze? What if I'm about to fall over a body?

My sister. What if she is here and I just can't see her? What if she's in trouble?

My pace quickens through the hall, back and forth, a blur of mirrors and windows from the corners of my eyes.

It's just me. My shaky voice, reflections and the noise. No one has come running to investigate. The quiet darkness was such a reprieve from the bustling court, but now I am left on edge, wishing whoever it is within the shadows would end the mystery and loneliness.

I turn to the mirror for answers but am met with something grazing my arm.

The hairs along my entire body stand and I shiver.

Someone touched my arm.

But there is nobody here.

EIGHT

A shadow crosses my path. The darkness plays tricks on me, blocking the only light from a window one second and passing my reflection the next. The golden statues hold their unlit candelabras high.

My limbs stiffen, waiting for the shadow's owner to become clear.

Someone *is* here. I feel it deep within my bones, though there is no face appearing from the pitch black. I look down to my locked knees, keeping me planted close to the mirrored wall, as if I'll be able to just jump straight through it and save myself.

A skirt brushes by the tips of my bare toes. The same way I imagined the ghosts of Josepha's stories. But this is *real*.

Biting my lips closed, I look back up.
Blackness.

I crane my neck to uncover the source of the shivers crawling up my spine, to see the hem of the skirt again as a gust of air blows in front of my face.

"Who—who are you?" I don't recognize my own voice, low with a rasp. As though something has taken hold of my throat.

No answer. Only *gurgling*.

I flinch at the noise, and from the depths of the darkness, she appears. Terror runs through me as I recognize the creamy yellow dress. The fire in her eyes.

Geneviève.

I can't speak. My breath stays trapped in my lungs, inescapable.

She sways while playing with her skirts, working her way toward me down the middle of the hall. "There you are, Marie," Geneviève sings, moving closer while I stay in place.

"Geneviève?" I wince. Saying her name feels impossible on my tongue.

"Who else would I be?" She giggles with the wink I love of hers.

Loved.

"But I found you. All that blood. All. That. Blood. And I watched as Alexandre carried you from the hedges." I pause, stunned by the impossibility I see with my own eyes.

"Sooo?" She smiles with a shrug.

"You're dead."

The accusation leaves my lips and instead of Geneviève laughing again, a wound blossoms across her throat. The same I saw when I found her in the hedges. Where the blade took her last breath of life.

Her arm reaches toward me before her head rolls back, exposing her neck. From her left ear to her right, a slit of red splits her throat open wider. The cut is horrendous, shaped like a smile. A wide, evil smile of folding flesh.

Waves of crimson spill from the wound, pours down her chest, and splatters against the floor. She coughs, choking on her own blood.

Gurgling.

I should turn and run to find that guard. Escape the horror only a few paces in front of me, but my feet are frozen in place. I clasp my hands over my mouth and swallow hard, praying for spit to wash away the dryness in my throat.

Josepha's haunting stories by the fire were *true*. Real. Somehow, I always knew they were; the fear they would send slithering down my back told me they were. I can still hear Josepha's voice whispering the story of Anne Boleyn, scaring me from leaving my bed at night, afraid the headless figure of Henry VIII's wife would take my head to replace hers.

Though, the reality of that horror standing before me as Geneviève is now, gurgling louder with each of my heaving breaths, never crossed my mind all those years ago. The omens were meant to be an unseen, bodiless essence nipping at my heels.

But this—*she*—is a very real body. One that is dead. One that smells of the earth she died on and the metallic blood she drowned in.

Geneviève's hair is wet and slick with blood, her red strands turned a dark crimson, matted to her temples, her cheeks, her shoulders. I am a heap of nothingness, still unable to pry my feet from the sticky, bloodied floor.

Hot tears stream down my face, cascading off my chin to my chest.

Ghosts are real.

My arms shiver as goosebumps appear along my flesh.

Her freckles are now indistinguishable from the splatter of her insides out. Her soft yellow dress stained and marred for all of eternity. Her death dress.

Geneviève's head rolls back down to face me and she smiles while the blood disappears. From the floor, the fabric, her skin. Her lips press together. When they open, I hear a faint plea. "Help me."

Her ashen hand extends toward me again and I squirm in my own skin.

She winks before her head lolls back once more and that invisible knife cuts across her throat as it did seconds ago. Shaking my head in denial, my feet finally wake up. I walk backward, legs trembling, so slowly as to not trip on my nightgown or have her chase after me.

Hurt leaches to my stomach, leaving her while she asks for help. But my fear consumes all.

The blood disappears again and she starts to follow me. The beating of my heart thrashes in my ears. I can't see anymore, the tears taking my vision. I blink repeatedly, not wanting to lose sight of her.

She abruptly stops, and crimson comes gushing out of her again.

I'm grateful to be barefoot, soles gripping onto the wood, stepping faster and faster while her head is yanked up toward the ceiling.

Why must this hallway be so long? Why did I stray so far from my chamber alone? Where has the guard gone?

Why is nobody here to save me?

Finally, I make it far enough to turn and run. I still can't scream. Something has captured my tongue, leaving me unable to speak. Stealing my words as Geneviève's life was stolen.

A strangling pain that matches my guilt.

NINE

My feet can't run fast enough. Each step echoes through the hall as I desperately try to distance myself from Geneviève. I risk a glance over my shoulder, and there she is. At the end of the Hall of Mirrors, head tilted back, the ghost of the girl I had only just begun to love.

I jolt myself from the terror, praying my feet don't freeze again. I've made it out of the hall, into a horrifying room—a great white carving greets me, a man on a wild horse, its eyes as pained as those in Apollo's fountain. Bronze statues circle round me, men with emotionless faces.

Their faces are so angry, so similar to those back home. Though at home, I always had Josepha there to save me.

She should be here for me now. My head pounds as I hold my breath, waves of confusion and sadness crashing into me.

Moonlight streams through the windows, illuminating the ceiling full of painted death—men in battle wielding swords and shields, bodies crumpled at their feet while beastly vultures cry out above them.

I pry my eyes from the scene above, searching for a door to lead away from the hall.

Away from the gurgling.

The gurgling.

She's still there. And now she is moving closer—skipping effortlessly across the wooden floor as though she has not a care in the world.

She looks alive. Alive as when I first met her.

"Poor Marie, another maze. Found her once, and now again."

My reflection in the bronzed face of a demon on the mantel flashes before me, and it's enough to bring on the voice. It never seems to miss an opportunity to taunt me.

I gulp down each panting breath. She sees me. She wants me.

"Marieeee," she beckons.

I'm moving again, through a door and into another space, this one darker than the last without as many windows. I can barely make out the walls of burgundy embellished in gold.

The tingle crawling up the back of my neck, tendrils of hair rising, signals that she is drawing near. I dare to turn around, hoping the disappearance of the gurgling sound means she isn't really there.

Please, *please* don't be there.

I slow enough to stay upright, then crane my neck. There's only the shadow of the space I've left behind me, soft moonlight shimmering in from all the windows.

Not a soul in sight. A relieved exhale slips free from my mouth as I turn back around.

My scream follows. Clawing its way up my throat.

My forehead comes in contact with a solid mass, dark and tall. I reach my hands up, to push myself away but am unable to step backward as arms envelope me.

This is how I die.

"I've got you." The soft voice of a boy whispers as his face lowers to meet mine.

I pull away, stumbling on my ankles as I walk backward. He's not wearing a guard's uniform. The white linen of his loose shirt shines in the little light from the glow of the moon, the bronze threads making up the fleur-de-lis pattern of his vest come to life. Strangest of all, he wears no powders. No tightly coiled wig pinned to his head. Only soft brown curls brushing along his forehead, and the ordinariness of him sets me at ease. He moves the curls to the side with a single finger and it hits me.

It is the boy.

From the handing over ceremony, and later in the halls. The boy who unleashed butterflies in my stomach that are better left caged.

"I remember you from the forest. Who-who are you?" I ask softly, voice a tremble.

"I'm so sorry. I did not mean to cause a fright, madame." He steps forward, offering a hand, extending it to me just as Geneviève did before her neck split in two.

Geneviève.

The driving force of my heart returns to my chest, my head, my ears. Still seated on the floor, I spin to see if she's upon me as I quickly rise to my feet, without accepting the boy's hand.

She isn't there. She isn't there.

"Are you well?" Concern fills his voice, smooth and deep.

I finally tilt my head up to truly see him. Breath hitches in my lungs when my gaze finds his eyes. More blue than the clearest tides, brighter than the cloudless sky, encircled by the faintest line of azure, and framed by dark lashes.

"I—" the words do not come. Spellbound by his hand encasing mine, the stranger's eyes unleash a flutter in my chest. That calming blue like a hazy daydream I could hold on to forever.

"Is someone after you?" he asks, checking behind each of my shoulders, his impossibly sharp jaw set with concern. He smells of sweet oranges, freshly picked.

"Geneviève." The chill from seeing her spirit is ever present in my veins.

The boy—who can't be much older than I—hangs his head low and runs a hand through his mess of hair. It reminds me of chocolate, and even within this hall in the dead of night, the movement of his rough fingers through the strands reveal hints of a caramel color. I catch the widening of my eyes, hoping he did not notice my study of him.

"I heard what happened. That you found her. How horrible that must have been for you," he says.

Tears well quickly. This stranger cares for *me*.

Hair catches on my swollen wet cheeks when I spin to look for Geneviève. "She was just here."

"I know. Just this morning I saw her, and now…she's gone," he sighs, not understanding that I mean she was here in these halls, standing before me mere *moments* ago.

The space around us finally comes back into focus. An unlit chandelier hangs overhead, a large black iron circle holding candlesticks gone cold. Portraits hang from the walls every few paces. The one closest to me is of a girl dressed in emerald, reading at the base of a tree while a boy lays his back upon the trunk's bark beside her, strumming on a guitar.

"No. I mean—" My lips slam shut. He will think the worst of me if I tell him there is a ghost of my friend, with blood trickling down her dress, chasing me in the dark hallways at night. He will think I have lost my mind to the grief of it all. But I haven't. She was there. As real and beautiful as the moment I met her.

"It's all well, madame." A bend in his knees brings him closer to my height. His eyes peer at my own through lowered brows—they are unkempt, yet I wouldn't change them for all the world.

He steps closer. My breath stops. I forget how to inhale altogether.

What is *wrong* with me?

"You are so pale, I would think you had just seen a ghost."

I don't answer, though everything screams within my soul to tell him that I *did* just see a ghost. The ghost of the girl I confided in mere hours ago, who made me feel hope when my old world was stripped away from me.

I nod slowly, expecting him to shout for the guards to come take me away, to rid Versailles of the mad woman.

He draws his teeth over his lower lip, the fullness of them disappearing into his mouth before he releases them again. They're so…inviting.

The moment of silence while we look at each other feels eternal. My heart, a ticking clock in my ribs. Does he think me mad? Of course he does. I just met this boy and am already speaking of ghosts.

But Geneviève *was* just here.

"I see them, too," he says, raising an eyebrow.

I repeat his words to myself, growing lightheaded as my ribs pull tight.

"Though," he continues, "they don't usually show up so quickly after their deaths to walk these halls." His jaw relaxes as he chuckles to himself, dimples pushing deeply beside his pillowed mouth that I really need to stop staring at.

"Don't laugh," I say.

Black spots blur my vision as I contemplate the magnitude of this information—had I been so foolish as to believe Geneviève was the only spirit within these halls? I stepped over the dead upon my arrival. Heard the whispers of killed women.

The truth grips me by the throat—*Versailles is haunted*.

Josepha's stories flood my memories, wiggling their way to the surface of my mind. Ghosts and ghouls, and the omens that follow me. The stench of death ripe on me, always.

"You are right. I'm sorry. I was just trying to make light."

"Who are you?" I demand, attempting to snap myself away from the reverie of those eyes of his. "You are dressed nothing like the other gentlemen of court." I regret my tone, so stark compared to his genuine softness, but don't back down.

"I beg your pardon." He bends at the waist, arms extending, like he's a bird with outstretched wings about to take flight. Hair swipes along his brow, and he peers up at me through it with those eyes. Those damned eyes. "My name is Étienne. It is a pleasure to make your acquaintance."

Étienne returns to standing, all the while keeping his gaze stuck to me, sweet like honey.

"Why weren't you in the gardens tonight…after…while everyone celebrated the wedding?" I ask.

"Who said I wasn't?"

My arms fold across my chest. "You cannot play coy with a dauphine."

He immediately falls into a bow again, this time even deeper. I fear his nose will touch the floor. "Your Majesty."

The laugh that tickles my tongue on its way out surprises me. The happy sound feels so *wrong* after all that has happened today. So foreign from the fright ripping through my insides just a moment ago. I move to him, motioning with my arm for him to stand back up, unable to keep from noticing the muscle beneath the thin white fabric of his shirt.

"There is no need for that. And please, call me Marie. I am just Marie." I like the sound of that. *Just Marie.* Stripped down and simple, yet pretty. It feels more *me*.

"I couldn't possibly—" he starts, but I quickly shield the words with a raised hand, palm flat, pointed in his direction.

"I insist. Just Marie."

He tilts his head ever so slightly, and agrees. "Well, *Marie*," the way his lips purse as he says my name causes me to look down immediately, to conceal a grin that can't be contained, "will you allow me the honor of walking you back to your bedchambers? I swear to protect you from any wandering ghosts."

I stare at a small table set against a window, a porcelain white vase inked in blue, holding bright yellow flowers, still full of life and beauty.

I shouldn't say yes. It would be scandalous to walk the halls at night with a gentleman.

Perhaps the boy in front of me isn't dangerous, but the thoughts clouding my mind *are*.

My gaze returns to Étienne's face, hesitant. There are a few freckles there, light and scattered with the precision of an artist. I hadn't noticed them until now, as a hint of peach sky enters the room, the rise of the sun a glimmer on the horizon. More hours than I thought have passed.

He is not my husband, yet the *want* to spend more time with Étienne stirs in my stomach like a hunger pain.

Maybe I should accept his offer. The thought of walking on my own, of coming face to face with Geneviève again, or other ghosts for that matter, is scarier than the judgment of others.

Yes.

I move to his side, so we both face the same direction. My night dress brushes against my knees and the room whirls around me, much less scary now draped with pink light.

"I would like that, thank you," I finally reply.

His dimples deepen again with a smile, but before he takes a step, he looks down to his side. To the narrow space between us. My eyes trail down and I watch the muscles in his hand twitch, his fingers reaching out to mine before quickly curling into a fist.

He knows the rules. He knows the risk.

Ladies of the court would gasp to see anyone courting come as close as grazing hands. And I'm not courting. I'm married. To another.

I am the dauphine. And the space between us now shall forever remain as it is—a gaping cavern symbolizing my duty. My body feels cold because of this. Hollowed.

I take a step forward, breathing in the scent of oranges lingering on his skin, and he follows. We fall into step together. It comes so naturally, as though we have known each other for an eternity. "Did you truly mean what you said about ghosts?" I ask.

"About protecting you from them?"

"That they're actually there at all…"

"Ah. Yes," he says with a faint whisper of hesitation in the way he draws out the two words. "I, seemingly like you, enjoy the peace that midnight beckons. But with that, I have been forced to reckon with seeing the souls who met their final fate on these grounds."

He is not making fun of me. His serious tone and hunched shoulders tell me he believes. I smile again, feeling a sliver less alone. "Do they not frighten you?"

"It's not so bad, just—open your eyes. Steer clear." He flashes a quick smile and a brow lifts in a perfect arch.

"If Mops were here, perhaps I would not be as afraid."

His chin nearly touches his shoulder when he looks over to me. Behind him is a tall window decorated with heavy curtains in the most hideous shade of light brown feigning to be gold. We pass another one identical to the last, and Étienne is still looking at me, waiting for explanation.

I like him looking at me.

"My dog," I say. "They took—I—I couldn't bring him with me to Versailles."

"I am sorry for that, Marie. I know how important pets are—how close to the heart we hold them."

"Yes," I say, holding back tears. "But that is the way it is meant to be. And now, I have this palace, and a happy future, and will make everyone proud."

I can hear his breath tremble as he takes a deep inhale. He abruptly comes to standing, and I stop with him. "The pictures they paint are not always as vibrant as we wish them to be. They lack luster. They hold darkness. And *you* deserve more than the terrible things that happen here and the expectation they place so heavily on your shoulders." His hands reach out, as if to put his fingers on the shoulders he speaks of. Instead, they fold in front of his chest—rubbing a thumb into his palm instead.

"I—"

The words will not leave my lips. Everything is going to be wonderful in the end. But the amount of death I've witnessed in a single day would send any sane girl running straight through the double doors out to the gardens we just passed, never to return.

But I am not any girl. I am Marie Antoinette. Bound by duty.

"How are you? Truly? I can't imagine the gruesome scene you came upon this evening. Is it true that you found…" I look up at Étienne when he trails off. His Adam's apple plunges as he swallows down a gulp of air.

It's puzzling to me this boy would ask how I am before getting the dirty details. He must be fifteen, maybe sixteen—and boys our age, they do not care about a girl's feelings. Boys our age care more about finding a dead thing and how it remains limp even when you poke it with a stick.

"I am—" the flashes of the tall, green hedges return, "I'm not sure. Overwhelmed? Tired?" My temples come to life with a painful pulsing. I should add that I am still feeling the effects of all the champagne, but I keep that to myself.

Overwhelmed. Tired. Drunk.

Is it possible these things could cause visions of ghosts? Traumatized by a day so far removed from reality of most other people—people not bred to and trained for royalty.

No.

She was *real*. Geneviève was there.

Étienne believes me. He's seen ghosts too.

"Anyone would be overwhelmed. You, Marie—You are quite impressive." Étienne's voice is soft and serious. I surrender to it.

I mutter "thank you," unsure what else to say in response to his compliment, while I take short, quick steps to keep up with him.

Our feet fall silently against the polished wood floor. I enjoy the void of swishing skirts and clicking heels. Hearing only Étienne's breath—in, out—fills me with warmth, comforting like the fires Josepha and I sat near all those late nights. I do hope she is well and knows that I will find her no matter what.

A pair of guards walk toward us and I falter. "Your Highness, is everything well?" the one with broad shoulders asks, the blue of their uniforms bright even in the darkness of the hall.

"Yes, thank you," I say softly. And I am well. Étienne is here.

Étienne looks to me and smiles, and we both bend our necks slightly to bid adieu before walking around the men. Their whispers echo behind us, and I swallow down the fear of how I will pay for being with another in the early hours of the morning.

I could lose everything.

I focus on my tiny hands, feeling shame grow hot within me. Shame that I will—or already have—let everyone down.

"I must admit, I'm a little embarrassed about my appearance. In your nightgown, you look like an angel right here on earth, gracing the halls of Versailles. I should be dressed in the finest to be in your presence."

"Nonsense," I laugh, my spirits lifted with just those few words. It makes him smile. "Such things are not necessary with me."

"The heavens shine down upon me if that is true." His long lashes flick up to the sky. "You're not like other girls at court, are you?"

"Louis said something very similar to me, actually," I say just as we arrive at my bedchamber. *Louis*. My stomach drops and I quickly move a step back from Étienne. My husband is on the other side of the door. I can hear his snores through the small opening to the room.

If I'm honest with myself, I don't want to move from Étienne's side. This stranger sparks such a curiosity in my soul, comforting and dangerous all at the same time.

"Thank you," I whisper. He knows immediately why I speak softly, his ocean eyes darting behind me to the door.

Étienne bows again, causing the corner of my mouth to rise into a grin. "The pleasure is mine." His volume is so low I must lean closer to hear. I love how he smells of oranges. They are my favorite. "Goodnight, Marie. And please, don't be so sad and scared. That smile is too beautiful to hide. Open your eyes and enjoy this new world."

My eyes widen and I bite my lower lip. His voice and his compliments shower over me like the most gorgeous rain under the summer sun. "Will I see you again soon?"

"It can't be soon enough that we roam these dark hallways together." Étienne nods then turns on a heel and walks off into the gloom.

I creep into my bedchamber, carefully closing the door shut before I slide down on to the floor. Though I am sitting still, gripping the doorknob, my heart gallops with the strength of a thousand horses. I peek through the keyhole, hoping to catch a glimpse of Étienne walking away.

He's already gone.

TEN

Sunlight glints off the knife. The slight movement of my finger refracts the light into my eye, blinding me momentarily with its brightness. Such a simple piece of metal holds so much power. Can do so much damage. Inflict death.

This is all it took for Geneviève to die. Someone holding a knife, able to end such a vivacious life.

My eyes burn, not from the light, but from last night's discovery—of her body, and then her ghost. The fear that some unknown man with a blade or vial of poison could get me too.

I clear my throat, needing to feel something physical to know this is not all some nightmare I can't wake from. Voices. Spirits. Visions that are as clear as the diamonds of my bracelet, drooping from my teeny wrist.

Or my dear sister. I bite my lip, guilt piercing through me. I didn't think of her at all while with Étienne—he had the ability to take all the terrible thoughts from my head. But I should be out there now searching for hidden places where she may be. Yet, I can't. And I mustn't cry in front of all these people.

Whispers pull my gaze away from the knife. There must be over one hundred souls crammed into the room to watch me and Louis eat our breakfast. This is the first time I've seen him today, he was missing from the bed this morning when I woke, and of course, he never uttered a word about our marriage not being consummated.

We eat in a room of white, embellished in way too much gold. There are carvings that trail in swoops along the wall near the top of the ceiling, twisting and turning into vines with little grapes. No doubt to represent Jesus, and how close royals are linked to the Holy. If they think Louis was chosen by God Himself to be King, I wonder if I am chosen as well.

If I am chosen by God too, then it must not be possible for omens to follow me anymore.

"You daydream too much," a voice in my ear croons while a hand brushes across my back.

Geneviève kneels down between where Louis and I sit on display, but nobody sees her. The sea of people look on as though the ghost of a murdered girl isn't there. And I must pretend too. Has she been here the whole time? How did I not see her before?

"Oh, sweet Marie. I promised we would be the best of friends." Her fingers dig into the tablecloth and the satin folds beneath her grip.

"I won't let you meet the same fa—" she chokes, a hand quickly covering her slit throat, fingers digging deeper into the tablecloth. "Fa—fate." A cough of blood sprays from her lips. I hold my breath while the shower of scarlet peppers across the feast on the table, forcing myself to not cause a scene.

My heart drops to see Geneviève like this, wiping the blood from her mouth with the back of her hand. Here with me, even in the afterlife. I put my utensils down, and place a hand to Geneviève's shoulder. She's so cold.

Madame Etiquette stares me down. She glares at the way my hand hovers in the air, unable to see my attempt to comfort the girl she cared so much for in life.

I automatically sit up straighter, snapping my hand back to the spread, grabbing a grape. It pops between my teeth. I wish Etiquette were as sweet as this fruit, and could soothe me, give me kinship. Not just rules.

"Those do look good," Louis says, picking out a grape that has tiny drops of Geneviève's blood. "Mmm," he says while my stomach churns, but I only watch as he grabs another, this one covered in blood.

Geneviève giggles, jumping to her feet and grabbing a grape for herself. "Guess I can't eat this, being dead and all." She giggles again.

It's not funny, I want to say to her.

"They really watch you closely, don't they?" She skips over to Victoire, practically touching nose to nose. Victoire's eyes only narrow to me, seeing through Geneviève. "Her eyes are so full of criticism. Look at her…a daughter of the king, intent on each bite you take."

Geneviève looks over her shoulder, her red hair moving in clumps, wet from blood. She is right. The pressure to follow the French court rules is a heavy weight upon my slender shoulders. If only that were the singular pressure. It is near impossible to show no reaction to Geneviève here now. And what a jest, for this room to only focus on how people eat while I feel paralyzed watching my murdered friend skip about.

I hesitate before picking up my croissant, afraid that I should be cutting it with the smallest knife instead of eating with my hands. The dough is sweet on my tongue, and I'm so hungry, yet I slow the gnashing of my jaw when I feel all the people around sinking their own teeth into me with their eyes.

Geneviève runs to Louis, bending over to plop her elbows down on the table, cradling her chin in her hands. "I told you, Marie. Look at the way he doesn't care about anything but shoveling food down his throat. Doesn't care that you're here on exhibit like an animal."

I think about last night, and the anticipation that filled the room before everyone left. My jaw clicks as it slides back and forth, grinding away the worry of those same people finding out I am still a virgin—a failure. A target grows wider on my back.

"These men are bad," Geneviève sings. "Bad, bad, bad. Don't drink from that cup, Marie. These men, with their poison, with their words. Abandoning daughters. Taking lives."

I should want to go to the bedchambers with him again tonight, but with Geneviève's warnings, the thought sets an aching dagger in my chest.

I don't want to be tethered to Versailles like all those long dead. I want to change things here.

And I don't want to die.

I inhale a breath between bites, prepared to break the silence in the room and ask him about his hunting plans for the day, but I think better of it and clap my mouth shut again. Every word I might say will be analyzed, and I don't know what chaos Geneviève can cause.

Geneviève rounds the table back to me, kissing me on the forehead. The cascade of her flesh, exposing the insides of her throat, ridged and pink, are so close I can smell the metallic tang of her blood. Yet I smile when her lips of ice press to my head.

In the night, I shall try to find her again so I can talk back, ask her who did this to her. Not stand here motionless as a statue amongst a crowd. I long for the day to pass and for all to give into sleep so I can explore the palace as it transforms into a dark tomb free of prying eyes and rules. Those few moments when I first left my bedchamber had been such a reprieve. To be lost in the silence, and enjoy the stars all to myself without worrying about how Victoire and Adélaïde want me to treat Madame DuBarry, or how I am probably one big disappointment to Madame Etiquette. Will she order blue bottles of poison be given to me if I fail as dauphine?

I long for the day to hurry through these ridiculous ceremonial duties so that I can hear the sound of my bare feet upon the floors again. To not have any eyes on me.

I hope to see Étienne again.

I wonder if he will be up, wandering the halls, hoping to see me.

I shake my head slightly, the weight of the wig on my head shifting and scratching painfully across my scalp. I think of him being near me again. His strong arms. Warm laugh. Butterflies dance in my stomach and I bite the inside of my cheek to stop myself from such thoughts.

The silver of Etiquette's ruby brooch catches the reflection of the sun as she makes her way toward the table. She is hard to miss with each step so poised. Her head, always pinned up straight toward the sky.

"We cut the skin. You'll watch them die. Pain from the past, now we laugh and cry."

Cold splices down my neck, my nerves unraveling into shivers. I look down at my plate. Most of my food is still there, but at least the voices are not.

Etiquette clears her throat when she reaches the table. Geneviève rests her head on Etiquette's shoulder, smiling. I wonder if Etiquette feels her there, and how close they really were in life.

I nod for Etiquette to approach and she leans in close to my ear to ensure not another soul hears what she says, not even Louis.

"I must let you know that a chambermaid with loose lips has shared with others that there was no blood in your marital bed as she changed the sheets this morning."

My shoulders jerk away from her. I feel my brows pinch together. "Why would there be—"

Her talons dig into my arm, yanking me back into her. "A marriage consummated brings blood to the linens. They know you did not attempt to make an heir to the throne."

Yes. Of course. Mother told me about the first time bringing blood. That I should not be scared when it happens and it is but another stage in becoming a woman. So it is no surprise there was no blood. Louis only wanted to sleep.

The room spins around me, all the faces melding into one. The shame of everyone knowing I was unable to fulfill my duty makes me ill. My first morning as dauphine and I shall be labeled a failure, the fires stoked by relentless rumors.

"I will try harder," I hiss between my teeth. Because I *do* want to fulfill my duty. Perhaps once my belly begins to swell with his child, Louis' tune will change and all my dreams will come true. We will rule together in bliss, and this will protect me.

If only I could catch his attention. I watch him swallow down another bite, then turn back to Etiquette.

Etiquette holds eye contact with me for an unforgettable beat, but her claws have released me. I fight the urge to rub my arm and send warmth back to the skin. Louis clears his throat and Etiquette disappears, Geneviève trailing behind her, while the rest of the people in the room look at my husband with bated breath.

Louis is finished. He pushes himself from the table and I follow suit. The chair scrapes across the floor immediately preceding the round of applause that erupts from our spectators. How utterly absurd to be commended for eating breakfast. My nose wrinkles, unable to contain my disgust with all of the ridiculousness. Everything here is about fanfare.

Mother used that to her advantage back home. Perhaps I can do the same.

If ever there was upsetting news she had to deliver to her people, she would soften the blow with extravagance. With a distracting celebration to remind the court of happy times.

And it worked. They all loved Mother.

That's it.

I will hold a party.

My toes ache as I stand and my weight shifts from the heel. The sapphire shoes are deliciously beautiful, with folds of lace topped with a perfectly tied ribbon, but the pain is searing. Holding back my wince and pretending nothing is wrong makes my stomach flop.

They will love me. I will be adored for throwing the most magnificent soirees and wearing the finest silk shoes. I will be the young, free-spirited future queen. Madame DuBarry will be put to shame in comparison to me. They will say my name in glee. No one will care that I haven't gotten with child right away.

Sweat builds on my brow waiting to leave, and I quickly swipe it away with the back of my hand, the need to discover the stories of ghosts and death that are kept locked away by tight lips. I need to have people like me and be on my side.

To tell their secrets. To find someone, anyone who can provide a direction toward my sister and keep me safe from a killer getting close. Maybe they see ghosts too.

There are answers, waiting for me behind the gold leaf, waiting within walls of damask to be uncovered.

Once I know more, I'll exorcize the palace of ghosts. I'll be the heroic knight of the court in a glittering dress. More importantly, I will free my dear friend, allow her to move on from this wretched place, where she spins and spits blood, to eternal happiness.

A pathway appears between the sea of people as Louis walks through the room to exit; I follow close to his heels. Women clutch at their skirts, attempting to pull the armature under all the fabric to create more room for us.

Were the women who were poisoned once in this room witness to the spectacle of royalty, only to be killed later that day? My pulse increases, a beating in my head demanding answers I know must exist here. What do these people know? The chatter is constantly on their tongues. I just need to pull the stories of poisons and murders from their mouths.

What better way to loosen lips than with the sweet bubbles of champagne?

I want to paint wider smiles on all those around us. Turn judgmental eyes that bite into my skull to a night of indulgence and distraction.

With answers, I can protect them. Surely the venom of fear coursing through me will seep out through my skin.

I am so much more than a wife. A bed warmer. A vessel for an heir.

More than Maria Antonia of Austria, the disappointing child with omens circling close.

I am *Marie Antoinette*. Smart and capable, ready to infiltrate their conversations and burrow my way to the truth, like a mouse intent on cheese.

The tiny crystals on Louis' shoes glitter as we spill into the empty hallway. The voice leaps from them into my unwilling ears.

"Primp and plan, play the charade, unbury the truth, and go insane."

It has been *days*.

Long days ticking by ever so slowly, my hopes of finding Josepha wilting with each passing moment that I search quiet places of the winding gardens and unlocked doors in the palace, coming up empty. Long days of facing the fact she must be gone, and did not come find me to at least say goodbye. Long days, followed by nights without rest, aimlessly wandering through halls and undiscovered rooms, with no sight of Geneviève. Or ghosts.

Or him.

Étienne.

A yawn stretches my mouth open wide. Exhaustion from sleepless nights and days full of party planning setting in. But it was all worth something, the fruits of the work and endless decisions now set out before me on the grounds under the shining sun. I bask in it, sitting on the steps overlooking the gardens, watching people frolic and laugh between rows of bright flowers and meticulously pruned and carved shrubbery.

The sound of joy is so much better than those whispers behind paper fans. There are so many people here, I wonder how they all fit inside the palace, and how strangely quiet the halls must be with everyone in the grass before me.

Scattered throughout the gardens are silver rolling carts holding cakes layered so high, it's as if they are reaching to the sky to tempt the Gods to take a lick of the bright blue frosting. Fresh strawberries and overflowing glasses of champagne dance throughout the crowds on platters carried by more servants than I can count.

It's a dream. A dream I created for *them*. And I watch it all from my seat on the stone stairs. Thinking how this moment could be even better were Mops sitting in my lap now, growling at the ladies with their dogs tightly held in their arms.

In the heart of it all reigns a fountain, water spraying high into the air unlike any I am accustomed to in Vienna. Little frogs of lead, water shooting in streams from their lips. They all circle around Apollo's mother, Latona. I remember her story from my mythology lessons—she turned peasants into frogs for insulting her. I giggle to myself, picturing all the ladies and gentlemen of the court turned to frogs, hopping around with their white wigs still intact.

They die of petulance. Of lower class and amongst their filth.

The king's words flood back to me as I remember sitting on the edge of Apollo's fountain. I know it's there, just beyond the hedges. Guilt begins to eat away at me like hundreds of insects crawling into my skin, removing my flesh pound by pound into their tiny little mouths.

I was so upset on my wedding night. Devastated for the king to see Geneviève's death as commonplace. Like she didn't even matter. Like so many women before her. How I was poked, and prodded, and *changed* to better suit society.

None of the women who drank from blue bottles mattered—not to them anyway.

And now here I am, the host of a grand outdoor garden party.

Geneviève would want me to move on and have fun. Enjoy living.

I remember her words so clearly.

I must relish the life still within me, not live for the dead.

At least I hope that is what Geneviève would want me to do. Anything else is a swill of vinegar, searing my tastebuds.

"All this work and you are not going to join in on the fun?" The voice out of nowhere makes my shoulders jolt up in fright.

"What a shame. Her party and she doesn't even have a drink in her hand," another voice, this one I recognize— Victoire. I laugh along with her and Adélaïde. I do quite like them, even when they speak of me like I'm not here. They're a bit odd, the way they play off each other like a game, bouncing a ball back and forth just for entertainment.

She plops down beside me, Adélaïde next to her. The hoops of their dresses are so obnoxiously large, I'm shocked they can sit at all.

"It's a great party though, I'll give her that." Adélaïde smiles at me, and I appreciate the praise.

Before I can thank her, Victoire jumps in. "It really is. *Marie Antoinette*—putting Versailles on the map with the most lavish celebration. The desserts, the music, the entertainers. All so *magnifique*. Those starving wretched souls in Paris have no idea what they are missing."

My chest shudders slightly. I hadn't thought of the spending. I just decided between options given to me, and picked the things I thought everyone else would like best, hoping to impress them.

The sisters laugh, squawking like birds held tightly in a child's arms trying to escape. I laugh along. Everything is wonderful, and people are happy. Their laughter alongside my own makes me feel like we are old friends, like the sunshine has brought forth a ray of hope.

"Speaking of wretched souls," Adélaïde touches the side of her mouth as she speaks, "I can't *believe* my father chose her to be by his side."

Victoire's eyes narrow on Madame DuBarry. Their hate for the woman is palpable. She's beautiful, in a mint-colored dress that sways in the warm breeze.

Something shatters between her and Chloé. Cobalt blue shards like sand at their feet. Chloé doubles over, coughing and wheezing. Nobody stops their merriment to help the poor girl, Madame DuBarry just waves over some ushers, who carry Chloé away. I hope they can get her some real help for that cough.

The king's laugh carries across the distance. Madame DuBarry seems to make him so happy, as though she has cast a spell on him. A witch I do not trust. Even if I wanted to, I couldn't, because I must side with Adélaïde and Victoire.

My friends.

I play with the buckle of my shoe as they continue despising their unofficial stepmother. "Villain" this, and "blinded our father" that. The brass of the closure is cool on my thumb, but I make the mistake of looking down into the reflection.

"The light of the sun, it makes you a fool. It casts the shadows, cloaking the truth."

I clear my throat, on edge at the voice's mention of what waits for me in the shadows. The truth of what this pompous court hides behind their champagne and tiny dogs. Who among them is targeting me?

This whole party was a way to get answers. And I need to know if others see ghosts, even if it breaks up Adélaïde and Victoire's laughter, full of snark. "Are there any ghost stories about Versailles?"

They become silent, attention fully falling onto me.

"Uh," Victoire grimaces, "what do you mean?"

I feel my face get hot, beyond the heat of the day, petrified to embarrass myself. "Oh, just that my sister would tell me stories of the palace I grew up in. I was wondering if there is anything similar here."

Adélaïde tugs at her ear, rubbing the lobe between her pointer finger and thumb. "You strange Austrians. Of course there are no such tales here in Versailles. It would not be very Godly to imagine ghosts in this place."

Victoire leans in. "You are French now, Marie. You really should not worry about such things."

She is right. I am French now. I have left Austria and all that was.

I must think of France. The people of *this* court. But how can I focus on the living when I am within a ghost story myself?

"What things?" Louis appears beside me, pressing a drink into my hand.

"Nothing. Just silly things that don't matter," I say quickly, thankful for Louis' divine timing. They both look at me like I have grown an extra head upon my shoulder. I'd run if it wouldn't make me appear even more peculiar to them, flee to suffocate by tears in my pillow.

There is no way I can ever tell them that I saw Geneviève. And I definitely can't tell my husband. My stomach hardens with embarrassment and darkness encircles me despite the brightness of the day.

I am still alone. Even with all I've done, they only see me as a prop for the dauphin, entertaining them with my silly little stories. Victoire and Adélaïde's next conversation will be about *me*. They'll gossip about how I talk of ghosts and how I am of no right mind to be in my position.

Mother will kill me.

On the verge of tears, I instead think of Étienne. I need to find him again. *He* believed me.

I take a sip of the champagne, the ever-flowing drink I've grown to love these past few days.

Louis takes a seat on the step beside me, leaving a gap between us. His hands touch the stone for only a moment to adjust before he claps away invisible dirt from them. He may have said that I'm unlike anyone he's ever met, but it is he who is a bit peculiar.

"I only come to tell you I am retiring for the evening. It has been a terribly long day conducting the most fascinating experiments on the inner workings beneath the flesh."

Louis' words make my heart drop, tumbling like a stone down an endless well. We need to produce an heir. The ultimate way for everyone to love me, to want to protect me more than the most precious gems, is to announce a baby boy is on the way.

That will never happen with Louis gone. *Always* gone.

I guess I must rely on myself. My ghosts. My Étienne.

"It's still early, Louis. I was hoping we could enjoy the festivities together," I say, angry at the meekness in my voice when all I want to do is scream. How can I possibly win over this world without my husband by my side? Women have no choice but to win people over, and we must use our husbands and fathers to do so. But Louis, he is *always* leaving me.

I watch Victoire's fingers tighten on her sister's knee, the form of it becoming clear even below all the layers of fabric. Adélaïde's eyes grow with glee. The anticipation of Louis' response sets them both aglow. I wonder how they arrived at being the way they are—enjoying drama as it unfolds. Spectators to the drama of the court, they hold the highest position of scandalmongers.

"A future king requires his rest." His words are abrupt. Matter of fact and not open to discussion. Enough to shut me up despite the screaming within growing louder. I'll have to talk with him about this later. Assure him that I am worthy of his love and companionship—of creating life. I dare not say anything right now, not in front of the sisters who will use it as fuel in their own social circles. They likely already know too much of our private affairs as it is.

"What is it you're working on, dear nephew?" Adélaïde asks. As though she is attempting to come to my rescue. As a friend would do.

Louis glowers at her. The wide brimmed hat atop his head casts shade over his eyes. "The study of medicine and the human body is not something I believe a woman would be able to begin to comprehend. Surely, the subject matter is too dark for you to even want to know about."

One of the hundred servers I dressed as well as royalty offers me a drink as he steadies one foot on the step next to me, the other two steps down. The silver platter holding the champagne glasses trembles ever so slightly from his hand attempting to hold it steady. I take one, and in its place is a circle of gleaming silver.

"A man with a blade, a man with a mission. He'll do as he needs, with exact precision."

I down my drink, ignoring the voice, tempted to throw the glass against the stone steps to shatter my rising anger. My Louis. He's not supposed to think of women this way. He is supposed to worship women. Worship *me* as an equal. Through the anger comes a boil of pure curiosity. *How dark could what he is working on be?*

He gets up then, wiping at the crushed plum velvet of his pants, not bothering to bid us adieu. I can't bear to watch him walk up the steps, and so I look back down toward the fountains, surrounded by perfectly trimmed bushes and meticulously placed flowers. All greenery is shaped into circles, surrounded by swirls, broken up only by walkways now filled with my party guests. It's all *so* marvelous. I only wish I could enjoy it without fear of omens and expectations. Without the crushing weight of my husband's abandonment.

I am constantly aware of people out the corner of my eye, hoping to spot blonde hair and a violet ribbon amongst the crowd. Or for a glimpse of blood on a cuff that will lead me to Geneviève's murderer.

"Did you hear poor Jean recovered?" Victoire asks her sister. My ears perk up at the mention of Jean. I remember Geneviève being so kind to him.

"I spoke to him this very morning," Adélaïde says with a sense of entitlement, hand on collarbone and head up straight. "I was beginning to think nobody would recover from that nasty disease."

"It is quite gross. So many of them crying from their beds. It makes my skin crawl," Victoire says with an exaggerated shiver of her shoulders.

Adélaïde fiddles with her tall hair. "As long as it's not one of us, isn't that right, Marie?"

I shrug, and look back to the gardens. I do not wish to think of these things.

Alexandre is surrounded by a flock of women who act like sheep. The shepherd smiles at them as he turns in place, his hair pulled into a thick black bow that trails down his back. They all giggle in delight, but the loudest of all is Anne.

Her sweet voice carries like a melody with a genuine laugh. She is infatuated with him. This poor chambermaid's broken heart, forgotten at the opportunity to receive attention from the guilty man that originally did the breaking. I don't blame her. That thumping in the chest, the one that lights a fire in the hollows of your stomach, is worth chasing. When Louis finally kisses me, I'm certain that flame will be stoked within me. I *need* that flame, for how am I to spend my life with someone who cannot give me that?

A flicker of Étienne's freckles comes to mind, and I press my lips tight.

No. Louis.

I try to think of my husband's face, but instead watch as Alexandre takes Anne's arm and they leave the rest of the swooning girls. For a brief moment, I smile for Anne. Until my teeth clench in protest. I don't like that boy. The way he laughed at me when I was introduced to Louis. Maybe that is why my husband is cold toward me. Alexandre got in his head and told him I was unworthy and unfit for his bed.

I can't think of such things. Not now.

"Shall we join the fun, then?" I say to the sisters, more an announcement than a question.

"About time!" Victoire says and I'm sure Adélaïde responds but I'm too far ahead of them now, running down the steps into the crowd.

A man nearly trips me as he skips down the steps, trying to impress a woman at the bottom. He catches me by my arm, and cowers into a bow the moment he recognizes my face.

"Pardon me," he says, and stares at me with wide eyes. There is a twinkle in them. The twinkle of a man that can so easily cut down a woman. My mind can't escape from what happened to Geneviève in these very gardens.

I flash him a saccharine smile and continue on, stealing a glass from the hands of an older gentleman. He protests at first, but then realizes it is me. The dauphine. And I like the way that feels. To do as I please. To have fun. To be powerful. I wink back at him, the way Geneviève would have winked at me after doing something like this.

Where is Étienne? I twirl through people, annoyed by the tightness of my corset, restricting me from further freedom. Yet another ridiculous expectation to alter our bodies for the gaze of men.

With each move I make in step to the orchestra's song, I search for Étienne. Imagining what he would look like under the curls of a white wig. How he would look in his finest.

I'm curious about him. The way he makes my heartbeat speed.

My vision blurs and my throat scratches, a sadness I try to hold down. I'll bet Étienne would tell me how well I did planning this party. He'd notice how much work I had to do. Unlike Louis, who didn't have enough time to compliment a single thing. My cheeks turn hot. Not one.

Madame DuBarry cuts in front of me and I burst into laughter, spittle nearly hitting her in the face. I can't talk to her. Can't explain that my popularity in court hinges upon ignoring her. Her face pinches in what I can only imagine is disappointment, and her eyes gloss as she turns towards the king.

I leave her then, heading in the opposite direction of the king. It no longer matters that it was me who made this grand event happen, and that there's free-flowing drink and revelry to enjoy. I won't enjoy them. Not really. Not when the grief imprinted on my heart fails to be wrapped by bandages of distraction. When I don't know which of them killed my friend, inching ever closer to killing me.

The omens.

"They are still with me," I whisper to Josepha under my breath, as though she is here. I long for her to be. "The omens have darkened to my death."

Not a soul hears.

This party was not some elaborate plan to be scolded. I was to make friends. I was to have a distraction from Geneviève. My sister. To get answers about the haunted halls of Versailles.

Fruitless. That's all this was.

All of it a grand misstep, only providing dizziness and disappointment.

ELEVEN

I scurry into the palace, more like a rat than a royal. I do not want to face the king after laughing in the face of Madame DuBarry.

A tear escapes from the corner of my eye. I don't want to be cruel to her. Her eyes are always kind, begging for me to break the silence with something. And she *seems* to care for her friend. I wonder why then would she give her that deadly blue bottle.

The king's reddened cheeks set me into action, but I should have left the party long ago. Before I embarrassed myself. Before I drank too much.

It's difficult to raise my dress high enough so as to not trip on the circled wire that makes the skirts so wide, all the while balancing on these heeled shoes.

"Damn the formalities," I say to no one. The race away from the king and his mistress has led me to a column at the entrance of a new hallway. I lean against it to remove my pale pink shoes.

My breath is fast now, burning in my chest as I run. Worsening the ache left from Louis stomping on my heart. "He is supposed to love me," I say to no one. "He is supposed to be there for me. But where is he now? Experiments, hunting, or bed."

"Or worse!" A high-pitched laugh turns to gurgling.

I turn my head and find myself staring into Geneviève's eyes. Crimson streams from the corner of each eye, but they remain wide, desperate, staring at me through a haze of cloudy white.

I stumble back into a wall but she stays on me, blood dripping onto both of us.

I feel less alone when she's here, my confidant returned, but her sudden appearances give me a jolt and my chest struggles to keep up. "Geneviève, what do I do? Please," I struggle to breathe, "what do I do?"

The gurgles turn to a rasp as she holds one hand to her throat and another out to me. Blood oozes from between her fingers. She touches my cheek, leaving it wet.

"Can't you see, Marie? Think of Chloé. She's gone now."

"Gone? She was just in the gardens," I whimper.

"Now she'll be on Louis' table. I know better now," she says, taking a pause as liquid bubbles in the back of her throat, choking her endlessly. She moves behind the statue, hidden, before she pokes her head out. I watch in awe.

"What do you know, Geneviève?"

She slowly walks around the statue, leaving a smear of blood as her fingers graze across the white stone. "Louis was ever lurking, waiting for each of us to find his table and have our flesh torn open. Louis doesn't care about any of us. Alexandre and his friends play with us while we are living, and the soon-to-be-king plays with our flesh and bones when we are dead. "

Geneviève is close now. Her face before mine, urging me to listen. "Look at me. So desperate for love, I let boys play me like a pawn. They all abandoned me though. They always do. And now, I am this."

She looks sadly down at her stained and torn gown.

And then she's gone.

A guard arrives beside me, panting, straightening his jacket before standing tall, hands at his sides. He must have run after me.

"Please," I cry, throwing down my shoes, watching them bounce off the marble. "I want to be alone."

"Madame," he starts, as his forehead wrinkles. Anne runs to his side, panting.

"No. I am dismissing you. You are dismissed," I say, seeing the pain in Anne's eyes. Etiquette must have sent her to watch me. To take the place of Geneviève. But Geneviève is still with me, and I need to get her back.

The young man in blue tugs on his ear before bowing and doing as I asked. Anne sucks in her bottom lip, and saunters after him.

Thankfully.

When I see them no longer, I call out to my friend. "Geneviève!" A muted cry.

"Come back, please!" I call once more, beginning to pace, fighting the wire hooping of my dress. In my efforts, I fall onto the side of my hip. Pain radiates down my leg as I push my hands against the black and white checkered floor. The cool marble on my palms clears my head a bit. Still, I have no idea where I am. I've run past countless rooms and through unfamiliar corridors. I'm starting to think I'll never learn all the spaces within Versailles.

My head buzzes as I pull myself back up to my feet, standing in front of the most beautiful statue of Aphrodite. Waves of stone fabric flow from her head down to her waist, her breasts exposed without a second thought. Gooseflesh up the back of my arms says that she is watching me despite her eyes being closed. Despite her being made from rock.

Only statues. They are only statues.

The hall is full of them, a long line on both sides, of stone figure after stone figure, all perfectly sculpted by some formidable artists.

"You must be Aphrodite," I step closer to the statue with the closed eyes. "Goddess of love."

I snort, then rub my fingers across my brow. How absurd of me to be talking to a statue. And yet my mouth opens again. "At least *you're* safe," I say and run a finger within the folds of the white stone fabric wrapped around her.

The Goddess of love. Does she know how wrong this has all gone? How my dreams have unraveled from reality, left frayed from the harsh knife of Versailles?

"I would wager that you were in love once. Then let down. Even the Goddess of love can't escape heartbreak." I scoff, hot air sighing from my nostrils. "Now you're stuck here, with all these other statues. They are too far away for you to touch them, yet close enough to haunt you."

A memory, only a few years old, of Josepha crying in the rose bushes hits me. Thorns among the red flowers cut at her knees while she filled her hands with her tear-soaked face.

She had fallen madly in love with a boy who brought fresh vegetables to Schönbrunn. His clothes were tattered, but his words were smooth. She risked so much by sneaking out with him under moonlight and he repaid her by falling in love with another girl. A girl who didn't have her future slated out for her, destined to be sent to another country to marry for foreign ties like Josepha and I were—like all our sisters were.

Josepha's plump cheeks and pink eyes are forever etched in my memory. She warned me that day to never fall in love and to protect my heart. She begged that I protect others from the pain that now seared through her heart. To save them.

I heard her words, but I didn't listen. A piece of me hopes she failed to heed her own advice and her disappearance was merely her running away with the love of her life. The hope of it all sets a fire within my chest. Love is happiness, kisses and caressed fingers mending even the most broken wings.

But here I am, sad that my husband does not love me, because I so desperately wanted to avoid my sister's advice. Still unable to find my sister. Being hunted by a killer.

I study Aphrodite's face and the way the curls of her hair dance freely in the imaginary wind. "I do wonder, is it possible that one day someone might love me? That they'll protect my heart? Or are the omens there, waiting in plain sight, for that love to be crushed like a tomato under a heel?"

Something tickles down my spine and settles on my low back. My breath sucks in fast, fear forcing a gasp. The soles of my feet squeak on the shiny floor as I spin to face what's behind me.

Expecting to see someone wielding a blade. I wonder if Geneviève saw the blade before it cut her throat.

"I didn't mean to cause a fright," a voice says close to my ear as hands rub up and down my shoulders.

I turn, pulse thumping.

The threat is not a spirit.

Rather, it is the boy who could cost me my place in Versailles. The role I was bred for. And excitement rolls through me at the sight of him. The fear of thinking it was the hidden assailant in the hedge maze floods from me like an unleashed dam the second his eyes meet mine. Those ocean eyes I've been searching out for days now.

The rules of the court are strict, and yet he touched me as if it were natural. Like I would be accepting of it. And I am.

His white linen sleeves are bunched up to the elbow, his arms now crossed. Each muscle in his forearms is tense. Strong.

The place he touched my shoulders only seconds ago tingles, aching for his hands to return.

"Étienne!" I yell, but my laugh is impossible to hide. "You scared me."

He *scares* me. Would I be hanged in the square for all to see if someone were able to read the thoughts I have about Étienne straight from my mind?

Thoughts of him holding my hands under silk sheets.

Thoughts of his hand with its rough edges cradling my chin, lifting it to meet his—

"My apologies." His arms uncross and he motions them back to where I was looking, back to the statues. "You know, it is a shame that they never talk back."

My chest caves in embarrassment. He must have heard me talking to Aphrodite—the statue. I was talking to stone. Mortified, my ears grow hot, unsure of what to say to him. I am such a fool.

"I've always thought there is an eerie life about them," he continues, "they are the watchers of all the insanity that goes on in this place. The ones who hold the secrets of the palace and know who has died, and by whose hand."

His mouth is turned up into a sly smile.

"You tease me," I smile back, taking a step toward him.

"Never." His forehead tilts down and those blue eyes are shadowed by the lashes he looks through. "You may be the one talking to them in this hallway on your own, but it is I who thinks they're alive in some way."

His words are comforting. The seriousness in his voice is a clear indication this is not some great jest. My smile deepens, and I take one more step toward him, so close now I could reach out and take hold of his hand.

"Accompany me for a walk. If you please," he says.

My answer is quick. "I'd love to." I feel so safe with Étienne, comforted by the way he sees me and takes me seriously. Not many have before.

If only the boy I am *allowed* to love would take me seriously. Would look at me the way Étienne does.

Étienne's eyes find mine and his dimples sink into his skin, kissed with a honeyed tint from the setting sun through the windows. It's as though I am the only thing he sees—that I'm the only girl in the world.

A laugh echoes through the hallway, bouncing off the arched ceilings. Three chambermaids round the corner, heads tilted to the ceiling with their joy while their feet move quickly. I take a step away from Étienne's just as they see us. They come to a halt and quickly curtsy.

"Please, don't stop your fun," I say, looking to Étienne then back at the three girls. Their plain cotton dresses look like they've been worn for days. "I want all these halls to be filled with joy."

They look at us with blushed cheeks and sweat dripping from their brow. They've been working hard to pull off the garden party. For *me*.

"Apologies. We are just on our way to the kitchens," the oldest looking girl says, though she herself looks younger than I.

"Don't let us stop you. And thank you for all you do," I say, nodding to them.

Étienne bends at the hip to bow. "Good day, ladies," he says. The chambermaids break into a fit of giggles as they run off. They must think he is as handsome as I do.

Their laughter carries down the halls, and a memory of Josepha shines brightly. We would often linger outside mother's office to peek at our elder sisters' potential suitors, then fall into fits of giggles as we shuffled back to our rooms once Mother would catch our faces between the door left ajar.

"Josepha and I used to laugh like that." I'm stunned that I said it aloud for Étienne to hear. I find myself opening up to him further, as though giving him the key to a diary I've kept well hidden. "I saw her. My sister, Josepha. She ran from me in the hedges."

"You saw her?" We continue our walk down the hall, past Greek goddesses and men of stone wielding swords.

"Yes, the night that—the night that—"

"Marie." His voice, soft as a whisper. Soothing. He doesn't require me to finish the sentence and face the horror of finding Geneviève, and I'm thankful for the unspoken pass.

"Josepha was singing 'feeee, fawww fummm, I smell the blood of an earthly man,' just as we sang as children playing hide and seek in the gardens."

"Why did she run from you?" he asks, the same question I've asked myself countless times since it happened. I run my fingers across my collarbone, contemplating while Étienne leads me through halls I've not yet seen.

"It makes no sense why she would run from me. She loves me. We were closer than any two sisters could be." I don't say that she could have met the killer first, that she fled, or worst of all, that she has been taken from me. I can't say the words, because the idea rips through my aching heart.

"There is a reason. We just have to figure it out," he says as the black and white checkered floor leads to a room of windows. I take a step, unsure of where we are headed, and realize that I am still barefoot.

"We?" I ask, my steps inching toward him, wanting his hand to touch my own.

Étienne stops walking, to turn to me with wide, serious eyes.

"We."

My cheekbones rise as a smile stretches across my face.

I rub at my temple, unsure what to say. Would my lips even move if I tried, so content in this joyous smile.

Laughing echoes from outside, and I turn from him to look beyond the white room and out giant glass doors leading to the garden. The party is still in full swing, even without me there.

For once, I do not care. For I am with Étienne.

The gold cherubs stationed above the doors look down on us. Violent stares from their angelic eyes, devilish smiles perched upon chubby cheeks.

My fingers crawl to the bridge of my nose and I pinch there for a moment.

Could this be another omen? A shred of happiness—a connection—that is destined to be ripped away from me? Is it happiness I should have in the first place?

It strikes me then, a blade dug deep into my gut, as I look back out at the sea of people in the gardens, their green and purple and fuchsia hats visible from even here.

The chambermaids who giggled at us just a few moments ago.

Perhaps they weren't chuckling about how cute Étienne is. Perhaps their laughs were a precursor to the gossip they were going to spread about me. They could be on their way to tell all those at the party that the dauphine is with a boy, alone in the halls.

I am with Étienne. Alone. And wanting.

The idea of the rumors that would ripple through court about my holding a hand that doesn't belong to Louis trickles into my mind. My hands cup around my mouth, the smile faded. Each breath pushes through my fingers loudly.

"What is it?" Étienne crouches low and all I can do is stare at him over my fingertips, feeling warm tears fall onto them. "Marie!"

"I'm sorry, Étienne. I must go." I say the words that I don't want to, but I must. I imagine Mother's face. What she would do if she received a letter explaining how I ruined everything she worked so hard for. That France would now go to war with Austria. Because of me.

"I can't let you leave like this." His voice cracks. "Not while you are upset. Please. *Please* tell me why you are crying."

"Those—those chambermaids will start stories. About *us*. They could have me hu—"

"Don't say that."

"They could! If we are seen together, alone," I pace back and forth in front of him, the hall a blur of gold around me.

"Then we won't be seen together."

His fingers find mine, and I breathe in his soft scent of fresh oranges. Our fingers intertwine effortlessly and I'm suddenly aware of my own heartbeat. I count along with each racing thrum. It plays a happy song.

It shouldn't. But it does.

And then we are running.

He leads me through Versailles like a delicate dance, along halls I have not traveled and rooms I've not yet seen. They are all much of the same until we reach a rounded door made of wooden slats. So different from the rest of the white and gold in the palace.

Plain, like me.

Étienne opens the small door with his shoulder, still clutching my hand. His thumb makes the smallest movement to caress my palm.

A touch from another.

My breath rushes in and out. I've longed for connection for so, so long.

The door shuts and he pulls me in tight, his hand moving from my hand to around my waist. I arch my back, leaning into his pull and raising my chin to meet his gaze. The back of my head grazes the closed door, the rest of Versailles a world away.

"Told you." He smiles. "We don't have to be seen together. This is a very large palace."

I feel my nerves tremble, but a sun kissed hair falls on Étienne's brow and I forget all else.

"I've come to this room before," he says. "When I needed to be alone. It's where artists work on sculptures unbeknown to the court and out of the way. I watch them create for hours at a time, chiseling rock into things of beauty."

My eyes flick behind him, only for a second, to see the space he speaks of.

"Shall we?" His hold on me slowly releases, but the place on my waist where his fingers caressed burns. I dare to set my hand upon the back of his arm as we continue to walk, not wanting to break our closeness completely.

I remain silent, staring at a hundred faces of stone. Their blank eyes bore into me and guilt twines up my spine.

The room is vast, with no ornaments or carvings on the walls like the rest of the palace. Rather, there are tables covered in mud and dust, statues covered in sheets as far as the eye can see. This truly isn't a place royalty uses, which eases any remaining tension in my shoulders.

I feel like a child discovering a brand new world as I explore the sculptors' studio. There's a tall statue in the corner, covered with a muddy canvas. A curiosity causes my hand to pull at the canvas, wanting to see who is covered. Perhaps a lover for Aphrodite, not yet revealed.

The figure, taller than me, comes crashing down with the canvas. I scream, jumping back so as to not be crushed from the weight of stone.

A head made of clay separates from its body when it hits the floor. I pick it up, staring at her closed eyes. "I'm so sorry," I say.

Étienne gently takes the sculpture from my hand. "I'm so sorry," I repeat through sniffles.

"Marie, you have nothing to apologize for."

But I do. Looking down at the decapitated figure reminds me of the trampling again. The woman I walked over, through her pools of blood, to escape into the confines of Versailles. Following the guards while a little boy cried.

I sob into cupped hands that cover my mouth. "I do have to apologize."

Étienne gently takes my hands into his own, pressing them to his chest. "There is no thing in this world that you could ever do wrong."

He doesn't know me. Doesn't know the omens that nip at my heels, clouding me with deep, dark, horrors. "People have died because of me," I say shakily.

"Oh, Marie," he presses my hands even closer to his chest, "you can't blame yourself for these things that happen."

"But the woman who died when I arrived. All those people trampled because I—"

"Perhaps it was a gift. Those people were suffering, and now they suffer no more," he says before moving my hands slowly to his mouth, kissing the top of my fingers ever so gently. We lock eyes, and I wonder how this boy can find so much good in me. How I cause ruin all around, yet he only sees light.

He coughs, breaking the silence and the intense longing in my heart. My hands fall to my side and I turn to pick up the statue again, move it back to its body as if to make it whole once more.

"I wasn't kidding when I said I thought there's a life to the statues," he says.

"There really is." I lovingly place the canvas over the statue and walk away. I find myself holding my breath as I run a finger along a table, lifting away a layer of clay dust. "If only they could tell us who killed Geneviève."

"Ah, I wish they could." He leans over and blows the dust off my finger. My temperature rises, hotter than a fever.

The room is sweltering without windows to the outside world, and I can barely stand to be in my corset anymore, pulling me in tight while sweat pools upon the fabric against my back.

A weight in my chest sets my heart racing as I think of the man chasing Geneviève. How he could leave her the way he did, the way her ghost will be forevermore.

"Evil," I whimper.

Étienne sighs and rubs his hands through his brown hair. "There is evil in this place, but you are safe with me."

The back of his fingers gently brush down my cheek then trail down to my collarbone. He watches each place he touches while I watch him. He makes his way to my hand and lifts it up to his mouth. Étienne kisses the tip of my finger, so softly, a fire sets ablaze within me as he lingers there.

His lips are wet, and the pressure of my finger gently parts them as he begins to speak. "Things could be better for you, Marie. With me. You can trust me."

I stare into his ocean eyes. "I know," I say. I know I can trust him. And the warmth in my stomach knows he is right about things being better. But that is someone else's life. Mine is here, destined for a crown.

When he lowers my hand back down to my side, a twinge of disappointment runs through me. I say nothing. His hands rub down my shoulders to my wrists, only the thin, pink cloth of my dress between his skin and my own.

I walk around the table, regretfully. But I know I need to distance myself from him for a moment. At least until the fluttering sensations in my chest slows.

A scream shatters the silence, a woman in pain somewhere outside these doors. I stay frozen, waiting to hear more.

"Please! It hurts!" A woman pleas, strangled between coughs. They are in the hallway, getting closer. Étienne and I look at each other, then we both look to the door.

"Quiet!" A gruff voice yells, followed by the yelp of the woman.

The round knob on the door begins to rattle, the woman crying just on the other side.

Étienne leaps across a table, sending the stone head of a woman crashing to the floor, crumbling to bits of rock and dust.

A rainfall of dust and fear.

"Who is in there?" The man's voice demands, as he bangs on the door.

"Help me!" The girl bellows.

Before I can move to do anything, Étienne pulls me close to him with an arm around my waist and we hide in a wardrobe. My heart urges me to help the girl, but I stay in Étienne's arms, surrounded by clay covered smocks.

The booms upon the door cease, and Étienne loosens his protective grip on me.

Relief rushes through my veins. They have left the door, but only God knows where he was taking that poor girl. "We have to help her," I whisper.

"We can't. I can only keep you safe."

"We are all going to die," I cry, allowing the tears to come. He holds me close and I can feel his breath in my hair.

"You're safe, Marie. I am here with you. Everlasting."

I know better, though.

Versailles is haunted. And so am I.

TWELVE

Warmth hits my face, sun peeking through the small crack of the fabric surrounding my bed.

My arms stretch above my head while I lay on my pillow, sleep still in my eyes. A smile grows, touching each ear, remembering last night with Étienne. I feel drunk, though I've not had a drop of alcohol.

The screech of metal on metal breaks the reverie and I jolt, sitting upright in the bed. Etiquette stands over me, still holding onto the curtains she just swung open.

There they are. The line of ladies in waiting, ready to dress me for the day.

"Good morning!" I sing, hopping off the bed, the floor cold on my toes. "I do apologize for you all getting up so early to come attend to me, but I don't think I'll be needing assistance."

Etiquette's hand claps down on her collarbone, while the other women look on with gaped mouths. "Marie, there is—"

"I do believe *I* am the dauphine. So, as I said, I do not require assistance today." I walk past them all, stifling a giggle at their slack jaws while I grab a simple peach dress from a plush armchair.

"As you wish," Etiquette says as my hands push through the arm holes of the thin cloth.

It feels great. Magnificent even. I practically skip out of the room, into the hall. It's as though I see Versailles in a whole new light—the palace of gold leaf and fleurs-de-lis on every wall, a masterpiece as it was built to be. The epitome of beauty, straight from the dreams of the Sun King. I laugh at a golden statue of a cherub as I pass, ignoring its leering grin.

Madame DuBarry appears from around a corner, and even she doesn't put a stop to my bubble of happiness. The moment she sees me, she curtsies, but there is something more…her face has gone pale.

Like she has seen a ghost.

Words nearly burst from my mouth, wanting to ask her if she has experienced the hauntings in these halls. Where Chloé is. How her cough is. My smile fades, remembering the woman screaming outside the studio door while Étienne and I hid. Could it have been her who cried for help while I remained quiet with Étienne's arms around me?

I cough, suppressing the guilt building at the back of my throat. I can't face Madame DuBarry. Conversation with her would only lead to thicker layers of guilt. As if that's not bad enough, the sisters would be furious if I speak to their stepmother. The careful chess pieces I've attempted to place socially within court would fall over. *I* would be over.

Her eyes grow to saucers, staring at me. She wants me to say something. To break the silence between us. I can't. Madame DuBarry looks over her shoulder, in the direction she just came from, then back at me. Her head slowly shakes from side to side.

What has she seen?

I can't stand here any longer, so I nod with a closed mouth, then move around her. I feel her eyes on me while I walk away.

As soon as I round the corner into another hallway, I come upon a wall of people, huddled close together, intent on a singular thing. There's a hum of voices, broken up by shouts of "let me see!" and "give it here!" and "how *scandalous.*"

I bounce on my toes, desperate to be a part of the action and to see what all the fuss is about. I push through their sweaty bodies, skin slick, no doubt from the blistering heat beaming through the windows. The stench of them all forces me to take shallow breaths as I continue to make my way to the object of everyone's interest.

I falter, scared it could be another dead body. There's laughter though; the closer I get to the source the more I hear. There wouldn't be people laughing over a dead body. No. No. Everything is alright. I let loose a long exhale through pursed lips and finally see it.

Alexandre waves a piece of parchment in the air. "Drawings never lie, friends!" he calls, and I realize that he is clearly adored by the growing crowd of more than fifty men and women of the court. They also seem to be enamored by whatever it is he holds in his hand. He passes it to a rather plump man, whose greasy fingers smudge the ink. His other hand touches his mouth as he laughs.

Alexandre spots me in the crowd, "make way for the dauphine, you scoundrels," he says, but there is a glimmer in his eye, my intuition stirring as I continue to push past the people that didn't pay mind to Alexandre's instructions or my presence.

He hands another paper to a woman with so much red lipstick it has coated her teeth. Alexandre grabs more pamphlets from the few other sheets scattered at his feet. I quickly snatch the newest one Alexandre's fist clenches to. He watches me with precision, like an eagle intent on his kill.

Uncrumpling the parchment reveals the last thing I thought I'd see. My bubble of joy now burst.

Me.

My hands tremble, my eyes straining to take in the details before me.

THE BUTCHER AND HIS BRIDE is sprawled across the top of the paper in large, bold black ink.

It's a crude drawing, with shaky lines and blocks of color outside the lines, but the likeness is there. My naked body sits upon a throne. I hold a hand mirror to look lovingly at myself while adjusting an extremely large wig on my head with the other hand. My small breasts are accentuated, and my stomach concaves, hollow and void of my duty. I'm wearing blue heels though—how kind to leave me some semblance of clothing.

My eyes trace through the drawing as my chest heaves with pent up breath, anger, and tears. Cakes and sweets lay about my cartoon throne, complete with a table of jewelry and dresses carelessly scattered in the background.

Louis sits on the edge of a smaller throne than mine, hunched over so his face will fit into his hands while he cries. Louis' large nose sticks out from between his fingers.

A golden cradle sits in front of him, mocking him with the absence of a child. In it only lay a large knife in a pool of blood.

Implying Louis is unhappy. A victim despite his status. And that I—that I am some sort of villain dripping with decadence. It is not true. Not in the least.

Worst of all, below the thrones lay a heap of bodies. Dozens of souls bleeding out while Louis and I ignore them below our feet.

Heat rises in my arms, my cheeks, my chest.

"Well, Marie," Alexandre says after giving me enough time to look at the paper, "I think it's one of my favorite pamphlets yet. Everyone else seems to like it too."

I shake my head at him, in utter disbelief that he would do such a thing to his best friend. His enjoyment in my misery, in spreading around a drawing as a sick joke, leaves me speechless. I turn, and push my way back out of the crowd. This is *treason*.

I attempt not to crinkle the paper any further as I run down the halls. My peach dress flows and creates a breeze on my legs as I hurry to the dauphins' chambers.

An usher stands in my path when I reach my destination. His navy-blue coat suddenly all I can see in front of me. I push him, but he does not waver. "I need to see my husband!" I scream, yet he still doesn't budge. "I order you to move! I am the dauphine!" I yell even louder this time.

Finally, the white and gold doors open. "What is going on?" Louis asks as the guard side steps out of my way.

"Did you see this?" I walk straight past Louis, letting myself into his chambers. "Why would he have us drawn as killers?" The word *killer* is heavy as lead in my belly.

He's on my heels by the time I turn back around to him, now in the center of his room, at the foot of his bed.

"I assure you, I have no clue as to what you are speaking of, if you could only calm—"

"*This*, Louis. This!" I push the pamphlet to his chest, the browned paper a stark contrast to the white ruffles of his shirt. I continue speaking as he takes the drawing from my hand and studies it. "*The Butcher and His Bride*! How can they say such things, while I grieve Geneviève's death? When I saw a poor boy's eyes drip tears on his mother's dead face, right on our doorstep when I arrived."

He clears his throat, but I continue. My rage a roaring sea of words. "They want an heir, but think all I do is stare at a mirror, in love with myself and the indulgences of the court. See all those desserts and dresses? This isn't me!"

A piece of me cracks when his response is laughter.

Louis points to the strawberries that line a tier of one of the cakes. "I know it's not you. But you must admit, the artist did a great job with his details. Look at how well he captured my nose."

I come completely undone then, tears falling like yolks seeping out from my shell. "You—you know it was Alexandre passing these around. It is treason, yet you laugh?" I cry.

"It is not treason. Alexandre did nothing wrong, he simply finds the humor in such things. He means no harm," he says and I grit my teeth, biting back my anger.

"Someone killed my friend! My sister is missing! The number of people dying from smallpox grows every single day! Yet this," I point at the pamphlet he holds, "this is what the focus is on? High society cares more of rumors above the sick and dying?"

"It is a drawing, Marie. Who cares about what the poor citizens in Paris think about—"

"The people of Paris. The court. They don't respect me, Louis! We must have a child. I must do my duty." My eyes sting from the strain of ever flowing tears. I will never have love with Louis. But I want to survive.

"Yes, I know it is our duty."

"I will be safe if we have a child. If I carry your baby, the heir, I won't end up in the hedges like —"

"You are safe here, Marie."

He crumples the paper into a small ball between his palms. Louis reminds me of a child as his tiny hand drops the pamphlet on the floor. He is too weak to truly keep me safe. Étienne is strong. He would have Alexandre's head for hurting me.

"This I promise you," Louis continues. "And you will eventually fulfill your role and have children."

"We should—"

"Just not right now," he says, taking a step across the wooden floors but failing to embrace me or even touch me. How could I have been such a fool? To think he would want me. He took me as his bride, but he doesn't want my voice, or mind, or even my flesh.

A lump in my throat is desperate to ask him why we can't have children *now*. Intuition screams in my belly to shut up, and I listen.

The fractures spread across my heart further, breaking me into tiny pieces. The rest of me is numb. Louis doesn't truly want to be with me. I am merely an obligation in his eyes. A fulfillment of his promise to the throne.

My dream of falling in love with him and being happy shattered forever.

The silence must be deafening to him. "Come. Rest for a moment," he says, ushering me to the other side of the room, and sits down on the emerald bench along the window. The sun hits the glass just right, a burst of white bouncing back its own reflection.

"Look what you've become, they pulled too hard. The dead are not at rest, left you covered in scars."

I know they aren't at rest. I know. *I know!*

I fiddle with my skirts and blink back tears. There may be no happiness here, but I must collect myself. Must keep myself safe from blue bottles and disappointing Mother more than I already have.

I fold my hands on my lap, intentionally studying them for a moment while I smother my emotions.

"I want the court to like me, and I so desperately want friends," I begin. "I can't do that without having a child, and I especially can't do that with your best friend handing pamphlets like this out."

"Madame DuBarry went through the exact same thing." He pats his hand down beside me, inviting me to take a seat. "And the drawings of her were horrendous."

I pick up my skirt and sit down beside him. "That is exactly what I mean. Look what pamphlets got her. She is hated by many and the source of ridicule. The only person by her side coughing in such fits I fear for her life." I swallow down the urge to mention the screaming of the woman in the halls, mere steps away from a wardrobe I cowered in.

Louis glares out the window, in a way I wish he would glare at me. I crave for him to touch me, to hold me tight in an embrace until I can fall asleep and pretend that none of this is even happening. That my husband could provide a true sense of safety.

"Marie, you must understand that the hunting and experiments are what keep me sane in this place," he says. What is easy for him is impossible for me. I am not able to live, not when I am drowning with fear.

"There is always gossip," he continues, "I am always disappointing someone. Stop worrying about pleasing everyone, for it is an impossible task, and you will fail. They are vipers, intent on striking, finding any weakness they can. You need to forget all the distractions and find something to do, a distraction for yourself, and fill your time with it in order to stay sane."

My teeth dig into the soft flesh of my tongue. Distractions. That is not what I need. That will not make the chatter in the court silence, or tame Alexandre, or make the ghosts of Versailles move on to the Heavens.

The corner of my eye twitches, and before I can stop them, the words fall. "Do you know what scares *me*? What riding horses through forests won't help me with? That I'll continue to see ghosts until I can stop the killer. That Geneviève haunts me, stalks me to show her throat sliced over and over again."

Louis' brows pinch together, creating two sharp lines between them as I continue. The floor creaks as I stand from beside him and begin to pace back and forth, realization spreading faster than any pamphlets ever could.

I've been too focused on political adoration and on ghosts. The real threat comes from flesh. "What of Geneviève, Louis? Why is nobody asking who killed her? There is a murderer in our midst and not a single person is afraid? Who is killing poor souls like my friend?"

Louis stands from the bench. His form is a mere silhouette of black with the sun shining behind him. His features come back to focus when he steps so close his breath warms the skin of my face. I swallow, half expecting he is going to kiss me, before that warm breath turns to sharp words. "Geneviève was a nobody. Mark my words, wife, there is no killer on the loose in Versailles. Geneviève's death was of her own doing and her death means nothing." His hand grips my elbow, forcing my arm to bend. "You sound absolutely mad talking of ghosts. You are to speak no more of this to another soul."

It hurts. The words spit from his mouth like venom, poisoning my veins. He truly believes Geneviève was nothing. He has no belief in me.

He releases me. Then steps back and claps his hands twice, dismissing me again. "Well, then. I must get my horse ready for today's ride." His volume is back to normal, a bounce in it that shirks away the disdain his previous sentence held.

Instead of kisses, he questioned my sanity and gave me orders of silence. I clasp at my stomach, pain writhing there, my devastation turning to sickness.

He brushes past me as he walks out of the room. I wobble from the contact, then remain motionless, staring out the window. The reflection of a scared girl looking back at me.

"There she laid, you will see, Josepha cries, she dies, she screams."

I turn from the window to quiet the voice, only to find a violet ribbon.

THIRTEEN

Intuition pulses in my stomach, causing bile to rise up my throat.

I take one step. Two. Slowly inching closer to the ribbon under Louis' desk. One end of the violet satin tucked into a crack between floorboards.

A violet ribbon, strayed from its owner with blonde hair. With the smallest drop of blood.

Josepha.

The light of Louis' chamber fades—a darkness cloaking the windows as a cloud passes by the sun, like the gloom quickly stealing all my hope. My throat goes dry as the back of my neck prickles with dread.

I crumple to the floor, and my head nearly hits the edge of the black table on my decent.

"Feee, fawww, fummm, I smell the blood of an earthly man." The memory of her voice sings, as clear as if she were sitting right beside me now.

Fingertips tickle up my sides like little spider legs, and I fold over with laughter. "Josepha," I cry.

"Shhhhh. Mother will hear us!" Her finger presses into her lips.

I wrap my arms atop her shoulders, pulling her in close. Taking in her rosewater scent. "You're better. Finally. I thought you would never get better."

"I missed you too. Now, come, I have stories," Josepha leans in close to whisper while she takes me by the hand.

We shuffle through the halls, trying our best to muffle happy giggles. My cheeks hurt from smiling—my sister looks as healthy as ever and my heart blossoms to have her back.

White nightgowns swish around our ankles while our feet pitter patter against the marble floor. We make it to our favorite fireplace and curl into each other. A natural position to find, familiar from many nights before.

"Where were we…before I got sick?" She asks.

"Henry VIII," I say with excitement, scooching in closer to her, keeping my voice down. I do not want Mother to ruin this moment.

"Oh, yes. His buttons always popped from his belly, and his breath smelled of spinach. He spun lies when he was done with Anne Boleyn, and while her neck was hacked at by a sword, he popped grape after grape into his mouth. He smiled, enjoying the thrill of the sword instead of the swift axe others would receive. His rotted teeth gnashed the grapes, and they burst in his mouth as Anne's throat burst with blood."

I feel my cheeks go cold despite the crackling fire. My hands tremble, but I don't stop Josepha, only watch her in the glow of orange light as she spins her frightening tale.

"Nights would pass after her brutal end, and he felt no remorse. He slept well in his soft sheets. But his rest soon came to an end," she

says, standing up and wobbling on tiptoe. Josepha pulls the blonde hair atop her head, tilting her neck to the side. "'Heeeeenry', Anne would whisper in her ghostly form. 'Look what you've done to me.'"

My hands clap to my mouth. Gooseflesh rises on the back of my arms.

Josepha sways back and forth, eyes wide and staring blankly. "'You killed me. You killed all of us.'"

"Josepha! You're scaring me!" I yell, and the memory dissolves so quickly I have no chance of hanging on to it.

Josepha is not here.

All that is left of her is this strip of fabric, in *Louis'* study, smooth as it meets the pinch of my fingers. I wrap it around my index, pondering how it got here. If this is a drop of her blood.

Why is it not with her now?

I deflate, sinking into the hard floor, shoulder meeting the table leg for support. The contact knocks over something atop the desk, a loud *clink* before the item bangs against the wood.

With the hair ribbon still held tight in my hands, I prop myself up, rising to my knees to see what fell.

A blue bottle. A fallen soldier weeping some strange dark liquid next to more blue bottles standing at attention behind it.

There's a marble mortar and pestle next to them, white and sparkling, yet filled with herbs and flowers crushed to flecks of orange and yellow and green and…something dark as night. I stir the dried concoction with the tip of my finger, and a violet petal surfaces.

Just the same as what lay on Geneviève.

Are they used in the poison too?

"I told you," Geneviève says, appearing from nothingness.

"This is the poison," I state, not even looking over to see the apparition of my friend.

"A concoction of death. See what they do? The remnants here, ready to be made again for more victims."

"For my sister?" I ask shakily.

She was here.

She was here and now she is not.

No, no, no, no. I don't know how to handle all of this.

The room spins around and I drop from my knees, landing hard onto my side, or my arm, I do not know.

Josepha is gone. She is really gone.

The floorboards are rough against my cheek, and I stare blankly at the wall before me. Wishing for this to all be false.

Geneviève's face is suddenly in front of my own, laying on the floor next to me. She tucks some of her wild red locks behind her ear then folds her hands as a cushion beneath the side of her face.

"You'll see your sister again, but we have to help everyone. This is only the beginning of the truth," she says. Her face is so muddied and bloody, but her green eyes still sparkle.

"A beginning…" the word stirs and solidifies. Geneviève smiles in silence, as if she can see my mind processing a direction. "The ribbon and the herbs. A start to proof."

"Yes," Geneviève sings while I push myself up to standing.

A large portrait of Louis hangs on the wall, and I am tempted to spit at it. "He called me mad," I tell Geneviève, "the boy supposed to love me thinks I'm *mad* and expects me to stay silent. Expects me to not collect the proof to cause his throne to come crashing down. He doesn't care about me. Doesn't need me. He's playing a role, just like me."

A wave of angry heat passes through me as I stare at the way his face winces. He's seated in a chair three times his size, and the artist captured a collection of dirt below his fingernails. A cabinet stands behind him, complete with shelves of square blue bottles.

The same as on the table beside me now.

Geneviève jumps up and down, clapping. "You're starting to see."

I bite down on my tongue, tears burning through my eyes. "It pains me that I ever thought Madame DuBarry was giving her friend poison…she was only being used as a pawn like the rest of us. A means to kill in plain sight of day. I *should* have been looking at the person who lay in my bed. Sits beside me at meals. The boy I dreamed about as I coveted his portrait on my way to Paris."

"…Louis and his experiments," she adds.

I take hold of a blue bottle, squeezing it tight. My fist rises, cocking back behind my ear, and I hurl the glass into the portrait of Louis. It feels *good*.

Geneviève laughs, and hands me another bottle.

I smile, staring into the beautiful cobalt glass, seeing the liquid wave within my grasp. "No wonder there are so many spirits of Versailles," I say. "Not mere flickering candle flames and disembodied footsteps. They….*you*…are trapped here by the very people supposed to protect them."

"They are too busy grounding a blend of herbs, designing death, and calling it science," she says.

"Designing death…like my sister's." Everything always comes back to her. To Josepha. My poor Josepha. I hold the ribbon so tight my fingernails pierce into my palms, tiny crescent indents of pain.

"Do you think they have her somewhere here?"

"Josepha." My voice cracks between the tears. Slowly feeding her these herbs, keeping her from me? Or is she—

I close my eyes, the tears stick to my lashes, as I continue to call her name. As if it will bring her back. It won't though. She's gone.

She is gone.

I drop down, my knees too unsteady to hold me upright. The cold floor presses into my wet cheeks, and I see myself in the shiny gold urn propped against the wall ahead, though the reflection could be mistaken for Josepha.

"The proof you seek, we hope you find. Look to God, to ghosts, to mind."

I cry harder, holding tight to the poison. Something happened to Josepha in this room. She was here with me— *finally*—and then she was not.

"How am I to stay in Versailles, with murderers in the gardens, poison in bedchambers, and ghosts in the halls?" I ask Geneviève.

"Marie?" A man answers as shoes scuff along the floor at a rapid pace. Then a boy drops down to the floor to have a closer look at the broken girl. "Marie, what is going on?"

The unsightly mole below his eye gives him away. I like that Alexandre has a flaw on this otherwise perfect face.

Geneviève strokes my hair, comforting me. "Act the part, Marie. Make him leave."

"Leave me be." I say to Alexandre, then turn my head, resting my other cheek on the wooden floorboard.

"Come on, Marie, it was only a drawing. A *joke*. No need to be so dramatic over a funny little pamphlet." His arms scoop beneath my armpits then, pulling me up with force.

"A drawing that fed hate to the court. Painting a larger target upon your back," Geneviève whispers. I feel her cold breath on my ear and it sends chills across the nape of my neck.

"*The Butcher and His Bride?*" My voice rises. "*That* was a joke?" Something snaps inside me, like a tree limb breaking from its trunk and shattering against the ground from its grand fall. "You think everything is fun and games, don't you Alexandre? All of it! This court, people's lives… all just a little game that you like to poke and prod at like a dead thing. Like little boys do."

He lets go of me and takes a step back while I remain sitting on the ground, arms limp at my sides like a ragdoll. Alexandre pulls back farther, a single brow arching up as he watches me, shocked from the unexpected outburst. I dig my fists into the floor below. I'm glad it makes him uncomfortable. "I'm trying to be kind! And yes, the pamphlet was fun and games…you *need* to learn to laugh a little.”

“You've made a fool of me. The buzzards are circling, and I will be their kill. My only friend gone, and next it could be me.” My bones tremble, and I cave into myself, making my body a small ball.

“Stand tall,” Geneviève demands.

I listen, my body slowly rising like some invisible force is lifting me up.

Alexandre runs his hands through his hair, clearly frustrated with me. He was trying to be nice. But it's all a damn act.

“He's a great actor. That's how he gets away with so much,” Geneviève reminds me.

“Do you always have access to Louis' chambers?” I ask Alexandre.

His brows knit together. “Yes, of course. Why?”

“Heaven knows my husband will let you do absolutely anything, anywhere,” I say as my heart thumps with force.

“Maybe they were in on it together. Everything a game—an extended hunting trip from the forests to the palace,” Geneviève says, her nose nearly touching Alexandre's cheek. He scratches the place her breath tickled his skin, unaware of her presence.

I can imagine it all now. Alexandre, running through the maze, both his hair and his blade glinting under the moonlight. Ending the sweet life of Geneviève. Then he found my sister and brought her here, where they'd be alone.

My chest caves and the corset digs into my ribcage. Alexandre towers above me, but I don't feel quite as small as I usually do.

It was all because I was chasing her. I led her right to him and then Josepha went running scared. Guilt turns the contents of my stomach.

My sister. My poor sister.

"Do you know *her*?" I scream and he shifts, another step away from me toward the middle of the room. At his blank look, I continue. "My sister. Did you hurt her? Just like Anne. Just like all the others you probably had killed because the sly tom cat was finished with his prey." I think of all the poisoned women discarded like soured milk.

I suck in a huge gulp of breath between my accusatory words. Mucus runs from my nose, and I leave it. Let it drip down my lips because I'm too hurt to care.

He grimaces, his *I'm too good for everyone* face growing stronger by the second, making me hate him even more. I've hated him since the moment I met him. Alexandre is a despicable human and the thoughts swimming in my mind about him behind all the mistreatment of women have suddenly become so clear.

"Marie—"

It makes sense now. He loved them to death.

"Geneviève," I cut him off, looking to the ghost of her. "Did he kill you? Is that why he was the one to carry you from the hedges? Hide lingering evidence?"

"Marie, who are you—"

I can't hear his lies, so whip the blue bottle toward his head. He ducks, and it hits Louis' portrait, black liquid running down his horrid face. "Was her death a warning? Are you here to kill me next? And then Anne?"

I feel my eyes bulging out from my skull as I yell louder. His own eyes are wide, as if he is shocked I have figured him out. That he can't fool me. Not any longer.

I know. I *know*.

"I—I would never," his words are slow. Callous. "You think it was easy for me to see her like that? To have her lifeless body in my hands?"

Yes. I say nothing out loud, just stare at him as he scrambles to speak in that slow, measured tone. I run to the table, arming myself with more bottles, threatening to cut that pretty face of his with shards of glass.

Geneviève's eyes roll in the back of her head, white blank stares like all the statues in Versailles. My mouth drops in horror.

"And I assure you, I don't even know who your sister is. And Anne—Anne is quite special to me. It's so hard, a chambermaid and a noble together, but I need her. I think I—"

"Liar!" I spit. He tilts his head, holding his lips into a tight line as he studies me and I watch Geneviève, frozen, blood rolling down her chest from her throat. "You hurt women. You hurt *me*. Those drawings—they are proof of your villainous soul! And now Josepha is gone. All that's left of her—" I don't finish the sentence. I just hold on tighter to the sacred ribbon in my hand.

"I am no villain!" he yells, arms extended while he turns slightly on his heel, searching the space I look to. "I really have no clue what you are talking about."

"Always lies with you," I whisper.

His palm presses into the flesh just above his eyebrow. "Perhaps I shall find Louis. It appears you've had too many drinks. That, or Austrians really are much stranger than I suspected. I'll help you, Marie, just stay here while I get Louis."

"Don't bother," I say, fists clenched. I charge through him to get to Geneviève, and he stumbles out of the way. "Just get out!"

He listens, and practically runs out of Louis' chamber.

"Geneviève. Please he's gone. Come back to me," I beg, holding her head in my hands. She chokes, blood thick on her tongue, and dissolves from the room like vapor from a kettle.

I want to curse God for taking Josepha and Geneviève, yet want to thank Him for finally making things clearer to me now. For having Geneviève here to help me see how wrong my dreams of Louis were.

I'm exhausted from it all and need to lay down. I have my answers, and next, I need a plan.

But for now, I only crave my pillow.

FOURTEEN

A swarm of bees waits for me.

I hear them, just outside the fabric encircling my bed. They are usually silent, waiting for Etiquette to whip open the curtains and get me out of my nightgown. But right now, they're loud and buzzing, their mouths thick with the honey of gossip—words I can't make out.

I open the curtains myself and Etiquette shuffles to my side. Ten or so chambermaids flutter closely behind her, chests heaving from quick breaths in place of their chatter. I wonder how long they have been awake for. Or how long I have been asleep for.

Since finding Josepha's ribbon.

I spent hours crying into my pillow last night. I'm positive that if I reached over now and touched the linens where my head just lay, it would still be soaked through.

Waking can be the worst moment of all—when your escape from the darkness of life into the darkness of night is ruined by the damn sun rising. When reality strikes its hardest blow.

"Marie," Etiquette grabs my hands. My first reaction is to flinch away, but I don't. Out of pure shock that she would hold me in any sort of way. "You have been asleep since yesterday afternoon. We have all been terribly concerned. You best have a good explanation for worrying us."

The chambermaids bounce up and down, trying to get a look at me. What is going on? Unease settles in my stomach, and I wiggle closer to the edge of the bed as though that will help.

"I am fine, Comtesse." I'm not fine. But I lie. "Are you? You all seem… a bit strange." I worry her pain over the loss of Geneviève may be getting the best of her.

"I'm afraid something has happened," her face smooths out, and I can't help but notice she has far less folds in her face when she isn't scowling. I hold in a breath to brace for what she is about to tell me. "There was another death in the palace last night."

"Another chambermaid?" My eyes search the room for Anne. I can't see her, but the sunshine is bright and I'm struggling to focus.

"Anne was—"

My heart sinks, plummets to my feet faster than I can catch it. "Please do not tell me that Anne is dead. Was it Alexandre? Did he murder that poor girl?" My voice strains and turns into a cry. "Geneviève too—"

The bees gasp at my accusation. A girl in green covers her mouth with both hands. Two of the eldest turn to each other and I can tell by their wide eyes they want to say something, but know they can't.

Etiquette moves closer beside me, our hips touching. Her hand pets along the side of my head. I lean into it. "Anne was not killed. She was there though. Asleep. She was the one to find him."

My heart makes it back up to my ribcage, revived by the relief of hearing Anne is alive.

Him.

It couldn't be Louis, could it? I swallow hard and stare back at Etiquette. "Who is 'him'?"

"Alexandre," she says softly.

Everything feels hazy. My eyes squint with confusion. How can Alexandre be dead if he is the killer? There are a million questions I want to ask, but when my mouth opens, nothing comes out.

"Anne woke next to him," Etiquette continues, "and his—I'm sorry to say this—but someone was intent on him losing his head."

"His head?"

"Excuse the crude image, but yes, it appears an axe was taken to his neck. The assailant hit only once, until Anne stirred and they ran off." Her hand lets go of mine to wipe the sweat from her brow. "So how you could think he had anything to do with Geneviève—"

The person I accused is dead. It had been so clear in my mind only yesterday. "I thought it made sense. He is so horrible to women. *Was.*"

"No, Marie. You should not say such things. Especially of those of such high standing in the court like Alexandre. He may have broken hearts, but he wouldn't lay a hand on them in such violent ways."

"What's the difference?" Geneviève creeps out from a billowing satin curtain. I close my eyes and draw a deep breath in. Her green eyes are back, along with her grin.

"There is a murderer among us though. Geneviève. Alexandre." I want to add my sister to the list. But I keep this hidden to myself, coveted. Perhaps because I can't handle saying her name again, or perhaps because I don't know how to explain the ribbon under the table in Louis' chamber. Ice trails down my spine as I look in the mirror behind Etiquette.

"Heartbreak is violence, can't save them all. They laugh, they die, articulated dolls."

"Pardon me madame." A mousy girl steps forward, brown hair pulled back messily, accentuating features that are small and scared. She curtsies before me, and I am shocked Etiquette doesn't snap to quiet her. "We are afraid and don't know what to do."

Every girl in the room nods, looking at me expectantly. So does Geneviève, watching these confessions while nodding and biting her lip.

Another breaks out from the rest to come closer to the bed. She can't be older than twelve with those black ringlets bouncing by her ears. "What if someone is after maids? Geneviève acted like one of us. She was like a sister. And what if it was supposed to be Anne last night instead of Alexandre? I fear the night now, madame." Her brow wrinkles with her worry, wanting to say more, but remembers the rules that have always been fed down her throat. She curtsies, then disappears beyond the skirts of the others who shift their weight from one uncomfortable heel to the other.

This is the first time I am *hearing* them. The bees. Beyond the buzzing, there are voices to faces. I am just like the other royals, easily accepting help from the less fortunate, without even giving notice to the fact they are humans. Guilt makes me shift on the bed again, until I can't take it anymore and stand up. For the first time, I really look at them.

"What happened exactly?" I ask.

There's a scratch at the door before anyone can answer my question, and Etiquette runs to it as it's opened by an usher outside.

Anne enters. Her body looks even smaller as her shoulders slump in a dirty nightgown, spattered with bits of red and brown like she's just been to war in the tomato garden. Her hair falls in front of her face in a dark mess of black.

Etiquette envelopes her with both arms as she leads Anne toward the rest of us standing in silence.

"I told you to take the day, Anne," Etiquette says to her as they walk across the room toward me. It is the last thing I expected her to say. To show such kindness. Despite how devastated Anne may feel, Etiquette always puts duty above all else—at least she does with me. "You need sleep."

"I know. I just, I can't be alone. And I can't sleep. He died because I slept," Anne says softly, her tears streaming down to her mouth. "I've been cleaning the blood for three hours now."

Her hands are stained red. The dirt I noticed before is her nightgown covered in the crust of Alexandre's blood. *She* was the one cleaning? Cold spreads through my core, and I place my hand above my belly button, afraid I may be sick. "Anne, I—I—" I can't find the words so I run to her.

I pull her away from Etiquette and bring her to the edge of my bed, wrapping my arms around her shaking shoulders, and her head falls down to my chest. Anne's soft, gorgeous hair is clumped together in places with what is left of Alexandre, but I continue to stroke my hand through it slowly. The same way Josepha did so many times for me when Mother was mean to me, or worse still, when someone close to us had died from drawn out and painful illnesses. It feels good to be that person for Anne now.

The rest of the chambermaids give us space, Etiquette included. It exposes the piece of her heart that cares more for the girls than for routine and order. They move across the blue and cream-colored carpet and watch us. Waiting for someone to break the uncomfortable quiet.

"He was worried about you, Marie," Anne says. I feel her jaw moving as it rests on my chest and I tighten my arm over her even more. I notice the small flower she clings to in her hand; the indigo veins are undeniable.

A violet.

I dare not ask her about it, but I am sure it must have been left with Alexandre, as violets were with Geneviève and the bottles. "He came to talk with me after he saw you, unsure what he should do. Something you said made him tell me just how much he loved me. How sorry he was for all the things he did because of the pressures of court. Who he thought he had to be and who he had to be with me instead of just being himself."

My teeth dig into my cheek, grinding the flesh inside my mouth raw. I can't believe I thought so horribly of him. How *good* he had been on the inside. He pretended to be one thing when he was truly someone else. A false façade to appease the impressions of the court. I knew he was a great actor, but I got his part wrong.

He was forbidden to love the person who made him feel alive. As I am forbidden to even allow Étienne to come to the forefront of my mind as he does so often.

As I begin to taste blood, I wonder who killed Geneviève and all the other women before I arrived. Anne continues to speak, but the thought and the fear doesn't escape me.

"It's my fault. For not waking up before it happened. For not helping him, or at least seeing who did this to him. We drank together in celebration of our plans, to *truly* be together, but I didn't think I drank enough to sleep so deeply."

"Don't blame yourself, Anne. You did nothing wrong," I say, and run my hand along her hair, though it keeps getting stuck on the knots that are thick and clumped with blood.

"How could I not?" She sniffles, and I'm relieved that I do not see her expression of sadness as she speaks. "Someone crept into his chamber and while he innocently lay upon his pillow they took an axe to his neck. An *axe*, Marie. I woke to his dead eyes staring at me, the cords of his throat spilling out, his body still tucked into the bedsheets. I tried to put him back together again with my hands. Shove the cords back in place. I—I tried—" She lets out a wail. A wail that the moon could hear. A wail that rattles my bones and rips us all into a thousand pieces.

The younger girl, who spoke of her fear before Anne arrived, breaks from the group of chambermaids and runs for the door, but vomit spills from her mouth before she can make it out.

I gently sit Anne up and hold her chin in my hands before wiping the tears from her pink cheeks. Her eyes are glossed—I see myself in the black circles of them.

"To bare, to bleed, to dance, to please. This Marie, is destiny."

It's the same thing the voice said before Geneviève told me of the poisoned ladies of Versailles. Heat swells in my veins as my heart beats faster.

This is not my destiny.

Nor will it be any of theirs.

I look over to my chambermaids. "I have failed you all." They immediately shake their heads in disagreement. "Please, allow me to apologize. I am sorry that you have all been treated so poorly. This will change. We have a killer among us. We are lucky poor Anne is still here. The killer is growing more brutal, first taking a knife to Geneviève, and now picking up an axe. The court didn't care about a maid, but they'll be damn sure to care about Alexandre, a man of royal standing. Geneviève wasn't a nobody, and I will be sure to remind everyone of that now."

Geneviève smiles and cheers. Maybe she will find peace if I can avenge her. If I do what I should have done in the first place. Stand up for her. Find her killer. My chest expands with the growing shame.

"Comtesse de Noailles, have the guards been sent to find Alexandre's killer?"

"Yes." She curtsies, though she need not to. "Louis was informed first thing this morning."

Louis. His best friend murdered. It hadn't dawned on me enough to care before, though it should have. But I will not run to him in this moment because the fear is like venom in my gut, wondering if his experiments truly do involve poison. He may poison women, but he wouldn't end his best friend.

"I will help." I swallow, knowing I must help even if it means getting close to a killer. Even if that killer is Louis. "I will make sure they are as determined as we are. We shall not live in the most beautiful palace in the world like frightful birds in a cage."

The buzzing begins again, and this time I don't mind it. Each girl approaches one at a time to embrace me in a hug.

I bathe in the warmth of their smiles.

FIFTEEN

They come from all around the world, smelling of sunshine and happiness. Tiny trees in perfect rows, a place of sanctuary just outside the palace walls. The lines of orange trees create the precise shape of an equal-armed cross, with a circular pool gleaming in the center.

I pluck the fruit from the closest tree and bring it to my nose, inhaling deeply. Oranges have always been my favorite. The way juice bursts from its flesh, sweet and citrus tickling my taste buds. This particular one will be delicious—I can tell by its tenderness beneath my fingertips—and I add it to the basket dangling from the crook of my elbow.

The orangery is a magic place at the break of dawn, before anyone stirs from their slumber. Though I love Geneviève being by my side, helping strengthen my spine, it is nice to have a moment's peace. If only I could stay here and eat orange after orange, laying by the pool under the rising sun every day.

I grab an orange from the basket and slice into the peel with my fingernails, lifting it to expose the white skin below, excited to get to the middle. From the corner of my eye, the pink sky reflects my own face off the oversized buckle on my shoe. Just for a single second, but it's enough.

"Tear into the flesh, peel it away, suck out the juice, then come and play."

My moment of delight is severed by the voice. How silly of me to think I could pretend that there is not someone trying to chop heads off and pouring poison down throats. That I have girls relying on me to right so many wrongs and to help them feel safe.

I ignore it and walk toward the center of the orangery, to the large pool. The surface of the water sparkles as it moves.

Moves.

Someone floats in the middle of the pool, a white nightgown dancing in the water while the body it clings to lay still.

I drop the basket of oranges, hopping over the fruit as they roll in my path.

The water is cold as my arms reach in and take hold of the girl's arms and pull her to the side of the stone pool. Her legs begin to kick and we both screech.

Through the splashes of water, I finally recognize her. "Anne! Thank heavens."

"My apologies for the fright," she says. We both slink down the side of the pool, resting our backs on the stone and panting.

"What were you doing?" I ask.

"It is quiet here in the mornings. I came to think, but found myself stepping into the water, then floating. And for a few moments I was—I was able to forget about everything." Anne buries her head into her hands, gasping between tears.

I rub her back in tiny circles. My heart aches for her.

"I am scared, Marie."

"I know." My palm slows on her drenched nightgown, before I admit, "I am too."

Anne's sweet face leaves her hands to study my face. "You are?"

"Of course. There is evil among us, lurking in plain sight, and we are left poor and defenseless."

She shakes her head in refusal to my words. "You are the dauphine. The most protected here, next to the king and dauphin."

"How can that be true when anyone who comes near me is quick to—" I don't want to say the word while Anne's tears for Alexandre still run warm on her cheeks. I let out a large exhale instead while I calculate what to say next, without admitting the truth that grows within me. "I think, perhaps, that Louis may know something. Alexandre was his best friend."

The name causes Anne to cry harder.

I lean over to grab two oranges. "Here. Let us eat while we grieve," I say, and she slowly takes the orange and turns it in her hands several times before finally peeling it open.

I do the same, separate a slice from the orange, and pop it into my mouth. Chewing. Thinking.

The skin is tough to break through, but my teeth keep at it until juice coats my tongue.

"You could ask Louis," she says between bites. "If you think he knows more, would he not tell you?"

"I fear not." I look around at the orange trees, beginning to cast longer shadows as the sun rises higher from the horizon. "He does not speak much to me when we are together. It seems he prefers the company of his horse or his study more."

I don't know why I am able to expose myself in such a way with Anne. She is as vulnerable as I am and perhaps that is why I spill so much of my mind to her.

"What if there was an event? A social obligation where he would have to speak with you?"

"There is so much chaos at balls, and he can move freely, avoiding me." I swallow.

We sit in silence, chewing our oranges.

"A play!" She jumps up and offers a hand out to me. I take it.

"Yes." Seeing a play come to life on stage always brought a sense of wonder and magic to my life. Could it help us now? Help *me*? "Louis would *have* to join me for a night at the theater."

I haven't seen him since Alexandre died not that many hours ago. I slowly walk to a tree next to the pool, grateful I haven't been forced to face Louis just yet. But I need to. I know this now. Fears be damned.

If he is too busy for me, despite all my efforts, perhaps this will work. Throwing a party isn't enough for him to stay around for. But if I were to bring a troupe to Versailles to perform, all the highest nobles would attend, and Louis would not be able to run off to go to bed early. He'd have to sit beside me for hours. He'd have to *talk* to me.

"You would be by his side, he could not leave without the eyes of the court chasing him, and you could ask him about my Alexandre. And the chambermaids. The theater could distract them from the current fright they feel," Anne says.

She is right. I feel responsible for them all. The cold chill they've begged me to warm. A chance to be lost in the revelry of the theater will provide a break from the tragedies, if only for a night.

"And they will be safe there. It will be wonderful."

Anne and I smile, a bond formed, a plan concocted.

"Have you heard the rumors of poison?" I whisper. She nods. "Madame DuBarry's friend constantly drinks from blue bottles. What if I ask Louis where she gets them from?"

"Oh, yes! It is a start. I will go speak with Etiquette about your wishes for a performance here," Anne hugs me, new life in her rising to the surface. I laugh, and encourage her to go.

I sit down on the edge of the pool, watching Anne leave. I set the orange peel down, and I giggle to myself, a lightness filling my chest as fast as the fruit fills my stomach.

I'll have the grandest show all of France has ever seen. There will be the finest acting troupe, endlessly flowing drinks, and cakes topped with these delicious oranges—I'll pick them myself.

Etiquette isn't here, but I can still hear her nagging in my head, *"Be careful of the spending. People will talk."*

Let them talk. It will be worth it. For the girls. For a lead.

It will force Louis to spend time with me. So that I may uncover secrets being hidden from me. He is the most powerful man next to the king. It was his best friend who was murdered, and he knew of the gossip surrounding Geneviève. He must know things. *Something* that will lead me down the right path. Even if that path leads me straight to him.

My stomach stirs. That path is one I do not want to wander, and I hope I am wrong, like I was wrong about Alexandre.

I hold my aching stomach, and try to focus on something else. All that comes to mind is Étienne. With a gathering comes another chance to see him.

What I wouldn't give to have his hand in mine right now. My indulgences hold a slight trace of guilt over me. I am married. But I did not choose Louis, and he most certainly does not seem to want me. Not the way I long for Étienne's skin to brush against my own. I should be banned from him altogether, a chaperone nearby at all times. But I'd much rather be pulled into his arms, hidden in the unseen room of clay and quiet. The longing is sweet and euphoric, like the way sugar makes me feel when it meets my tongue after the first bite of a cherry pink macaron.

Someone clears their throat behind me. I turn to find a guard with a silver platter held out to me, a single envelope atop it. "Thank you," I say to the boy, who bows slightly before leaving me with the letter.

I would know the handwriting anywhere. *Mother.*

I want so badly to be excited to hear from her, but I know her words will only make the blood in my veins pump faster. She'll remind me of all I've forgotten—all she expects me to do.

My hands shake, but the paper tears easily and I unfold it to read her swirls of ink. There is no greeting, no well wishes.

> *I have received word of your misbehavior with the court, Marie. Your fantasies. You must leave all you left in Vienna. Versailles is your life now.*
>
> *I continue to hear of your failure to meet your marital duties. Whatever you are doing wrong to keep your husband away, you must correct. This shall be your greatest focus.*
>
> *France is to be at the centre of everything. No longer are you the impish girl playing with her dog all day. You now have responsibilities.*
>
> *You are to also open up to Madame DuBarry and speak with her. Become her best friend.*
>
> *I am too busy to deal with you while disease continues to sweep through Vienna.*
>
> *Do not disappoint me.*

The paper of instruction—without a scrap of love—crumples into a small ball within my palm.

She does not understand, and hurts me with the mere mention of Mops, not even bothering to let me know how my sweet pup is.

These are the moments when the cannonball-sized hole in my heart is reopened by Josepha's absence. Mother would slice through me with her words, and Josepha would be there, ready to bandage the hurt. Josepha would understand and care for my feelings above all else.

Mother must be hearing from her little henchmen, the ears she has listening throughout Versailles, the small trivial things. There is so much more at play in the grandest palace in the world. I may have been sent here with the goal to marry and have babies, but the absence of that is not my fault. *I* am not the disappointment.

It's maddening. Louis is left to his own devices, gallivanting as he pleases while the burden of blame is placed on my head. I'm the one who must spring into action, fix things, smooth the rough edges of Versailles left from men's vicious hand.

But my plan…my plan will fix it all. The theater and my heroism will shine a light upon me, even brighter than that of their ever precious Sun King.

I smile. The theater is the perfect place for all to see that I am trying. That I am the one attempting conversation and trying to please Louis.

I will get close to Louis and Madame DuBarry, but not for the sake of Mother. I will ensure that the entire court will be my biggest fans, so that they may have the loosest lips. And it all starts at the theater.

The greatest play to find a killer.

The fresh new theater is made up of layers, topped onto another, just like a deliciously scrumptious cake. There is the orchestra on the floor, surrounded by stacked balconies, all looking onto the grand stage. Two pillars, marbled with soft pink and gray, and thicker than any tree trunks I've laid eyes on, frame the stage on each side. They are so smooth, as though someone painstakingly spent hours rubbing away at any sign of grit; complete disregard for wearing their own fingernails down to the quick.

I requested a minimum of fifty trees from the orangery be moved inside the theater. I inspected them earlier, ensuring each was pulled far enough from walls and seats to give the green leaves enough space to breathe. I can still smell the faint scent of oranges on my fingertips. It adds to the magic of the theater.

Built only this year, it feels like it was created for me. As if Versailles knew my heart would soar to be in this magnificent room, cut flat on one end by its focal point. My favorite color of blue, just a shade brighter than a robin's egg, is used for the swag curtains over the stage, cascading down with velvety folds like a waterfall I could dive into and be lost in forever.

My jaw clenches tight when I see him. Alexandre peers out from the crack of the curtains, a head held by his own headless body. His eyes roam until they meet my own and he starts muttering, but I can't read his lips from this distance. My teeth chatter at the sight of blood cascading from where his neck should be, while he tries to tell me something. His face is desperate, before disappearing back behind the stage.

If nothing else, seeing him is a reminder of why I am here. I may have hated him for his vile way of running his fingers along my back and speaking of women to impress Louis, but no soul should face such a horrific fate.

I focus back on the theater, and notice that there are many women drinking from blue bottles. Only women…not a single man. Ladies suckling small doses of poison, each drop bringing them closer to death. It makes my head spin, my ears filled with the sound of a ticking clock.

I can't help but scan the space for Étienne, not that I'd be able to run to him if he were here. From where I look, he's not. I exhale my disappointment. I have other things to focus on. Me and Louis. Louis and me.

We, of course, have the best spot in the house, the balcony looking dead center upon the action. *We,* if Louis ever shows up, that is. It's just me, cooling my anger with a satin white fan. I wave it up and down in short flicks of my wrist. A clear indication to the guests that I am hot, bothered, and flustered. Let them know—they should be witness to the fact that I am not the enemy here. I am not the cause of the clean bedsheets.

Louis is ruining everything. *Again.*

As people take their seats and the theater fills to the brim, I'm supposed to be asking him questions. Which questions, I do not know. But something that will encourage a secret—a clue—to spill out of his mouth. I need time to warm him to me, to make him trust me. The want for him to love me feels like a piece of glass under my skin, healed over. My duty should be top of mind. Pain pounds in my temple. How can I lay with the man who fills the blue bottles? I suck in my lips, forcing myself to keep dry eyes. My only choice right now is to put on a charade, just as the actors will be tonight.

Those *on time* appear to be enjoying the affair. They have all dressed in their finest. The women have tall feathers that flit in the air with their every movement stuck into powdered hair. Their dresses, all shiny satin in the most glorious shades of pinks and peaches, you'd think you could take a bite of them. Even the men are dripping with jewels, wearing jackets with lace trimmed cuffs and collars. They are dressed for my party. All so gorgeous to impress *me*.

Some of those that linger below wave up at me with saccharine smiles on their faces. I wish I could feel joy at their acknowledgement of me, of the wonderful party I have thrown, but it is impossible through the stone walls of anger Louis' absence has built. Agitation pressing my fingernails into my palm. I need to talk to him. This was to be my chance.

The soft velvet drapes swooping down around our section of the balcony, not for privacy, but for indulgence, are the same fiery red I feel inside. But then I catch a glimpse of some of the chambermaids in the audience. They weave through the gowns and feathers of the rich, blending in beautifully as I suggested. They act like they are there to assist, to provide, to charm. They force smiles to who they need to, but otherwise, they rest on columns and walls, ready for a break. Ready to watch the show. But ever watchful. They are my eyes and ears, for I trust no one but them.

The dancing flames from hundreds of candles cast a glow over the entire theater. The light reflects off the framing of my balcony box, a wire of golden waves.

"Double, double, toil and trouble, your plans are falling all to rubble."

If I could strangle the voice, I would. Reciting Shakespeare and the horrible witches who sing of doomed fate. My fate is not doomed. Damn the omens. *Damn the omens.*

The thick blue curtains concealing the stage, lined with gold fringe and tassels, begin to move, pulled apart by people tugging on massive ropes behind the scenes. The audience claps, ready for the show to begin.

Louis finally takes his seat beside me, chin tucked into his chest. I clench my teeth so hard I fear they could shatter. I lean to my left, close to his ear, and hiss, "Where have you been?"

"I had some things to take care of," he states, looking straight ahead where the acting troupe starts to take the stage. I could explode with anger right now. I've done so much to make tonight happen in such a short amount of time. But I must tamper the anger welling within, and remain sweet with him.

"Oh, yes. I have been busy as well, husband," I begin, "my chambermaids have had an awful cough as of late."

He nods, not bothering to look at me. "I am sorry to hear."

I become distracted by two of the actors who are dressed as Louis and I, dancing before us in a strange reflection of our first meeting in the forest. I had not expected anyone to be playing us. A flutter of excitement in my chest quickly fades when I see that the man playing me is large, stomping around with a disheveled wig, purposefully off kilter. Like he's—*I'm*—drunk. He stumbles forward past paper trees, landing on the wooden stage face first.

How dare they. This was supposed to be a comedy show. I gave the troupe explicit instructions to put a funny show on for the court, to distract them through laughter. I was not to be the *subject* of the laughter.

And oh, do they laugh. I can barely hear the orchestra's instruments rising up from the pit to the dozen glittering crystal chandeliers hanging from the ceiling anymore. Pinpricks pierce through my lungs, making it impossible to breathe. Like my insides are collapsing on themselves, just as the world outside my body is collapsing on me.

I turn to see the king laughing a few seats down, his daughters slapping their knees and lifting their heads to the sky. Their mouths releasing ear piercing squeals of glee—Victoire and Adélaïde, my supposed friends, laughing at my expense.

Beside the king is Madame DuBarry. Her hand softly on his knee as it bounces, her mouth closed, in a straight line. She must sense me looking at her, for she turns to meet my eyes. Her solemn expression does not waver. It almost looks as though she is about to cry.

Chloé is behind her, hands on her friend's shoulders. She looks over to me, her eyes haunting and hollow. My head tilts, in wonderment that she isn't coughing.

They've killed her too.

She begins coughing then, blood filling her hand as she moves it away from her mouth. Chloé collapses, convulsing on the floor, fighting for breath. Not another soul notices her bloodied and writhing on the floor. Another ghost in a loop of agony. My eyes sting in pain, still trying to play a part in front of Louis.

I turn away from her quickly, back to the disgusting display on stage.

"Louis, one of my chambermaids coughs like Chloé."

"Such a shame about her," he says.

Louis already knew she died.

"I have something that may help your chambermaid. A special elixir. I have none with me now, but will get you a bottle for your maid."

I freeze. A part of me squirms, not wanting to face the truth.

"Thank you, Louis. That is very kind."

"Very good, now watch the show," he instructs.

"What is in the elixir?" I try.

"Nothing more than syrups, and flowers, and herbs. Enough now, let us watch."

My fingers curl into the arms of the chair.

All of Etiquette's words of warning begin swirling in my head as the actor picks out an oversized ruby necklace from one actor, and moves across the stage to grab a bird made of red feathers and stuffing from another actor, shoving it into the mess of hair on his head. *My* hair. Etiquette warned of the spending. It was all for the people of Paris though. Not truly for me.

The volume of giggles from the ungrateful court rises as the man pretending to be me swipes his finger through a towering wedding cake, and sucks a gob of icing off while rolling his head back in pure enjoyment.

He screams with his best attempt at a female voice as the rest of the troupe, dressed in black, wave branches of evergreen at him while he runs back and forth across the stage. Like he's running through hedges. My neck snaps straight up, attentive and waiting. I swallow, hoping that what I know is next does not come.

No. They can't be.

I begin to tremble through my core, loosening my corset.

They wouldn't.

He screams again, and falls on a pile of yellow fabrics. Fabrics covering a woman with blood squirting from her neck. He stands and then falls over in the blood, over and over, all the while screaming with his hands flailing at the sides of his face dramatically.

They did. They are acting out my finding of Geneviève's lifeless body.

A flash of her green eyes looking up in horror as her killer slashed her throat fills my mind. Her hands up trying to stop the hand holding the blade. She must have been so terribly scared. An ache sets deep within my heart.

Geneviève takes hold of my hand, kneeling before me right here in the theater. I almost say her name, but bite my tongue, remembering Louis is beside me.

"All is well now," she whispers, then places the side of her head on my lap. Her frizzy red hair has tiny twigs and flecks of mud and blood matted in it. "You must not relive this moment further, my dear friend."

I push myself back into my seat, as if the little space it gives me from the stage will help my restricted breathing. Geneviève disappears again as I do.

And then I hear *his* laugh beside me. Louis'. His silly little laugh, like a donkey losing air—a gasping nasally sound that sets my nerves on edge as tears slice through my eyeballs. Of course he wouldn't think to stand tall and stop this from happening. I instinctively look for Étienne, knowing he would jump across balconies to save me, as he leaped to rescue me from Geneviève. He would stop the jeering crowd now, all the people filled with hate for me. I am trying to help them, to save them, yet I am only met with betrayal.

I look ahead again, the brass instruments within the orchestra reflect the horror on stage.

"Oh Marie, just you wait. The next scene we play is where we decapitate."

My hairs stand along my arm as shivers hurry across my skin.

"It wouldn't happen like that," Louis says, surprise settling along my bones, that he would acknowledge my existence, "once she was dead, blood wouldn't be squirting out like that. But the effect they use to make it look like a fountain of red is quite entertaining." He smiles. *Smiles.* What is wrong with this boy I married? It's evil. *He* is evil.

"How would you know? You weren't there, Louis." Though he *is* right, the blood did not spray in spurts when I found her. It pooled.

His smile widens, like the devil himself is wearing Louis' face. "My experiments of course. When I dissect a fresh corpse, the blood is thick and rises up and out of the cut skin, but only enough for it to spill out on my table." His hands move to his own neck, flicking his wrists like he is invisibly performing said experiment. My stomach churns.

"How could you—*why* would you want to do that? Why disturb a body in such horrible ways? The dead deserve rest," I whisper to him, while the actors dance about at a garden party. Actors dressed as frogs spit water from their mouths like the Latona fountain I enjoyed that day. The troupe is managing to suffocate all my joy. How could they have possibly heard of everything that has happened at the palace since my arrival?

This is treason. Plain and simple. Louis lets everything go, just like the pamphlet. As long as it makes him laugh.

The contrast to the strangling the court is on women, disposing of those with no use, punishing them cruelly with calloused hands and opened legs. It lights a flame in my belly.

"It's fascinating, Marie. To learn the way the body works. How our veins pump blood to our hearts." There is a sense of pleasure in his voice, pure pride, like a little boy shooting a rabbit for the first time. "You'll have to join me sometime. See it all for yourself." The acrid taste of vinegar rises from my throat, but I swallow it down with wincing eyes.

An invitation to his study, to the place where he cuts through flesh, could give me the clues I seek.

For me. For the girls.

"Yes, Perhaps you're right, Louis. Being by your side while you study would help me understand your interests better. I would like that very much. Thank you for the invitation." My fingernails dig into the arms of the theater chair as I turn my attention back to the stage.

Intuition bubbles with the venom still strong in my belly. Louis couldn't be responsible for the death, the need for cadavers above all else.

Could he?

Two actors lay in a bed—a man snoring loudly beside a tiny girl curled up in the blankets. There's a hush over the crowd watching the scene unfold. They gasp when a man carrying an axe tiptoes across the stage. He lifts it high above his head, bringing it down with a foul swoop just as the girl turns on her side and starts snoring. The axe lands in the bed and feathers fly up. The audience laughs in a riot. He tries again to strike the girl, but this time the man adjusts within the sheets, taking the blow in the neck to cause another fountain of red to burst from his body.

Some ladies in the front row scream as fake blood splatters on their pretty ruffled dresses—there's much more with Alexandre's death than there was with Geneviève's. The rest of the crowd lights up with glee and applause. I worry for the chambermaids, having to watch their nightmare reenacted, but I luckily don't see them when I peer down—I hope they fled at the first sign of this all going terribly, terribly wrong.

Alexandre.

I can see his handsome face now, content in slumber within his golden framed bed, nearly severed from the rest of his body. He didn't even see the axe falling, or have a chance to stop the blow. It took but a second for the crisp white sheets to be stained in crimson. Just like the spectacle unfolding in front of us now within this opulent theater. A stark contrast between what is on stage and the angels and winged horses painted on the ceiling.

I peer out one of the many circular windows lining the top of the room, staring out at the moon to try to forget everything. It's futile though, as the moonlight shines through the glass, carrying with it the insistent voice.

"This is an act, a simple play. We know their fate, more will die today."

SIXTEEN

Hairy legs traipse across the stage, the man playing me lifting his skirts up well over the knees. His wig has come completely undone now, loose coils of white poking out in every direction. He grabs Alexandre's severed head, made of melon, and stares into it lovingly. I shudder.

"Oh! Another death! Let's have a party!" He cries with glee, then throws the head into the air where it spins in circles, spraying fake blood across the beautiful blue curtains, before making a cringing *splat* on the stage floor.

The orchestra stops playing. Silence follows for less than a breath before the creaking of chairs fills the theater. Everyone has turned in their seats to look up at me. To see my reaction. Even Louis, who found a handkerchief to wipe away his spittles of laughter, glares at me. Waiting.

I stand and walk to the edge of the balcony, pushing my palms into the cold, hard banister. And I laugh. A fake, disingenuous, cough of hilarity forces its way through my chest and out of my mouth. And I linger there, let the laugh continue while they all gape at me with their horrid, powdered faces.

A man in one of the adjacent boxes to mine wheezes a laugh and suddenly the whole room is swirling with the sound of laughter and the smell of sweat and oranges.

The need to escape strangles me, fingers digging into the soft flesh of my neck. Standing tall to be what they want of me, while they mock my pain, is a cruel type of torture. I must be strong on the outside, clinging to the needs of duty to the crown and the girls, but on the inside I am cracked china, shards of porcelain poking into my organs.

I recede slowly, and lean over to Louis. "I must fix my powder, dear husband. Do excuse me," I whisper.

He waves his dirty handkerchief my way without looking, his gaze already back on the male version of me running around on the stage drinking champagne. Another shard of porcelain breaks inside me.

Louis will never be who I thought he was going to be. Who I think he should be. I swallow the realization down as I speed walk out of our box, down walkways that wind through the back of other boxes.

One of my chambermaids tries to keep step with me, and I can barely make out her brassy hair through my tears. "Please, leave me," I say.

A guard comes rushing over to us, so old I am surprised he moves so quickly.

"Both of you. All of you. I need just a moment to… powder my nose." The back of my hand rises to my mouth, trying to muffle the crack of my voice.

They stop as I continue forward. When I reach a space lined with ruby red velvet I pause for a moment, searching the room to ensure I'm alone before folding over with my arms on my knees to catch my breath. The sounds of the play, the *parody*, still reach my ears enough to taunt me. But not enough to cloak the sound behind me.

Drip. Drip. Drip.

My blood runs cold, pumping furiously to and from my heart.

Drip. Drip. Drip.

I slowly turn around and see Alexandre. His insides coming out, causing the dripping sound. He looks so angry, and he suddenly takes off, a headless body running through people without them even noticing.

I hold my breath—and the scream struggling to rip through my throat—and run after him. He flees through an open door that leads to the stairwell I came up through. I don't bother closing the door behind me.

I miss a step and cry in pain when my ankle twists in an unnatural angle as the rest of my body is pulled down the last few stairs. I land on my bottom, staring back up at that open door. My pulse is so strong now, like my heart is going to vomit itself onto the floor in front of me.

Alexandre is long gone now. I only wanted to know what he was trying to say. *Why did he run?*

The tears finally come. In the dark tomb of the stairwell I cry.

I cry over my plan being a failure. I cry over the way everyone sees me—how they poke and prod and twist and hate. I cry over the fact that my true love fairytale was all but a figment of my imagination.

My elbows dig into my thighs to support my head in my hands. My fingertips press into my forehead while my palms fill with tears. Everything turns to black, consumed with the pain of disappointment, and time becomes foreign. Minutes—or possibly hours—pass before I hear voices growing louder. People must be piling out of the theater. The show complete.

But I do have the promise of joining Louis' experiments and that he is the one who provides the bottles. I hang on to that sliver of a win while I move as fast as my sore ankle will allow me, desperate to find a place where I can be completely alone.

Every single statue I pass on the way to my room seems to watch me. I keep pushing on, toward my room, ignoring the statues, the people who pass with wide eyes—I must look a fright with my puffy face and slight limp, the fear in my belly directing my movements, sure that my death will meet me around each corner.

I made it. I made it, I made it, I made it.

My room.

I sit on the edge of my bed, wiping a trail of mucus from my face with the back of my hand. The reflection of my skirts in the glass of a cabinet catches my eye.

"Keep running you fool, be careful the axe. You can not escape, you can not relax."

"Shut up. *Shut up,*" I curse the voice through gritted

teeth, yet follow it, carefully moving from the bed to the cabinet. Beside it, the wallpaper is disrupted, a faint line tracing a strange shape in the wall.

Curious.

I lean in closer, nose nearly touching the wall.

My finger follows along the line, a groove scored deeply. It is done with such expertise. The plump pink flowers of the wallpaper undisturbed by the slight gap. A trick of the eye so impressive I managed to miss it after all these nights in my room.

With a deep inhale, I finally push my hip against it, opening a secret door.

The corridor is quiet and dark, lit by a few flickering candles on the wall that carry the scent of smoke and burning tallow. It is alarmingly dull and dusty for Versailles, which means it will never see the eyes of the public, or those who need impressing—a secret passageway, but for whom or to where?

I take timid steps across the plain wooden floor and stare at the white plaster, such a stark contrast from the bright hues and carved golds that are on the other side of the same walls.

There are wooden doors along the narrow passage. I shuffle forward just a bit more, questioning whether or not to peer into a room to see who else is connected to the corridor, who else knows its secrets.

I must be in a hallway of hidden doors, connecting bedchambers and ballrooms.

I still for a moment, focusing on my breath. Inhale. Exhale. There is no need to go looking into other rooms. I was searching for quiet. For peace. For solitude. And I've found it.

I feel my intuition tug at me again, and I grab onto my belly as my heart leaps. Is it one of Louis' men? Here to reach out to me—to murder me? My hairs are on end, a chill settling on the back of my neck.

I can't take this anymore. The fear is going to be the death of me, and I am too young to die.

I can do this. *I can do this.*

"Who is there?" I whisper. "Show yourself."

Silence. I listen closely, but only hear the crackling of the flames from the candles mounted to the walls.

A hand closes over my mouth. Saliva builds on my tongue, a tingling in my head urging me to run. I attempt to shift my feet against the plain stone floor when an arm wraps around my waist, covering my hands that lay on my stomach. A scream attempts to push through their palm, but it comes out a mere whimper.

It's my turn. My time to die. I'm going to lose my head.

"Shh," a voice brushes beside my ear. "It's only me. It's Étienne."

His hands move away slowly as my shoulders decompress with relief and my thundering heart slows.

"I'm so sorry," he says, "I didn't want to scare you, and make you scream. Not while we are in here. We can't be found in these corridors."

"How did you know—"

"I hate to admit it, but I came looking for you in your bedchamber and saw the open door in the wall." His lips turn into a sheepish smile, and it immediately makes me forget he scared the life out of me. "It was then that I heard you talking to yourself again."

"I thought the person who killed Geneviève and Alexandre may have been here."

"You are brave," he says, brows raising. "But please. Do not look for trouble, I can not stand the thought of you being killed."

I look into his blue eyes. "I feel so close to death already."

He kisses my forehead tenderly. "I will do all I can to keep you safe, and in this life and the next, I will be with you everlasting."

I suck in my top lip and cry. Here is someone who truly cares for me, despite all my flaws.

He closes the space between us even farther, the white linen of his shirt shifting with his movement. He is so informal compared to the rest of the court, and it carries an ease with it. Like he is a fresh breath of air in the midst of my suffocation.

His collar is open, the hint of his strong chest a tease in every way imaginable. He takes my hand then, but I don't take my eyes from him, moving up from his neck to his dimpled chin, to the lips I long for.

Étienne is everything I wished for as a child. A boy who would see through the gowns and powder, the titles and duties, and would love me for me. A boy who would want to be beside *me*, no matter what that would mean facing.

I even wished for soft brown curls of hair. Deep dimples beside a kind smile. And eyes I could lose myself in.

And here he is, standing in front of me in this hidden space within a glittering palace. It's as though I dreamed Étienne into existence.

I place my hand on his chest, and look up at him, losing myself in the eyes I had always wished I'd find. With the hand that holds onto his tightly, I pull down slowly, begging him to lower his face to mine. He does, just as I lift my chin. He waits for me, unmoving. The air swelling between us as my heart sings.

And then I kiss him.

SEVENTEEN

Étienne's kiss sparks a heat in me.

His lips, soft and wet, are a perfect fit with mine. Slowly, his kisses trail down my chin to my neck, just below my ear. His tongue flickers across my skin and I gasp as goosebumps spread across me with a delightful chill.

His fingers dance down my side, sending shivers through me. His hand settles on my low back and I arch into it, my head tilted to the sky. I close my eyes and lose myself in every second of these new sensations, a lightness in my head I've never felt before.

I wish desperately for him to pull at the ribbons holding my corset in place. Instead, his hand pulls me in tight to his body and he kisses me again.

This is it.

What I have always dreamed of. Come to life in the most unexpected ways. A boy who wants *me*. My body. My soul.

My obsession with all the people of Versailles accepting and adoring me falls away like petals from a rose—softly, effortlessly. All I need now is Étienne's love. And it feels good. So good.

My eyes flutter open when Étienne spins me around, hands high in the air, and we laugh. Our own little party in our own little dark, secret passageway. He takes a step forward, pressing himself against my body just hard enough that I take a step behind me, my back gently pinned against the wall as those devastating ocean eyes stare into mine.

He cups my jaw with cool hands, and his kisses become deeper. Wanting. Urgent. I bring my hands to his, resting atop them.

"Marie!" he yells.

No, not Étienne. *Louis*.

The dazzling light before my eyes winks out and all I am left with is a chill—a freezing cold that numbs my skin, my bones, my blood. I turn into a statue in this passageway that has given me all I ever wanted. Just another figure of stone in Versailles.

"Marie!" Louis says again, louder this time. I can feel him standing behind us now.

I want to cry, to beg Louis for forgiveness, while at the same time keeping Étienne wrapped in my arms and on my lips.

But Étienne is gone.

He's…gone.

My chest rises and falls as I look up, searching for the face that was just there. My arms suspended in the air where his hands just were. My back arched, waiting for more kisses.

Étienne has vanished. *How—*

Louis pulls my arm down, spinning me in place. Hard. Abrasive. Not the joyful spin I shared with Étienne a moment ago. "What are you doing here, Marie?" Louis' face is red, brow dripping with sweat. He's angry. Of course he's angry. To find his bride kissing another. I pat down on my mussed dress. Quickly smooth out my hair. But I can't hide my pink swollen lips.

"How did you know—"

"Know of the passageways?" He won't let me speak. "I know everything about this palace. And these corridors are strictly to be used for quick escapes. So what are you doing here alone?"

Alone? My head spins in a cloud of confusion. He didn't see Étienne. I stumble over my sore ankle, landing into Louis' arms. He looks at me with confusion, brows knit together and mouth wide open. I pull away from him, looking around the hallways, searching.

There is no way Étienne could have run away fast enough for Louis to not have seen him. It's as though he vanished into nothingness. Just as Geneviève does.

Geneviève's *ghost.*

My chest tightens, and I replay my stolen kisses with Étienne in my head.

The shivers he gave me. The cold hands. The goosebumps.

The disappearing.

I collapse, my body unable to take its own weight. Louis continues to look down on me as I cry into the back of my hand.

It can't be true. Not him.

The thick ache in my throat travels down to my heart, drowning it in black tar, never wanting to beat for another again.

Étienne is dead.

I've fallen in love with his ghost.

EIGHTEEN

Everything goes cold. My fingers, my head, my heart.

Just like Étienne.

"Marie?" Louis says, his head tilting toward a shoulder with concern as I sit before him, my dress a grand heap around me, crying uncontrollably as I try to make sense of it all.

Make it make sense.

He walks closer. The garnet of his ring catches the little traces of orange light in the hallway, and I know I am going to hear it. The voice. I hold my breath, readying myself.

"Kissing death and chasing stars, he is dead, still broke your heart."

Louis moves to me and offers a hand. The lace ruffles of his shirt brush along my wrist as he pulls me up.

"What are you doing here?" Louis asks again. I blurt out the single note of a laugh behind the tears. He doesn't ask *what is wrong* or *how can I help you*, only what I am doing in a place I shouldn't be. Why I'm not following the *rules*. He quirks his head at me, bewildered by my response.

I begin to inch toward the wall, clinging to it with my hands as my back presses into it. My heart is rapid with fear, alone in this space with Louis.

Through hitched breath and an aching chest, I gather myself to move. To speak. I open my mouth, but nothing comes out. He already accused me of being mad. Any word that falls from my mouth must be exact, must explain away my hysterics—he can't think I am mad. Because I'm not. I'm heartbroken. But I can't tell him that either.

"Marie, please talk to me. You never returned to the show. And now I find you here, alone?" He asks again.

Alone. I want to be alone.

I swallow, knowing I should answer him. A thrumming ache in my chest tempts me to confess everything. How horrible I think he is, how Versailles is haunted, how I was kissing a ghost just before he arrived.

I bite my lip, the imprint of Étienne's touch still lingering there. How ridiculous. It's all so ridiculous, and that's exactly what Louis would think. What the entire court would think as they threw me into the streets without a second thought, the dauphine who disgraced all of Paris and Austria. Maybe I won't make it to the streets at all. My eyes dart to Louis' hands, hoping he wields no weapon or poison.

Mother. The realization hits me like a bolt of lightning. The ripples from my actions will stretch far and wide.

I can't do that to Mother. And I can't abandon the chambermaids. I am the only person they can turn to, and I have promised I would fix things for them. Save them from a killer, even if that is…*him.*

So I hide it all away. The true way I feel must remain stuffed in a chest, with the key thrown into the vast ocean. Put on yet another act so that I can scurry from here, no longer trapped like a rat.

"I'm sorry," I say in a sweet voice. "I think all the sounds of the theater caused my head to hammer. And then I found this passageway through my bedchamber and it was so quiet, I stayed. To—to let my head settle a bit. It hit again as you came in. I am sorry for the tears. It is just so very, very painful."

My fingers find my temples, and I close my eyes, feigning a headache. My wince deepens, hoping he will accept my explanation as truth.

He's quiet. A hum vibrates in my ears, filling the space. He has to believe me. Please, just speak.

"Yes, well, I did find the orchestra a little too loud myself. I shall speak with someone about this." He puts his hands on his small hips, accepting my lie. It leaves a sour taste in my mouth, knowing he doesn't care enough to see through my story.

"That would be lovely, thank you, Louis." I blink repeatedly to stave off more tears. "I do think I need some air now."

"Maybe some sleep would help," he counters. His voice has become much sweeter than when he demanded answers from me. I breathe a sigh of relief knowing I have successfully appeased him.

"I think you are right. As soon as I can get some fresh air on my face, I will return to my chambers and sleep away this headache," I say, trying my best not to sound argumentative. I'll play sweet, but I will go wherever I wish. I will decide what I do, and that is not to go to sleep. I will find Étienne and make sense of everything. Be in my corner against Louis and all the others.

"Very well." He begins to step aside, but I'm already there, brushing past him. It takes great restraint not to let my feet lead me quickly through the hidden door into my room. I have to appear calm to Louis.

I don't look back. I control my destiny. I haven't before, but I will try now.

Each slow step is agonizing, but by the time I walk out of the palace and into the courtyard, I'm ready to take flight. A welcome breeze dries the tears on my face.

A giant statue looms in the distance, nestled beside a hedge, marking a corner between pathways of dirt. I step toward it, and as I get closer it seems even larger as if coming to life. But it isn't. Just a carved white stone shaped into a muscular man holding a sword and shield.

The shield is detailed with the head of Medusa. She's screaming while the snakes bite in mid air. The scream looks painful, as if her jaw is about to rip apart. She looks like a monster. The full transformation of her myth complete—a beautiful girl decayed to rot. What others had done to her, made her become something she was not. The lump in my throat is dry and stuck there.

I can not let the chambermaids change because of the vile nature of men.

My fingers run along the scales of the snake, the marble carved to raised edges to create Medusa's hair. I can hear the hissing from behind their venomous teeth. It makes me take a quick breath, and I smell something sharp like copper.

A flash of Geneviève running in the palace halls in front of me, giving me the grand tour, greets me happily. She was so joyful, almost prideful, to introduce me to the court as we giggled through my new home, sunlight pouring in all around us.

Did she run in front of her killer? Did he run behind her as I did that fateful day?

I don't like the thought, but I must face it. I have to do *something*. My stomach drops in protest.

I move past the statue, brushing my hand against the dark green boughs of the hedges. Perhaps…perhaps if I trace her steps, there will be a piece of her left behind.

I stumble back when Geneviève pops out from the corner of the upcoming hedge, laughing at my fright.

"Why will you not tell me who killed you?" I ask bluntly. "Please, tell me."

"You already know," she says. Geneviève uses a finger to signal she wants me to come closer before turning. I follow her deeper into the maze. She becomes childlike, skipping through the maze while I try to keep up.

I wish for Étienne to appear. To help me. He promised he would help me. I bite the inside of my cheek, angry at myself for wishing this after learning who—*what* he truly is.

This is the same route where I chased after my sister. I banish the tears threatening to spill at the thought of shadows. "I'll figure this all out, Josepha," I promise to the quiet night sky. "I'll save you. I'm going to save everyone." My hands tremble, clutching my aching stomach. I have to try. Nobody else can die.

"Here's where you found me," Geneviève giggles. An urgent need to be in this spot takes over, and I lay down on my belly, relishing the cool earth upon my hands and cheek.

A spark leaps from the dirt, just within the hedges, and I gasp in fear that it may cause a fire.

No—not a spark. I pull myself closer with my elbows, dragging my body toward the light below the green boughs.

A blade. The metal caught the moonlight and tricked my eye.

Geneviève begins spinning all around me. She has transformed into someone else completely, a dead girl far removed from the smart, vivacious, bull headed girl I once knew.

I smell the copper, stronger than ever as I dig pebbles away with my fingernails. My arms are scratched from hundreds of tiny branches, but I continue.

I bring the blade up to my eyes and realize it is a knife. *A knife covered in blood.*

A space between the splotches of crimson dried brown, the metal catches the light again, a sharp slice of white against the silver.

"It slices through the perfect spot, she begged, she pled, but the blood wouldn't stop."

I drop it, and it scratches when it lands and bounces into the hedge. Vomit rises to my tongue. I don't want to think about her last breath. What happened to her once she was cut. No. I can't. I allow the tears to come, accepting that I am one of the fountains here, a never-ending stream of water flowing out of me, only falling into dirt and blood in place of crystalline pools.

Yet I continue to stare at it, unmoving. This could be the answer. With the murder weapon I only need to link it to its owner. I can't wait to show it to Étienne, and to find the killer *together*.

But then I remember—the pain is hollow and endless. I don't know that I can bear to see him, as much as I want to, now that I know the truth.

He's a ghost. A *ghost*.

I am alone. Étienne and I will never be together.

"Marie! Marie!"

I look around the sea of green. I hear Louis, but he isn't here yet. I have time. I fumble to the fallen knife and cut my hands on the pebbles around it, trying to pick it up quickly. I stuff it into the bosom of my dress. My breath is so fast it dries and burns my throat, and the knife cuts into my skin. I flinch but don't show pain on my face.

"Marie, there you are." Louis' voice is calm as he picks me up from under my arms. Just as he did when he found me in this same spot sitting over Geneviève. "Come to bed."

"I—I—" My sniffling stops me from saying more before he cuts me off.

"You are being hysterical. Which a dauphine may not be. An ache in the head is nothing compared to all those who suffer from real illnesses. Now come, I shall put you to bed."

NINETEEN

"My dear heavens!" The shrill voice grates my nerves, waking me from a deep sleep. "What have you *done*?"

Blankets slither down my body as Etiquette yanks them off me. I slowly sit up, propping myself with palms pressing into the mattress behind me.

"Look at this mess!" She snaps, attempting to brush dirt from the white sheets with one hand into another. The bed is full of pebbles and muck, and I'm as confused as Etiquette. How did these remnants of nature make their way into my bed?

And then I realize my dress is the origin of filth. It's the same I wore last night—digging at dirt, finding then hiding the blade that killed Geneviève.

The knife.

I pat myself and feel the place it hides at the side of my ribcage. I smile, happy to still have the thing I shall use as proof against…

I fell asleep in it once Louis returned me to my chambers. Why didn't he kill me when he had the perfect opportunity? A hand goes to my mouth, realizing that he must have worse plans for me. But what can be worse than this hell?

"I—"

"Marie," she says before the shock leaches from her body and seems to droop, her motions stilling like a wound doll running out of turns. Stops cleaning. Stops scolding. I quiet as Etiquette takes a seat beside me, though it is more of a perch with her navy dress cinched so tightly it constricts the bend of her waist.

I watch her wrinkled hand move to just above my knee. It worries me. The way her gray hair mattes to her face, framing sorrowful eyes. How she doesn't care about the dirt soiling her own dress by sitting beside me.

Something has happened. My intuition is growing stronger, wilder. I *know* something is wrong.

The tiny rosebuds lining Etiquette's silver hair pin shine just enough to provoke the voice to sing in my ear.

"That poor little mouse, you already know, she couldn't survive another blow. And yet we smash, and dim her glow."

My fists tighten, hoping that Etiquette doesn't say what I fear she might.

"Something happened last night. I know you were unwell, but while you were with Louis, the most unspeakable—" I look around the room as she speaks, searching for the bees when I notice there is no buzzing. Where are all the chambermaids?

"Comtesse, where are the girls?" I ask, staring wide at her.

"Marie, Anne is dead."

"No—" My fists tighten, digging my nails into my palms. The truth I don't want to hear spoken from Etiquette's mouth is unbearable. I can't take anymore. I suffered enough, people dying and only last night having my heart shattered by Étienne.

Our necks both whip to the left as a cart rolls in, an usher bringing a towering display of sweets. The old man, dressed stiffly in a forest green jacket over white stockings, catches us watching him and knows well enough to excuse himself from the room, quickly.

My head shakes in disbelief.

Blood and beauty. Chaos and cakes.

"She was found dead just outside a theater box," Etiquette continues.

"The show was meant to get answers. Find out more about the killer. It was all Anne's idea." My words are monotone. I relax my fists and stand up, walking across the room to the cart of treats. Focusing on the buttery frosting and bright red cherries to keep out imaginings of how Anne's life ended. But then I see a sugared violet, with soft purple petals and a splash of yellow at its center, all coated in sugar. Something so sweet, so beautiful, now a reminder of all the death in Versailles.

"I know, Marie. The girls all know, too. This was not

your fault." Etiquette remains on the edge of my bed, pebbles gathering around her thighs.

I pick a cherry from the top of a small round cake and pop it in my mouth. It's tart, causing my lips to pucker while I chew. My teeth gnash down hard, taking my frustrations out on the flesh of the fruit.

Anyone close to me, anyone I start to care for…why must they be killed? I will never bond with another one of the chambermaids again. Not with anyone. Not until I can find the murderer and kill them myself. Nobody should have to pay with their life for being near me.

I yelp, accidentally biting my tongue, but welcome the metallic taste of blood that pools from it. Focus on the pain of the flesh instead of the ache in my soul.

I have doomed them all. The omens are stuck to me, like leeches from a dark, murky lake.

"Who would have killed Anne? She was so timid, so sweet," I ask Etiquette, though I know she has no answers.

"I suspect that it is a commoner, angry at the crown for overspending. Someone who attends court, and has watchful eyes." Her leg begins bouncing in place below her fidgeting hands. "Angry at *you*."

I swallow the cherry and drops of my blood down. "At me?"

"The acting troupe knew too much about you, Marie." Etiquette doesn't look at me as she speaks. Instead, she focuses her attention down at her thumb kneading the palm of the opposite hand. "Knew too many of the things meant to be kept private between royal blood. But they knew. Which means the people on the streets of Paris are aware of the murders. Of the overspending. And they're dying too,

Marie. Terrible, horrible deaths as they waste away to nothing, skin stuck to bones from starvation. It worries me to know there are so many eyes on you, Marie."

Those poor souls. Families desperate for bread. I suck in my lower lip. I would never want anyone to starve to death. What a sad thing to waste away to nothing only because of something as arbitrary as money. Any mother would kill to save her child from such a fate. They'd kill me.

"Are they after me, Comtesse?" I ask, my lip now trembling.

She falls silent, still staring at her own hands, speckled with age spots.

I'll never get away from the omens. *Never.* Pressure builds in my eyes, but I ignore it and rearrange the orange, purple and green macarons by color on a golden platter. "It's the terrible things that happen. They know I am surrounded by omens and destruction. And then there's this. The desserts. The parties. The gowns. All adding to their view of me." Trying to impress the court has done me no favors in the eyes of the rest of the city. My heart feels like it is shrinking, growing smaller and smaller so it doesn't have to face any of this.

"The rumors were spread by someone of high standing, likely exaggerating everything into something much bigger than it had to be. The expectation on your head as dauphine is to spend, to show the finer side of Parisian life, to live in the lavish walls of Versailles." Etiquette tries to make me feel better, but it doesn't work. My frown deepens as I continue sliding macarons across metal, my fingertips adding just enough pressure to the smooth pastry to leave small indents.

"Who is spreading such lies?" I ask. My stomach falls as I remember the hundreds who filled the square upon my arrival. But instead of happy and awestruck, they're angry and out for blood. The new dauphine they had high hopes for only bringing them more death and despair.

I *know* Etiquette is wrong. People still die in the streets of Paris, but it is here, in the golden sun that is Versailles, where omens have come to play. Lurking eyes toying with me like a kitten with string, cutting apart anyone that I begin to care for—I am the reason Geneviève and Anne are dead.

I feel the room closing in on me, my head light, and eyes searching for someone who might be after me now. Waiting in secret passageways, waiting for the perfect moment to attack.

"I don't know. I don't know who is blaming you. Using you as the scapegoat for all of France."

Both Etiquette and I jump when Louis bursts through the door. Etiquette falls into a low curtsy and scurries out behind him.

"How are you this morning, wife?" he asks, but continues before I answer, "I am coming to check on you before I hunt for the day. I will be gone until sunset."

He can't be serious. He is going to run off… *again*. In the midst of all that is happening. "I am not well, Louis. Did you hear—?"

"Of another chambermaid? Yes, my apologies. You'll be well in my absence. Stay in the palace and close to the guard," Louis instructs.

Geneviève is behind me, gurgling, sinking her fingernails into my shoulders. "Don't let him leave," she says.

"No! Don't go," I yelp to Louis and he stops. Waiting.

"What is it," he asks.

"Why did he come find you last night?" Geneviève asks, her mouth pressing into my hair by my ear. "Has he honestly been hunting on his horse all this time, or has he been hunting girls?"

I gulp. "I—" I can't ask him any of the things Geneviève encourages me to say.

"And why, oh, why would he kill his best friend? Because he chose Anne over duty? Does the same fate wait for you?" Geneviève says, and my heart feels as if it is going to give out.

None of this makes sense, and so many questions spin in my head, making me dizzy. But I take a step back, wanting distance between us.

"Marie, why are you so ashen? Are you not well?"

Étienne appears behind him. I freeze in place as water fills my eyes. The most beautiful boy is back, but he's…different. His skin is grey with blossoms of purple reaching up his neck. His lips are dark blue. His whole body bloated. There is a large wound on the side of his head, as though he has been struck by some blunt object, leaving a part of his skull concave and bloody.

Étienne's indigo mouth forms a small grin, his top lip the perfect shape of an *m* I ache to kiss again. I hate myself for it. He's dead. *He's dead.*

But I wish it wasn't true. More than anything.

Louis takes a step toward me. "Marie, why are you trembling?"

Étienne stays behind Louis, and finally his sweet voice

leaves his mouth. "Act scared, and upset about the rumors. Make him feel like you trust him."

I nod, yes. Louis thinks it is for him.

"You look so scared. Sit. Please. Tell me what is wrong. Marie?" Louis waits for my answer. My heart gallops uncontrollably, but I manage to keep calm, focusing on Louis. Étienne just over his shoulder, tempting me to ask all the questions flooding my mind. Why he didn't tell me he is a ghost. Why he made me love him.

I pinch my eyes shut as tight as I can, and when I open them again, he is gone. A piece of me misses him already, but the rest of me knows he has to go.

"I don't know, Louis. I don't know if someone wants me dead too," I start to speak fast, the world catching up with me.

"No need to worry about that." He grabs one of the green macarons and takes a bite, smacking the creamy pastry in his mouth as he talks, paying no mind to my panic. "I have increased the royal guard."

Geneviève circles the perimeter of the room, running her hand along the walls. Like her memory is lost and she is but a shell of who she used to be.

"And what of the rumors people are spreading about me? You must tell me who is saying I spend more than anyone, that I'm immersed in decadence. I am no worse than the rest of *you*." My brows narrow with anger and accusations.

He raises an eyebrow at me. The way my teachers once did when I was a child and I became emotional. Heaven forbid a child show their feelings. "If you can promise to calm yourself, to not be so hysterical as you were last night, I will tell you."

I could punch him. I could punch him square in his ugly, bulbous nose and make it even more crooked. My lungs fill with air and I hold it there. Hold the heat in so I can hold back the words and the fury I want to unleash on this boy. My husband.

"Of course. I promise," I say with a wide, saccharine smile.

How could anyone be so cold and cruel? Especially to the person they are supposed to cherish and build a family with. How could he be in such a fine mood, running off to the forest, and laughing at the actors playing out his best friend's death on stage?

He steps closer, his eyes tracing me from head to toe. "You do look a fright. You will have to be cleaned up. Fresh dress. New wig. I will speak with Comtesse de—"

My spine stiffens. "There is someone in this court spreading lies about me. Your *wife*. The future queen of your country. And you know who. You said you know everything. Tell me who it is."

"Oh, they mean no harm." He stuffs a purple macaron in his mouth this time; his chomping makes me sick.

They.

"I've tried to speak with them about their chatter, but they don't listen, ever under the protection of Grandfather. Their *daddy*. Victoire and Adélaïde live for gossip. It's all they have. Quite sad, really."

I back up from him with slow, steady steps. He doesn't notice how his words are like a sword in my stomach, puncturing straight through to the other side of my body.

My mind races with all the snubs I have given toward Madame DuBarry, how I'd greet others and pretend she was invisible. I just stood there over and over again laughing with Victoire and Adélaïde when it was *them* creating rumors all this time. I got caught up in the sisters' pull in court, the way their lips fly with fever, tall tales and poison.

"I see." I shake my head, waiting for Louis to take his eyes off the dessert cart and acknowledge me. Of course, I can't say anything about his aunts. Can't curse them as I so desperately want to right now.

"They're vile," Geneviève says from across the room. "The whole family. I'm sorry I didn't see things clearly, Marie."

He finally looks up, and must see the sadness in me. If there is any sliver of humanity within him, he *must* see my disappointment.

"But they have nothing to do with the murders, which are quite a nuisance for me, might I add. The killings have sent the whole court into a tizzy and I do not like it."

Poor Louis. How inconvenient of lives to end and cause him to be uncomfortable.

He rubs his chin, thinking. "I have an idea. We shall have a fireworks party tonight. It will be a great show, and will distract everyone. Fireworks, drink, food…maybe it will even help your mood, Marie."

I bite my tongue, more blood spilling into my mouth.

"What about the spending? The rumors?"

"Shhh," Geneviève hisses. "Play along. Focus on the rumors."

This time Louis picks up a pink macaron and licks the side of it. Then he studies the way it is two pieces made whole. "No matter. I am the dauphin of France and I will do as I please. I can get away with these things. I am always observing every little thing, so you need not worry about it. Trust me. And to me, the court being happy is all that matters. I will set the wheels in motion, and see you tonight."

Louis walks away, the dessert still in his hand, leaving me at the foot of my bed on my own

"We were right here," Geneviève sings. "I told you."

I remember being in this same spot while Geneviève told me about how she found Louis to be strange. I can imagine her as she was perfectly, pink in her cheeks and worry in her eyes.

She whispers the same thing now as she did then.

"Sometimes he scares me a little bit. Always creeping. Lurking around in the shadows observing us all."

Creeping.

Lurking.

Observing us all.

A tingling spreads across my limbs as suspicion solidifies.

TWENTY

The sky glitters with twinkling pinpricks of light, like a million fireflies taking flight.

Only they aren't fireflies. Or stars. The sparks of white spreading across the sky over Versailles are from the fireworks set off, one after another. Louis' hopes of distracting the court from the stench of death with a show of fire working as brilliantly as the light in the night sky before us.

My mouth hangs open in awe as the cascading fireworks fall into the air high above the hedge line, erupting into streaming stars, like the branches of a willow weeping. Each explosion casts a quick flash of light over the fountains and statues, and sounds like a barrage of firearms shooting with phantom bullets.

I love it. The smell of fire. The way each firework leaves an imprint of smoke for a few seconds before the next firework takes its place. I inhale the beauty of the spectacle, caught in the daydream, until I catch Louis in my peripheral and my reality smacks me in the face. It would be the perfect moment if only things turned out differently for us. We could watch the show holding hands. But now I think he never really cared. Even before I arrived. I am merely the next step he was forced to fulfill—to him, I am not a person of flesh and bone.

Is this why I'm still alive? The ties to our countries most important, but he ensures that I shall not be happy, and that all around me are doomed to die?

He will never love me and I will never love him. But we will forever be man and wife in the eyes of God and Paris. The ache rolls through me like storm clouds ready to break open. A rumble of thunder in my ribcage as I think of Étienne—the dream of happiness with him is dead.

Be with the dead. Be with a killer. Neither side of the scale weighs in my favor.

"You are welcome to join me in my study tomorrow," Louis says to me without turning his head in my direction. His eyes reflect the sparkling fireworks.

"A chance to catch a little rat, to see him laugh and skin the cat."

I smile. For the first time, the voice slithering its way to my ears from reflections makes me grin, beckoning an opportunity.

"To see one of your experiments?" I ask.

"You did say you wanted to see what I do. How I study the complexities of the human body." He turns away from the fireworks to look at me with a lifted brow. His powdered hair is too large for his small head, and makes me wonder how I ever thought there was potential in him. "Unless you have changed your mind?"

"I have not changed my mind," I say quickly. "I would love to know more about you and the things you love, Louis." I smile up at him, selling myself. Because I *do* want to know everything about him—everything that will cause his demise. With access to his study I could find evidence. Maybe the axe that ended Alexandre, or a knife set that will be missing the blade that cut Geneviève's throat.

"Very well. You shall be there first thing. And bring a strong stomach and will, Marie. I do not have patience for drama in my study." His eyes are already back on the fireworks, scolding me from the side of his mouth.

"The strongest," I yell, as another blast of fire rises up to the stars.

Someone knocks an elbow into me, and I barely catch myself from falling over in these ghastly heels.

"Marie, you have done it again!" Victoire announces as she tries to get close after nearly sending me tumbling.

Victoire and Adélaïde wriggle in place, trying to be at the center of everything, like the snakes in the grass they are. They wear matching serpent green gowns and their red lipstick is painted on so thick and beyond the lines of their mouths that they look like court jesters, not daughters of the king.

I feel the heat in my cheeks from their mere presence. "This is Louis' parade," I state plainly.

"Oh, we know you're the one behind it all," Adélaïde says.

I'm sure you do, Adélaïde. Or that's what you will whisper to anyone who will listen to you and your putrid sister. Instead of saying the words aloud, I swallow, shaking my head slowly and focusing back on the fireworks.

Play nice. I must *play nice.* If I draw attention to myself I won't be able to uncover the secrets I'm desperate to know.

A flash of sparks fall in the darkness, raining down on an open space just beyond a fountain. As if the gardens are abruptly emptied, there's just him.

Étienne.

His unkempt hair dances in the wind as he raises an arm, waving at me. My breath is crushed in my lungs as he smiles and motions for me to come to him. This new version of him, forever frozen, blue and puffed.

What kind or torturous death caused him to look so? Images of him losing breath speed through my mind, bringing tears to my eyes.

I want to run into his arms and pretend I never found out he's a spirit of Versailles. And while I'm tucked safely against his chest, I want to yell at him for leaving me alone with Louis, devastated.

"Please excuse me. I will be right back," I say—more to Louis than Victoire and Adélaïde—before picking up the mint green skirts of my dress and walking toward the boy who broke my heart, but still owns it.

The *pitter patter* in my chest unleashes butterflies in my stomach as I close the distance between me and Étienne.

A *bang* whirs past my ear. Heat, followed by screams,

slices through the air, stopping me dead on my path. What—

More screams. Panic.

What's happening?

I spin in place, the balls of my feet creating friction against the dirt, searching for the source of such pandemonium.

I look for Étienne. He is already gone. It's suffocating— to keep losing him.

The fireworks are aimed at us instead of the moon.

"To the ballroom!" Someone cries as loud as they can to be heard over the stampede.

Hornets of fire fly toward the people running to the palace for safety. Orange bombs of flame ignite dozens of trees in the garden.

A tall man pushes past me—practically through me— in a blur. I fall so fast, my neck whips back with a white-hot bolt of pain. My head narrowly misses smashing against the ground. I lower myself down gently, attempting to catch my breath. I watch my chest rise and fall. *One. Two. Three.*

I turn onto my side to get up and run with the rest of the people. As my cheek rolls to the ground, I come face to face with an old man screaming as fire singes his hair and the skin on his forehead bubbles red hot. I gasp in pain, as though I feel the burning on my own skin.

I can't help him. I have to run.

I have to run.

I cough, the world around me now thick with black smoke and the smell of burning flesh. As I stumble along half blinded and half choking, I find bodies in the dirt—their once glittering outfits now charred black. One after another.

As I reach a set of glass doors, I catch a glimpse of blonde hair.

Josepha.

"Josepha!" I scream amidst the chaos. She's freed from the shadows. She's still here for me. Relief surges through my smoke-filled lungs.

Her hands are around her own throat as she glares at me with frantic eyes. I double over, gagging on the smoke in my own throat, and when I look back up, she is gone.

She was trying to tell me something. *Damn it, Josepha.* Despite the sadness thrumming through my veins from all the death around me, an opportunity crystalizes. It slowly forms in my head, a distraction from the living nightmare the fireworks have caused, and a step toward answers without the presence of Louis. To search compartments that are kept hidden.

While everyone recovers from the night, busy mending the burnt and the scared, I can sneak away to Louis' study.

I am not afraid. I am not afraid.

I lie to myself. The room is so dark. Especially without Étienne by my side.

Onyx cherubs sitting on an armoire by a grand mirror are covered with creamy white wax as they hold candlesticks burned down to nubs. A faint blue flame encircles the remaining short wicks.

Combined with the light of shrubs and trees still aflame outside blazing through the window, it's enough to see the white sheet draped over a form laying upon the table in the middle of the room. My heart stills. I know what it is. *Who* it is.

Don't get distracted, Marie. I scold myself. *Don't allow the tide of pain to sweep you away.*

Find evidence. Find something. Anything.

I turn my attention to walls made of bookshelves, hidden behind glass and gold. Hidden like this room has been from me. All of court knows where it is—just beside his bedchamber—but nobody is allowed to lay eyes upon it without Louis' coveted invitation.

There is so much to go through to search for clues, and I don't know how long I have. Louis could return to his study at any moment.

He could do anything in this room and get away with it. He could do anything in all of Versailles and he would be protected by his precious crown.

A part of me wants so badly to believe that I am wrong about him. Like I had been about Alexandre. That Etiquette is right and a commoner is to blame—some poor, hungry soul exacting revenge on the royal family. That the knots tied in my stomach are wrong and will soon unravel to prove he is no killer. That my husband is innocent.

But the shiver that chatters my bones from just being in this room tells me otherwise.

With hesitation, I tiptoe to the armoire and slowly open

a cupboard, hoping I'll find a clue right away and can escape before being caught. As the wood *creaks* open, the orange light flickers from the cherub holding still my candle. I lean closer to make out words, but it silences as a new sound echoes through the room.

A grating sound of metal. Dragging. A low-pitched *scrape* echoing toward me.

A chill courses through my veins, all hairs on my body standing on edge.

Behind me.

Something is coming.

Behind the cherub, the mirror shows nothing in the reflection, only the sound of the voice.

"There we creep, behind their back. But don't forget the screeching axe."

I brave turning around.

Nothing.

But the sound continues, bouncing off the walls, calling to me from the hall just outside the study. The metal on stone is unnerving. Like an axe being dragged across the marble floors.

An axe. No. *No.*

My thoughts become a scramble. I look around the room for a place to hide. The voice taunts me as my eyes scan across the glass of the bookshelves.

"Tick. Tock. Time is up. The blade is here. Accept the fear."

I won't. I will not lose my head. I'm going to get out of here. Maybe if I can run fast enough out of the room, I can find a different hallway before the axe finds my neck.

It's getting louder. I have no time. *I have no time.*

An exhale escapes my mouth through pursed lips, preparing to unfreeze myself and take my best chance. I just have to run around the table, and through the door. That's all. Then I'll have options with corridors and doorways.

I trip on the sheet, revealing what lays underneath. I look at what I have been trying to avoid. The tiny feet sticking out from one end of the white linen. Toes turned blue. I whimper and my pulse races at the sight of the corpse.

From Anne.

The sound of the axe outside the door joins the moan that escapes my lips. A beautiful woman appears beside me and a scream scrapes through my throat. I jump to the side, tripping on my skirts, but catch myself on an armchair and claw my way up it, back to my feet.

I'm scared it is Louis, come for me, so force myself to be quiet.

This is only the body of Anne. The skin and bone that is no longer her.

"Marieeee…" A girl in pink—a *spirit*—calls to me. A wave of shock crashes through me, staring at the girl who is usually coughing. Chloé. She did not survive the contents of the blue bottle. And now—now she's dead.

She reaches an arm out. Oh God.

Oh God. I press a hand to the pounding in my ribcage.

"Chloé, please. I want to help," I say, and take a step back. And another.

"Run," she says pointing to the door and starts coughing uncontrollably.

The air fills with scraping metal, and cries of pain between calling out my name. The river of blood falls from Chloé's mouth, pooling on the floor.

A hand touches my low back. A familiar touch.

Drip. Drip. Drip.

I feel hot breath on my lobe.

I slowly turn my head, my whole body trembling.

Alexandre.

He smiles an evil grin despite the cords hacked out of his neck. His hand begins to run up and down my spine. His mouth moves, but I hear no words.

"Run!" Chloé yells and charges me.

Warm liquid drips down my leg, trailing into my shoes. My urine turns cold within seconds.

TWENTY-ONE

One flies when fright has them by the throat.

The horror of Alexandre's icy touch on my back sent me out of the study with a speed I've not known before. As though the normal frost that found my feet turned to fire instead.

I forgot all about my search for evidence against my husband as the ghosts closed in on me. Instead, I fled to a ballroom to be amongst the living. Even if the living were covered with burns from the fireworks disaster and the air still smelled of smoke and singed skin. At least I was away from spirits who breathed only days ago.

I trembled amongst the sea of distraught courtiers on unsteady legs, covered in urine.

Nobody noticed.

The court is calm this morning, now the fires are out, but there are still those who are mourning.

I do feel for them. Understand the pain that comes from loss.

And a piece of me is suspicious about the whole ordeal. Knowing the power Louis has and his desire for cadavers to examine.

I stare at him now, thankful for the light filling the room with sunshine, making the study much different than it was only a few hours ago.

Louis appears relaxed in a simple linen shirt and brown pants, an apron of canvas covering him from neck to shin. The walls are bright white, there is a golden carving of a God on a chariot, and the bookshelves are topped with urns and stone busts of kings. No sign of Alexandre, nor Chloé calling my name.

In the center of the room, below a grand chandelier of twinkling crystal, she is exposed. Skin gray with blooms of purple. The sheet that I tripped on only hours ago is crumpled on the floor, shoved under the cherry wood table.

Anne's face is peaceful. Not like what is just below it. The remnants of what was her throat now a mash of insides pulverized like ground meat.

The ghost of Anne stands over her own body. It is chilling to see the body and soul together. She doesn't acknowledge me, just looks down with deep sadness. Her life was cut too short.

Her presence is yet another reminder that I must stop the madness. Louis can't do this to *us*.

He, or whoever helped him, must have been brimming with hatred—a blackened heart intent on death. The leg of the theater chair, smashing down on her neck over and over again, until her head was close to separating from her body. As I look at her now, I can't tell if it's attached still or not.

None of this makes sense. A small mousy girl, who once poured her heart out to me, now motionless on this table that must be stained in layer upon layer of blood. She was so kind to me as I bathed the night of the wedding. So sweet. She didn't deserve to end up here.

I imagine all of the other chambermaids that greet me at the foot of my bed every morning. It is the only way I can stomach standing over Anne's body, next to Louis who is holding a long slender knife over her chest.

There's green on his sterile table. A plant. I lean in closer than I want to what is left of Anne. She's looking down at the same thing—a violet, complete with its scalloped leaves.

"Ah, yes. When the guards brought me to her body in the theater, there were a few violets placed gently over her heart. Very peculiar."

Liar, I think, but say, "I wonder where they are from."

But I know. The violets are left with the dead. A pretty little bow for a body gone cold. The same flower used to mask the taste of poisons.

"I make sure the bodies are stored in the cellar on ice," Louis is quick to change the subject and I clench my jaw tightly. "To keep them fresh. Evermore important as of late with the increasing number of bodies in Versailles. Otherwise they will rot away and be eaten by maggots before I have a chance to dissect," he says as the silver slices through her dead flesh. I anticipate it to be the opening of a dam overflowing with viscous red liquid. Instead, a mass of deep crimson marbled with white and yellow lays below the thick layer of skin. It shines like glass against the light pouring in from the window.

"Listen to Mother, don't you forget. I'll be here forever, inside of your head."

I grow queasy from the voice coupled with the stench of death and alcohol in the room.

"You see, it is all so intricate once you peel back layers," Louis says, pulling her skin farther up from her chest until it is folded inside out, the edge nearly reaching the crook of her arm.

He is no doctor. He is not saving her. There is no reason for him to do this. Only intrigue and *enjoyment*. I push down on my belly, attempting to restrict the sick from rising up.

The bile betrays me, touching my tongue as the thought of Geneviève on this same table strikes me. Was she here? Cut open by Louis, her insides on display for him. Did Alexandre's body meet the same fate at the hand of his friend?

Louis puts down the knife and rolls his sleeves up, painting them red from the blood on his hands. "Are you not well?"

Damn it. Louis noticed my hands. He will send me away if I can't control my feelings, but it is near impossible to contain being horrified to my core.

"Yes, yes. Just this corset. They really do tie them tight." My fingers grip the sides of my waist, and I take deep breaths to draw his attention there instead of the blood I'm sure has drained from my face. White as the discarded sheet.

"Good. Because this is where it gets interesting. The bones lay below all this muscle." He rubs at the smooth muscle gently, almost lovingly. "It's incredible how we have a skeleton that holds us up while also acting like a shield to protect the parts that make us live." Louis' other hand dives into Anne's open chest with the tiny knife, cutting away at the muscle, curdles of yellow rolling along with the blade. He laughs while he tries to get to bone, like a butcher slicing meat—pleased with himself.

My throat is dry. I rub my tongue along the roof of my mouth, encouraging saliva to build so I can swallow it down along with the terror.

"Just like a clock, we have all these parts that connect and work in perfect harmony."

"Like a symphony," I whisper.

"Yes!" He beams at me, happy and shocked at the same time. "Exactly like that. Like an orchestra has all the different sections and they each have their parts to play…if one fails, they all fail."

I nod my head. I've impressed him with three words. I don't want to mess that up. He turns back to his work. My friend.

I try to focus on the room again. Blending in with the books of maroon, copper, and green is a shelf with bottles. Tiny, sapphire blue bottles. Dozens of them lined up, and all missing paper labels. They shine brightly now that the sun is in the room.

"Done with a girl, now drink it down. The end of her world, we all fall down."

I close my eyes, praying tears won't fall. Not in front of Louis. Not in front of my husband who has a room for corpses and poisons. Are one of those bottles for me? If I fail to birth a baby boy, will I be deemed useless and marked for liquid death?

"Excuse me, Your Highness." An usher in bright blue enters the room with a bow, balancing a platter in his hand. I can recognize the movement of the ink from here. "I have a letter for the dauphine."

"Yes, yes, come in," Louis instructs, not taking his attention away from the unbeating heart hidden within Anne. The poor heart of a girl who gave so much to a boy she loved. And now they are both dead.

Don't cry. *Do…not…cry.*

I walk to the usher and take the letter from the silver. He bows at me this time.

It is indeed from Mother. "Louis, I shall take this in another room, if that is suitable."

"Do come back," he says.

The usher follows me out and I can feel his eyes on me.

"Thank you for the letter," I say to the empty space in front of me, knowing he is close enough to my backside to hear. "That will be all."

His feet make a scratching noise against the floor as he turns to leave. I am relieved he did not insist, for my stomach is still lurching from watching Louis doing the unspeakable to Anne's body. Nobody can see the sick fall at my feet. It would get back to my husband and I would not be granted entry back in the study.

I walk farther into the empty hallway, full of pillars of marble that connect all of Louis' chambers. I lean against one, the stone cold on my back, while I feel the sun's heat kiss my face from outside the floor to ceiling windows. I close my eyes to embrace it. To ground myself in the warmth on my skin instead of the chill in my bones. To really pull myself out of that study—though the door to it is still in sight—thankful the letter came in the moment it did.

I rip the paper and pull out the latest from Mother.

I fear for you, daughter.

Those in Paris grow concerned.

The news of a growing number of bodies in Versailles has reached Austria. Your siblings now worry for you too.

Death as well as no news of pregnancy has your brother planning travels to right your wrongs.

In the meantime, get control. Versailles is your home now and you must not allow such terrible things to happen. Those poor souls.

Do better.

Be better.

I am watching,

Mother

I leave my place in the sun, and continue to read her words as I walk back towards Louis' study. I don't want to go back, but I know I must.

The weight of my world is mounting quickly, higher than the baker's layered cakes and heavier than stone. Mother's letter only added to it all.

So few words. It always takes her so few words to seep under my skin. I walk straight into a wall, caught up in my own head. My toe kicks a panel outlined with gold paint and I leap back as something falls out at my feet.

An axe.

Covered in blood and gleaming.

TWENTY-TWO

The undeniable truth comes crashing down with the axe.

Louis is the killer.

I was right.

His all-important hunting, the thrill he gets chasing after animals and ending their lives. The experiments, fascinated with consuming as much as he can of the human body. Geneviève's warnings that I brushed away like dust.

The omens didn't follow me, they were already here.

Mother's letter crumples into my sweaty palm as I stare at the sharp blade at my toes.

His best friend. This is what ended Alexandre's life. A bead of sweat tickles my temple as it trails down my face.

I hear footsteps against the marble floor, echoing through Louis' chamber hallway, and I panic. Stuffing the letter down the front of my dress and dropping to my knees, I grab hold of the wretched device of death and cram it back in the little hidden compartment in the wall. My mind flashes back to Geneviève pulling out the green bottle of champagne for me on that first day in Versailles.

With as much calm as I can muster, I create space between myself and the axe. I'll come back for it at night. When I can hide amongst the shadows—an axe crusted in blood will surely draw attention in the light of day.

But a knife won't.

The memory of Geneviève's dead body, crumpled like the letter hidden in my bosom, races through my mind. I try to push it away, make it dull. Focus on going back to the hedges to get the knife. My pace quickens, searching for a door, forgetting all about returning to the study and the terrible boy in it, elbows deep in my friend's cadaver.

I'll find a safe space to hide the axe and knife, to give me enough time to decipher a connection between them and Louis. And then what? What do I do once I can prove he did it? Is it treason, when I am his wife? When the truth is as clear as the crystal they drink their wine from?

I find a door of glass, opening directly onto the gardens. When I push it open, I see my reflection, a girl with sad, swollen eyes and gaunt cheekbones. The face of a different girl than the one who arrived in Versailles—one whose bubble of hope burst into flames.

"They'll force your jaw, extract the truth. Can't take it now, you'll lose the crown."

The air is heavy, clouds pushing down from the gray sky, a storm ready to unleash its fury on the palace. The gravel crunches underfoot with each step I take, my legs moving with growing determination the closer I get to the maze.

My teeth dig into my gums with such force it hurts near as bad as the braces once did. The pressure standing in place of my anger from the voice promising my life will end if I accuse Louis.

But *I will.*

If it's a chance to ensure no other chambermaids have to die, then take my life, Louis. I shall risk it, for what is my life to be now anyway, without love and freedom, trapped in the haunted halls of Versailles? I spit on the dirt as I pass the Apollo fountain.

And then I catch her watching me, sitting on the edge of the fountain wall, in a velvety dress the color of a summer sunset.

"Madame DuBarry," I call to her as I slow to walk over. She nearly stumbles into the water from my address, then scrambles to stand before me.

Chloé is by her side, coughing into the back of her hand. The sound is incessant, hurting my ears.

When I arrive at DuBarry's side, my chest is heaving, attempting to catch my breath. My hand rubs at my hairline, the other on my waist.

She sniffles, and quickly dabs her eye with a white handkerchief covered with remnants of her makeup. "Your Highness," she says with a curtsy. "Please, forgive my appearance. Chloé—"

The fountain at our side creates a mist around us, the sound filling the air in place of Madame DuBarry's unfinished sentence. The water matches the churning in my mind. I don't understand why she is so upset. Wasn't it *her* who gave Chloé the blue bottle?

Chloé was slowly dying through bouts of hacking coughs as I watched Madame DuBarry shove the bottle into her hands again and again.

"But—what about the blue bottles you gave her?" I move my hand to my hip. My brows pinch with confusion as I study Madame DuBarry, who falls back to the edge of the fountain, her skirt brushing past mine as she sits.

She inhales deeply through her small nose, a beauty mark to the side of it revealed below the smeared white powder. "I know. I gave her so much after Louis gave them to me. He said they would help her. But they *didn't*. She only got worse. And now—now she is gone."

Louis.

I had been so cruel to Madame DuBarry, at first thinking she was poisoning her own friend. But she was a victim too—swallowing the lies Louis fed her just as fast as Chloé consumed liquid death.

"I am sorry," I say. Her shoulder shudders with each of her sobs as I place a hand there to comfort her. "I was wrong about so many things. I should not have ignored you, or laughed at you. I believed the stories instead of learning the truth for myself. And I was blind. So very, very blind. Will you ever forgive me?"

Her hand touches lightly against her collarbone. "Yes, of course," she says, then looks up at me with wide, swollen eyes.

"I am sorry too."

"No need for that. I don't deserve it." And I don't. Not from her. "And thank you for your kindness. I do hope we can have tea soon."

"I would like that." Madame DuBarry attempts to smile. I wish I spoke sooner. Apologizing to her feels good. And I must make amends with anyone I have hurt from being so caught up in court and impressing the wrong people—my husband and his aunts.

"As would I. I must leave now though, but I shall find you later," I say and she responds with a nod. I can almost hear Victoire and Adélaïde's disgust as I walk away from her and enter into the hedge maze. I hope they vomit in their mouths and enjoy the taste when they learn of my new friendship with Madame DuBarry.

My hand reaches out, allowing my fingertips to brush along the branches of the evergreens. I am getting to know the maze now. The turns I must take. The little markers that tell me where I am so as to not get lost. The boughs are soft like the touch of Étienne. I miss the way his hands felt on mine. I realize now that they were always cold, but the racing of my heart and the hope of a kiss distracted me from that. From *all* the clues.

But I see now. I see everything. And I am going to make sure the court and all of Paris see it too. That Versailles is haunted by the souls Louis has trapped there. The souls that the king, the Sun King, and the fathers before them have surely trapped there too.

I fall to my knees to retrieve the knife as I did to hide the axe. I dig in the spot I found Geneviève on my wedding night, scooping dirt aside with my bare hands, ignoring the dust it sweeps all over my dress.

It's not there. My hiding spot is empty.

I rock back and forth, digging all around. Where is it? Where *is* it?

I have it already of course. I've lived this moment before. Found the knife and slipped it in my dress, but where did it go?

I feel like a complete fool.

How can my memory fail me?

A pain in the back of my throat builds—I need this knife. This is my evidence. This and the axe are going to save us all. *Somehow.* But I'm a childish girl, misplacing something so important like it were some old and ragged toy.

I slam a fist on the ground, and stones imprint into the side of my hand.

What did I do with it?

"Marieeeeee," someone sings my name in a sweet tone, directly in my ear. I fall onto my side, skin crawling. I heard that voice only last night, in the study.

Chloé sits where I was just digging, her arm pushed up against the hedges. She holds out a bottle, indigo glass with a chip on its brim.

"We drank. We float." She sings sweetly, yet the haunting words leave my legs shaky, unable to move. I remember the blue bottles in Louis' chamber. The poison. The girls who died.

Chloé's ghost, with a heart-shaped face and black hair falling from beneath a powdered wig, stretches her arms out farther to show me inside her bottle, but it's too dark to see what is inside. "We drank. We float."

"Float?" I whisper, not sure what she means.

She shifts towards me in a jerking motion. Coughing louder and louder, her throat ripping to shreds. A tear streams from my eye.

Her nose almost touches mine, and I can feel her dead breath through all the hacking on my face—it makes mine shake. She lifts the glass just above our heads. Her neck snaps to the side and she looks at the bottom of the bottle.

"Below. Below," she sings and chokes, and I fight my urge to flee. She's trying to give me answers. I need to ignore the trembling her presence sends through my bones.

"We drank. We float. Below. Below," her haunting voice sings again. She looks back up at the tiny bottle, then at me. Her eyes are gray and wild.

"Run!" She screams then disappears.

I turn my head to the sky as the first raindrops begin to fall.

TWENTY-THREE

A drink can be a friend, yet your worst enemy.

My mattress is hard beneath me, bed still made, the sheets pulled tight. I stare above, at the tassels on the curtains, one strand of silk yarn after another after another—a brown color trying to be gold like the rest of Versailles. My body is motionless while my mind spins madly out of control.

Etiquette escorted the chambermaids from my room once I returned from the gardens. She said something about sadness and duty, but my head was in too much of a fog to make sense of her words.

Now, I think of the green bottles of ever flowing champagne on my wedding day, and at parties since. The sweetness on my lips and the tickle in my mouth as I drank from the crystal glasses. A friend—offering distraction and a faint and welcome numbing. A comfort to get through the horrors unfolding in my life.

I've been lucky though. That a few extra drops from a cobalt bottle did not find my cup. Not like Chloé. Whatever she was drinking became her foe. A boy simply drip, drip, dropped the perfect amount of tincture to poison her.

We drank. I can only assume the poison that ended her life. How many is 'we'? How long have these killings been happening for?

We float. The words replaying in my head make me shiver all over again.

Below. Below. I don't understand. *Below* what?

What does she want me to know? And why couldn't she tell me something useful? Like how to stop more from dying.

"Oh God," I whisper. The sound is hollow in the dark room.

I pick up my hand mirror from the side table, and look into it, only seeing the dark circles under my eyes. I'm so tired.

"Will the axe still be where I left it? Have I lost all hope of bringing truth to this court and stopping these poor girls from dying? From saving my own life?"

"Enough, Marie. No more lies. Listen, listen, stop all those who cry."

I throw the mirror down and stare into nothingness. Pain shoots through the tips of my fingers, waking me to the realization of my tight grip on the rose-embroidered blanket, lifting my nails up from their beds. I release them quickly, and fold my hands over my belly, focusing on the way it expands and deflates with each fast breath I take.

Scritch. Scritch. Scritch.

My eyes dart to the door. I remember Geneviève showing me the one fingernail she grew extra long in order to scratch on the doors of royals. The beating of my heart takes off, like a spooked horse bolting, leaving nothing but dust in its wake.

Scriiiiiitch.

I sit up and swing my legs slowly off the edge of the bed, not taking my eyes from the door.

Scriiiiiitch.

The sound makes me cringe and my shoulders and fists tighten. It sounds like a fingernail, digging into the wood of the door, dragging from top to bottom.

"Who is there?" I muster the courage to ask, but am met with silence. Maybe it is all in my head. Maybe I am just tired and overwhelmed and need to sleep. "Announce yourself," I say, trying one last time.

Scriiiiiiiiiitch.

I jump at the returning sound, and just as quickly decide to face what lies beyond the door.

Scritch. Scritch. Scritch.

Their movements are faster the closer I get to the sound. Summoning bravery, my fingers wrap around the golden doorknob, and pull.

Nothing.

There is no hand. No one scratching at the door incessantly. No trace of fingernails caked with dirt below them.

That can't be. I heard it. *I heard them.*

Holding steady to the edge of the door, I take a step out and peek my head out the corner, scanning both sides of the hallway.

Nothing.

After a moment I step back across the threshold to my chamber and close the door, placing my palm and forehead against it. Confusion and terror wage war in my head. I listen for the scratching to return. Still, nothing.

My brow rubs against the wood as I shake my head. There is too much to worry about, a great puzzle to be solved to save the chambermaids and myself. I do not have time for the noises of the night. Pushing myself from the door and lifting my chin with determination, I spin to return to my bed.

A loud gasp catches in my throat when I see her, sitting in a white nightdress cross-legged on the mattress, smiling at me. Both of my hands fold over my mouth, containing a scream of disbelief.

Blonde hair tied into a bow made of violet ribbon. She got her ribbon back. And she's here. She's here.

Josepha.

I can barely see her in the shadows, and run to her side, jump into her arms. She laughs, the same warm laugh I have longed to hear for so long.

"It is time, Maria," she says my name. My real name before coming here.

"Time for what? You're here now! You can help me with everything." My mind races faster than the words can come out.

"Maria," she gently presses her hand to my cheek. "Remember. It is time to remember."

I place my hand on the back of hers, holding on to this moment. But it doesn't last long.

A wrenching sob rips through me as the memory shakes me like an earthquake. Her eyes begin to swell, and a festering wound grows quickly upon her cheek.

"Josepha," I say and press her hand closer into my cheek. "Please! *Please* tell me," I beg.

"I died, Maria."

I hear her clearly, but I don't want to. My lip trembles as I cry and it feels like a cannon has hit me square in the chest. "No…you—you left home. You didn't want to marry."

"That's what you wanted to remember. But you were there while the pox took hold of me and made me suffer in agony. You've grown so much since then." Josepha smiles. Bile stings my throat, the touch of her wound infested hands wet and thick like syrup.

This can't be.

No. No.

Not my sister too. The devastation aches unbearably in my heart.

The wound on her face widens, a sliver of blue left visible below her skin, like a crescent moon behind clouds. It flashes with orange from the flame of a candle.

"You peek, you see, and then you find. I'm always yours, you're always mine."

The voice.

Reflections.

I remember watching Josepha through the door. Mother told me to go to my room. But I couldn't. I had to be there for Josepha. She was always there for me.

She was on her bed, surrounded by people—family, doctors, friends. And she was screaming in pain. I couldn't see her from where I stood in the doorway, but I could watch her from the long oval mirror on the wall opposite where she lay. It reflected the way her body was flung halfway off the end of the bed, her back arched while she writhed in pain. She kicked her legs violently, but men's hands held her wrists down.

A last fight at life before the disease took her.

And then she gave up.

Josepha fell limp and her head dangled off the bed, her throat long and exposed toward the ceiling. I continued watching the mirror until finally her eyes met mine in the reflection.

She was gone.

I face the buried memories of Mother telling me to stop living in a fantasy. A fantasy that Josepha was alive and ran away.

Josepha is dead. She was always dead.

And now, this is her ghost. Yet another here to shatter any remnants of my heart that was left. "You're a—a spirit. A ghost." Not a question. *Not anymore.* "Just like the stories you told me by the fires when I was little. The hauntings of the palace."

"And now I haunt you," she exhales out of her nose and grins, "I just couldn't leave without you facing the truth."

Josepha's contact with my face breaks as she convulses onto her back, her eyes bulge while she looks up at the ceiling. The girl I grew up with, the girl so full of heart and life, now fixed with her head cocked at an unnatural angle, with blisters covering her body.

"Josepha," I cry, trying to pull her back up, hold her within my arms. Her mouth splits open, popping the pustules one by one. Blood and puss spilling from her skin in spurts, dropping onto the sheets threaded with gold.

She opens her mouth, but the sound that comes out is garbled, as though marbles are swirling around on her tongue. Drool falls out the side of bruised lips. My stomach heaves.

"How can I help you? Help me save you!" I beg in the flickering candlelight.

She stops convulsing, and looks at me, trying her best to smile. Josepha's once porcelain skin is now a shade of gray and violet just a touch lighter than her ribbon. And red. So much red.

Her mouth is full of pink spit that continues to pour from her lips. Her face is covered in wounds. Red festering mounds of bleeding flesh spread like wildfire across her cheeks, nose, chin. Her eyes are so swollen she must have been beaten within an inch of her life. I wonder how she can even see me.

"I love you," I say, studying the way each angry circle of red erupts with a white puss. I choke. The stale stench of sickness and decay is overwhelming. But I remain with my sister, desperate for answers.

"I love you too." I hear the words even though it sounds like she is choking on her own tongue. Despair spins uncontrollably within me. My tears are hot as they fall from my eyes and onto flesh which smells of blood and vomit.

"You were the last thing I saw. Your little face peeking in through the door. Thank you for that."

I shake my head. Breathing so hard my lungs feel like they have caught flame and I'll drown in the smoke. My sister presses a hand on my chest and leans in to kiss my cheek. I look down.

Through the tears in my eyes, I watch her sweat and blood drip onto my lap.

It's all that's left of her when I look back up.

Josepha is gone.

TWENTY-FOUR

I tread through blankets like they are waves on the sea.

"Come back!" My hands swim through the air where Josepha sat in front of me. She was *just here*. "Please. Don't leave me."

The words trail off as I crumple into the bedding, smothering my tears with fabric, drowning in everything that has happened. Even before I arrived at Versailles, my sister was gone. I want her back. Even if the sight of her blood and wounds made my stomach stir.

I couldn't save her.

"Come back…come…back." My plea is muffled and unheard. The loneliness swells in my lungs, and I feel as though I'm being pulled underwater like an anchor, without a last breath.

All I've ever loved are nothing but imprints upon my memory now; ghosts that haunt me because I cared for them so much.

Thunder rumbles, shaking the windows, and I go to them. The tears that continue to fall are salty as they reach my lips, and I sniffle as best I can, but it is no use. I swing the double doors open and am met with a sheet of rain that is deafening. The first step onto the balcony soaks me completely. The scents of the gardens intensify in the storm, the earth absorbing water from the heavens.

I focus on the comforting smell as I take a few more steps out and find the railing. My hands slip on the gold of it, and I must tighten my grip to stay up straight.

I tilt my face to the sky and close my eyes, allowing the raindrops to crash down on my skin. The violence of the thunderstorm is a welcome reprieve from the reality of my sad, desolate life. A game of politics, where I am a mere piece on the chess board, moved around carelessly by those in power. What I wouldn't give to be the chess master.

If I had power, things would be different.

I run my hands through drenched hair and look down at the vastness of Versailles. So large. So beautiful. So much potential.

And then I scream, as loud as I can, until I feel it deep in my belly. I wonder if anyone can hear me, considering the speed at which the rain pelts against the palace.

"Come back!" I scream again. Praying that Josepha hears me. Étienne. Geneviève. I can accept it all. That they are dead. That I'm truly lonely amongst the living.

But I still need them to help me fuel this fire within me now. I *will* right these wrongs. And all those who have caused harm shall pay their dues.

A crack of lightning illuminates the gardens, but it looks different now. I have a difficult time accepting what I see with my own eyes. A trick of the mind, a mirage that will dissipate by morning.

But it is real. *Hundreds* of ghosts, strolling through hedges, sitting by fountains, walking aimlessly through the place they died. The palace where they were killed.

Like the ghosts of a garden party long forgotten.

Women who weren't helped when they were sick, women who bled out as they birthed child upon child, women poisoned because they were no longer of use to a man, mistresses who threatened a marriage.

Another crack of lightning brightens their faces. Pale and sad. They all look up at me at the same time, slowly beginning to walk toward the balcony.

Toward *me*. So slow.

So, so slow.

My heart echoes in my ribcage as the thunder echoes through the night sky.

Their eyes are sunken, and their cheeks are hollow. Their dresses cling to their bodies in the rain, the same as mine does.

Two young girls hold hands while they saunter through the grass. I assume they are sisters, with matching orange dresses and blonde curls down to the waist. I can't tell if they are twins by their faces, covered in wounds like Josepha's. Red, swollen, bleeding. I touch my own face, imagining how painful they must have felt in life. How so many have suffered from disease. How many have suffered at the hands of those in power.

Power is the disease in these haunted halls.

Fear begins to strangle me as slowly as they all walk. There's so much sorrow in the faces peering up at the balcony.

"I'm sorry," I say to them, but not loud enough to cut through the storm. "I'll end all who did this to you. I will. I will…" I have to. For these girls who came before me and still linger here, a piece of them forever bound to the French court. For the girls who are chambermaids, who deserve more than to be chopped apart by a ruthless boy. And for me, and all that has been done to me to bring me here.

I can save us all.

"It is time, my friend." I shed my skin as I jump in fright. I thought I was alone. But maybe I never was.

I turn to her. Still wearing the yellow dress covered in scarlet. The sound of gurgling no longer escapes her exposed throat, but her veins are purple and angry, crawling up her neck and face like they are trying to find where to take root. Drenched in blood and rain, the scent of metallic earth fills my nostrils.

"Geneviève," I whisper. A rasp in my chest shakes me.

"I—I'm so scared," I stumble with my words but try to hold my ground. This is what I've needed to face. All the running—for nothing. "I've been so scared, Geneviève."

"You deserve better," she winks, and I remember her as she was. A girl who spat in the face of rules and expectation, yet made so many love her at the same time. Except the person who killed her.

"I should have listened." I cover my face with my hands, crying into them, not sure where the rain ends and the tears begin. Shame flashes through me brighter than any lightning bolt.

Ice meets the back of my neck, and I drop my arms. She's behind me, consoling *me*. Geneviève's fingertips graze across my skin, and the chill reawakens the need to know everything about her last moments. "How—how did he—"

"You can't be scared anymore." She steps in front of me as she cuts me off. Her throat is gaping wide. Her red hair wild and she wears a feverish grin. Her hand finds mine, and in the pouring rain, we smile at each other. Because she's right. I can no longer be scared. Not anymore. All that fear has transformed to anger. The way they transformed me into what they needed me to be—good enough.

The fire builds in me, hot enough to withstand any storm, stoked by all the women ended too soon, all the deaths, all the horrible things Louis has done, and all that was stripped from me.

The twinkle of Geneviève's eye lights up her entire face. I follow her lead when her gaze falls to my hand, palm held upward toward the sky, holding a knife that glimmers as rain falls upon it.

The blade that killed her.

"Take the power in your hand, stab and kill the precious man."

TWENTY-FIVE

The handle of the knife in my hand feels oddly exhilarating. I had it ready the whole time. I knew what to do.

A blade that scared me before, now a coveted instrument that could be used for divine justice. My fingers curl around it completely, and I watch Geneviève dissolve in the rain.

"Thank you," I say to her, wondering if she can hear now that her form is gone from in front of me.

I return to my room and carefully place the blade down at the edge of my bed. Raindrops sit on it like water beads upon rose petals. I don't know what my next steps are—what am I going to do? I push down the words of the voice. It can't be right. Not again. Its eerie words are getting harder to face.

I shall kill no one. Not even Louis. But I will make him pay. *Somehow.*

My clothes are difficult to peel off as I shiver, and for once, I actually wish someone was here to help me with undressing. I cross the room naked, my feet squeaking on the hardwood, and find a dress in my wardrobe. A pale, yellow chiffon, one that feels like soft clouds as I pull it over my damp, clammy skin. No corset. No powders. Just me and the beautiful fabric that reminds me of Geneviève.

I tiptoe back to my bed, pushing aside the heavy curtains with a hand. I watch the knife. "Who do you belong to?" I ask it. My eyes burn, but they shed no more tears. I feel as though I'm a well; dried up, unable to cry ever again. But the pain will forever linger, unable to be released.

"Are you Louis'?" I say, picking it up and nearly cutting myself as it slips in my fingers. Lifting it to my face, I study it. The sharp edges, the glistening silver, the small sprout of lavender carved in the handle that I did not notice before. I press the tip into the bed of my finger, spinning it gently as my eyes squint.

What else have I missed?

A lump in my throat builds, remembering this tiny knife is what killed my friend. Something so delicate cut through her and ended her like she was nothing. I can't think about that now. I have to figure out what to do next.

I drop it in the small pocket cut into my skirts. But then feel something else there. More metal. I leave the blade and pull out—

The portrait of Louis. The painted boy I thought I'd spend every night with, talking about what we would name our children, right before we made love. My hands grasp onto the cold silver encapsulating the small, circular canvas. I stare into his cold eyes, knowing better. Stupid girl.

Stupid girl.

A million lies I told myself, in order to believe in love. In order to believe in anything that would mean I was adored. If they loved me, maybe they wouldn't leave me, abandon me like Josepha did. Or my mother. The court's constant emotional somersaults would land them at my feet, a future queen to worship.

Fantasy. A fantasy I lived in with a hopeful heart, excusing and ignoring reality. Until that reality started to pile up in the form of blood and bones—the flesh of the innocent at my feet instead of worship. Dizziness rushes from my head down my arms. Versailles, rotten with the stench of death is not fully to blame, but my faith in the fantasy which numbed me to the outside world.

Thunder cracks outside, and I shudder.

I brush the painting with my thumb, wanting to smear away Louis' smug look that not so long ago I thought was charming. There's been no real investigation by the guard. Of course there wouldn't be. Louis is the ruler of this palace, second to the king. He's protected at all costs—the name of the future king must not be soiled.

I see everything so much clearer now. My daydreams— once supple flowers full of color and beauty—are now brittle and broken, fallen to the ground, never to be revived.

I will not live in a fantasy. I can face the truth.

But I'll need help.

If I am to have a chance at connecting Louis to the killings, it will require the help of someone who knows of the hidden hallways of Versailles. Who has access anywhere without being seen. And who would do anything for me.

I place my fingers on my lips as I walk across my chamber toward the door, remembering his kiss.

Etiquette greets me on the other side. The bags under her eyes droop near as low as the tip of her nose. Blue and tired. Her hand touches the side of my head, pressing gently against my blonde hair. "Are you quite alright, Marie? I thought I heard screaming."

She peeks over my shoulder to my dark empty room. She won't find anything there. The ghosts of my sister and my friend have left.

"I am splendid." I bend at the waist, breaking contact between us, wiping down my dress against my thighs to straighten it. "Much better from earlier. I do appreciate your concern."

"Where are you going at such a frightful hour?" Etiquette pulls the corners of her emerald shawl tight to her chest.

"I like to walk at night. The quiet helps me think." It is a half lie. I do like to walk, but this time it isn't for the quiet, but to reunite with a boy and get his help.

"Would you like company?"

"Perhaps not this evening, but I *would* like to walk with you another time," I say. This time the truth. Etiquette has lost people she loves too. Who am I to be as cold as she was when we first met?

"Very well. We shall do that." She cracks a slight smile, then takes a step to the side, knowing I want to leave the threshold of my room and begin my stroll.

"Get some rest, Madame," I say softly. "I fear you need it as much as I."

We half curtsy at each other, then continue in opposite directions.

I wander what feels like all of the palace in my search for Étienne, hopeful that he will appear as he has before, will sense I am looking for him. I'm grateful to not have the watching eyes of the court on me, save a few guards who nod and let me continue. Their eyes are wide, no doubt excited to tell Louis of my movements.

As soon as the storm ends I venture outside, walking up and down pathways, circling in the dirt full of puddles and wet statues shining under stars.

Large, angled walls made of round stones welcome me into the ballroom grove, a most spectacular outdoor amphitheater. Even the people of Austria spoke highly of the architectural achievement, combining the grandeur of interior within nature.

I stand at the center, dirt under my feet, spinning in the circle that surrounds me. Tiers of seating look like perfectly sculpted hedges with stone underneath. The side of the grove is a masterpiece—cascading water over stairs made of pebbles and shells. Eight levels pour forth a continuous flow of water, adorned with golden urns larger than me. Fountains spray up from the front, sides, and back, as though the water itself is playing a symphony for me. I am in awe, and feel lighter than I should.

My heart stops.

Étienne appears at the top step, and slowly descends through the manicured waterfall, each step bringing him closer to me. He is still so beautiful. Though I now see him as he was in death, with gray and purple skin, and those dark blue lips, I still think he is beautiful.

My fingers trace along my collarbone, waiting nervously. Unsure what to say to him. Not sure how to fight the urges of both yelling at him for not telling me he was of the spirit realm and of throwing my arms around him. The conflicting impulses run through the corners of my brain.

As he nears, his smile turns grave. "I should have told you."

"Yes—well—" I stammer.

"I died some time ago. But Marie, that doesn't change how I feel. I may as well have a heart right here," he folds his hands on his chest, now only a small step from me, "a phantom beat playing whenever I think of you. Whenever I see you."

Happiness surges through me. He loves me. *He loves me.*

But he needs to know how his disappearing made me feel as well, so I hide my smile. "You left me there. In the corridor. Looking like a fool kissing at air. You left me with *him*," the last word is sour.

"I was the fool. I'll never leave you—" his arm reaches across the distance between us as he takes a step forward. I move back, which silences him. Still not decided on how to feel. There is a part of me that he broke—a piece I don't know is capable of healing again.

I need him, though. I shall bandage my heart and ask him for the help I so desperately need. The chambermaids are relying on me. And I need to handle Louis before he comes after me. It's only a matter of time.

We stare into each other's eyes, while his hands knead at his sides.

I decide.

My arms wrap over his shoulders and his hands find their way around me, lifting me into the air. I nuzzle my face into the crook of his cold neck and he kisses my head.

"I love you," he says. My feet find the ground again, but I hold strong to the nape of his neck. I kiss him in response.

The fountains seem to grow louder, the cold air just a touch warmer, and the scent of oranges billow from the orangery. I found love in this hopeless place after all. A love I'm not sure I can truly have.

I slowly part my lips from his and walk to one of the amphitheater seats. He joins me, a hand on my shaking knee. "What happened to you? How did you—"

"Die?" he finishes my thought. I nod sheepishly, suddenly a coward. "It was all because of a dog."

"A dog?" How does one die like that?

"A girl I cared very much about was given a puppy, who she adored, but he had a tendency to run off. He would send us on wild goose chases through forests and the palace and flower fields."

I bite my lower lip at the mention of him caring for another girl. I don't want to hear him speak of another, but stay quiet. I want to know as much as he will share. I am so tired of secrets. Sadness is worth the truth.

"One day, he took us all the way out to the creek where we would meet to get away from the business of court." Étienne's jaw tightens and he closes his eyes. "It's like I'm back there even now. I can smell the damp earth and hear the rushing water between the dog's barking."

His pain is palpable. I can't imagine reliving your death on repeat—seeing the last moments you lived. I scooch closer to him on the mossy stair and rub his back. Round and round in small circles, just like Josepha used to do for me when I was upset.

Étienne clears his throat. "He ran out on a tree that fell across the water. I froze when he got too far. But she was so worried about her dog, and I couldn't bear to see her scared. She had much loss in her life already, and I would not allow her to lose something so precious to her."

I hold my breath, afraid I know exactly what he is about to say. I can see it in my head as he tells it, the tremble in his voice making it so real even to me. His unsteady feet on the wood of the tree, the water waiting below. The poor girl worried for her dog. I imagine how I would have cried had it been my Mops; I hate the sinking feeling that greets my stomach.

"So I went farther across the log, and the pup was barking away at the very tip of it, as if talking to the swift water below. But I saved him. I did it. Her smile was brighter than any sun in the sky as I handed the furry scoundrel to her."

"A hero," I whisper to him. He grins, but moves his hands from my lap to his head, fingers digging through his hair.

"For a moment. Until my foot slipped, and I found myself falling. Really falling. Where time stills just enough for you to feel like you're floating. I landed hard." Étienne's fingers shake uncontrollably as they move away from his head, holding them in front of himself for me to see.

The tips of his fingers are covered in thick, sticky crimson. It stains the skin around his nails, and I now see the swollen space of his scalp where the blood drains from. A sharp pain slices through my chest, devastated that his life ended only from trying to do good for another. He died out of love.

My Étienne. He is *good*.

He is of the spirit world, but his heart is still as good as it was when he was living.

"I love you, too," I say, holding his hands in mine, not caring about the blood. "Everlasting."

"Everlasting." Étienne pulls me in, an all-consuming embrace I could stay in for days. More comforting than any hearth, even with the chill of his skin. I relax into his steady breaths.

"Chloé. She is a ghost. She tried to tell me something about a cup and being below. *We drank. We Float. Below. Below.*" I sing it just the way she did. It still scares me. "I think she's talking about the girls who were given poison. I think—I think Louis did it. He's at the center of it all."

"Marie," Étienne says, releasing his tender hold on me. My breath hitches at the quiver of his chin. It has the faintest cleft that matches the dimples in his cheeks. I could stare at him for hours and not grow bored. "I don't want you to put yourself in any danger—"

"But I must. He'll continue to kill. I need to figure out what Chloé was telling me." I stand and pace, matching my feet to the swirling thoughts in my mind. "I will find where they float. I have the blade that killed Geneviève. I know where the axe is hidden—the one he killed his own best friend with."

Étienne falls silent. All I hear are the fountains and my teeth, which have begun to chatter as the night goes colder. It is getting very late.

"Will you help me?" I finally ask.

Étienne saunters to the cascading wall of water and is lost looking at it for a moment. His finger reaches out to one of the streams spouting out from the ground. He touches it, displacing the water. "Louis is obsessed with these fountains, as was the Sun King. He had elaborate systems built below ground from Paris to Versailles in order to have enough water for this grand spectacle."

I think of the secret corridors behind my bedchamber. How that is mirrored below the earth. Water systems sneaking underneath our feet right now.

"Below! That could be it, Étienne!" I leap into the air, bouncing from one foot to another.

"We must go underground."

TWENTY-SIX

Beneath Versailles is an entirely different world. No gold. No powders. No judging eyes.

I had not seen the grove Étienne took me through before tonight. Hedges lined with trellis, and no statues to be seen. We push farther and farther within the lush greens to a cherry red door draped by overhanging branches. It opens to a stairwell of darkness, with candelabras hanging in wait at the entrance, ready for us to grab before our descent.

The underground is a labyrinth of its own, with the stinging smell of copper, rotting fruit, and human waste. Tunnels as large as the hallways of Versailles are flooded with murky water that seeps up the bare stone walls.

Étienne holds my hand steady as we slosh through the water, and I thank heavens I am not alone in this dark tomb, the only source of light the candelabras we each hold shakily.

It's enough to see the archways, almost perfect half circles every few paces—the way to keep the tunnel from caving in from the world above. The arches appear to be circular because of their reflection on the water, and it's like Étienne and I are walking through a strange hallway of hoops with moving liquid at our feet—alone, save the echoes of dripping water and the cries of rats.

I have a difficult time breathing between the stale stench.

I wonder what lays ahead of us in the darkness outside the glow of candlelight. I'm thankful Étienne is with me—I needed him to brave the *below*.

"I hate this." His words repeat as they bounce off the cavernous walls.

"Me too," I say, using as much strength in my legs as I can in order to move the soaked chiffon of my dress another step farther.

He lowers to a whisper. "No—I mean, well, I hate the water. I know I can't die for a second time, but being knee deep in it is not exactly pleasant."

He drowned. Of course the place I've taken him is a living nightmare for Étienne. My face flushes with guilt, I can feel the heat of it. "I'm sorry, this is my fault—"

Étienne stops walking and gently pulls on my hand, signaling for me to stop and turn to him as his body rotates toward mine. Our candelabras nearly kiss when we face each other.

"This," he looks in both directions, into the hollow darkness surrounding us, "is not your fault. I trust ghouls far more than I trust the crown."

"But bringing you here, I didn't consider—"

His head tilts to the side, and he sighs with a smile. "There is nothing I wouldn't do for you, Marie. I have shown it before, and now, I'll show you again. You save people. You've saved me."

A flutter in my belly makes me smile back at him. He really does see me as his queen—to face something so dark, just for me, shows me how much he truly adores me. Not like Louis. Not like the entire court of Versailles who laughed in my face as the acting troupe made fun of me.

Before I have a chance to respond, I spot something floating behind him. Slowly moving with the flow of water, straight for us.

Perhaps garbage discarded into the sewers—I can't tell in this dim light. I squint harder.

Could it be someone who followed us?

Someone.

My eyes grow wide and my jaw drops open.

"Marie?" Étienne searches my eyes before finally looking over his shoulder. Turning toward what I now make out as a lump of fabric floating.

A pink dress.

We float.

I splash through the water toward the body with my candelabra held high in the air, ignoring the pounding drum below my ribs.

"Help me!" I call to Étienne as I try to pull her face out of the water with a single hand. He quickly joins me and we hoist her up by the cloth of the dress clinging to her shoulders.

She's so heavy—I grunt as my fingers strain.

It's Chloé.

I know her beautiful face, even through the puff of her features. A little black bug crawls out of one gray eye and I scream, stumbling back. Her head makes a *plop* back down into the water when Étienne lets her go to place a hand on my back.

"I'm so sorry," I call to Chloé's body, staring at her still back as the mass of pink floats away. I move candles through the air, looking for her ghost. I wonder where her spirit is in this moment. Likely at Madame DuBarry's side, always staying with the person she loves.

"I don't know. When we die, we don't stay with our body. It becomes just flesh, proof of what we leave behind."

"Proof," I whisper. "This is proof of bodies being dumped under Versailles."

"I would imagine only those of high standing would know of such a place, so hidden from the world above, void of even the sun," Étienne says.

"Like Louis."

Étienne's mouth presses into a straight line, and he inhales deeply, expanding his chest.

The sadness is swallowing me up. Sadness and disappointment in my ridiculous fantasies and the horrible reality floating in the water.

I've been such a child.

I think of how small I felt sitting with Chloé, her hands

above us as we looked at the bottom of the blue bottle of poison. Her words haven't stopped playing in my head since.

"*We* drank. *We* float. There must be more bodies." I start walking again, ignoring the weight of my dress trying to pull me down.

"Let's push forward," he says, but I catch the way his Adam's apple bobs when he swallows.

The water is freezing, but a fever builds in me now. I am determined to find all of the bodies and bring them out of this wretched, damp coffin.

I will expose Louis in the light.

The putrid stink grows stronger the farther we venture through, and we follow the scent whenever the tunnels separate into two. We stay silent along the way, so I can hold my breath as much as possible.

It doesn't take us very long to find them. A mass of bodies, piled in the water against the wall, their sheer weight holding them in place. Vomit cascades down my yellow dress, then into the surface of the water infested with decay.

"Oh, Marie," is all Étienne can muster. I can't even manage that much, the aftertaste of my own sick stinging my tongue.

Louis makes them drink, carves them up, then throws them here. My *husband*.

My family sent me here to marry and I lied to myself to make it feel a bit better. I wanted to love him and see the best. The thought sends another piercing pain to my stomach.

All these bodies. At least a hundred of them. I want to know what happened to each and every one of them. Know who their families are so I can try to make this all right. What they endured is sickeningly wrong. I gather my courage and squeeze Étienne's hand, before passing him my candelabra and slowly wading toward the mountain of dead.

I walk around, studying them all. So many have the mark of Louis' knife, their cut open chest where he once dove inside to study their hearts and bones. Some appear to have a second skin, the top layer so waterlogged it has lifted from their bodies, encapsulating them in a white transparent film. Others are purple, their faces so swollen, it looks like they've been beaten with stones—but it is really their bodies returning to the water, becoming one with it.

My skin crawls, like there are a million bugs scurrying over me.

"Are you alright?" Étienne asks.

I'm not, *of course* I'm not. The acts of my husband are vile, so much worse that I could have ever known. But I nod yes anyway.

The bodies near the bottom have decayed down to bone. Some just skeletons with silk dresses barely clinging on to ribcages. One girl's skin is mush, her face being eaten away from the mouth up, her teeth and jaw gleaming in the orange light without lips and skin to conceal them.

Another has been ravaged by disease, illness taking root in her as it did my sister. Maggots writhe and wriggle inside her mouth, making their way out and down her chin.

They are all like abandoned dolls, falling apart at the seams, body parts broken and loose as an eye button would.

As I move around the pile, ignoring all else, even my own shaking knees, I find a yellow dress just like the one I'm wearing.

Geneviève.

Or, what is left of my friend anyway. Étienne's hand falls on my shoulder and he thankfully stays silent. I wouldn't hear a word he said if he attempted to talk.

I crouch down in the water, and run my hand along the red hair that sprawls out from her scalp in knotted clumps. Seeing her final resting place breaks me, as though a thousand twigs are painfully snapping in place of my bones.

My tears fall fast as I rip myself away from her. Knowing that I will never be able to bring her back. That only her body and ghost now remain.

And then I find Anne. Mousy Anne. Her sweet little button nose just above the horror that remains of her neck. How could anyone smash her neck to pulp like this? My sobs are endless, echoing through all the tunnels. I just saw her in Louis' study, and already she has been discarded like this. Carelessly.

I look for Alexandre, but it is only women here.

Of course. For why would women deserve better than a watery grave?

TWENTY-SEVEN

Étienne screams.

I whip around to find him surrounded by women, their hands wrapped around his waist and arms. His knuckles are white from holding the candelabras. All their mouths are moving, creating an indistinguishable sound, haunted voices attempting to be heard.

"Étienne!" I yell and begin to run to him, clutching at my skirts, trying to lift them from the water so I can move faster. Then I notice the women holding him, hundreds surrounding him, are those whose bodies lay behind me. The ghosts of the dead come to join us after all.

"I'll find you! Everlasting!" he screams, just as a pale hand slithers across his face and covers his mouth. The poisoned women swarm him, and as the candelabras drop from his hands, the tunnels fall into darkness.

Pure darkness like the pits of hell must be.

With the candles snuffed, the underbelly of Versailles leaves me blind.

The ghosts whisper louder—a sharp buzz like cicadas piercing my ears.

In the pitch black, a hand brushes against my arm. I move back as fast as I can, sloshing in the water, my lungs tightening like a violin string pulled so hard it snaps.

Why are they doing this? I am only in this place *for them*. Searching for proof. To find answers and bring them justice after death. I am after *their* killer.

My stomach flips. Is Étienne safe?

"Where is Étienne?" I ask, but am left unanswered. "Please. I'm—I'm trying to help you!" I try as I continue moving. Their unseen hands grab at me, one at a time, toying with me. "*Please*," I cry, spit falling from my mouth as fast as tears from my eyes.

I drop onto the pile of dead bodies, my palms pressing into the various degrees of rot. Skin soft and squishing through my fingers, like an orange. With hands behind my back, lifting myself into a bridge, I walk backwards up the bodies. I don't need light to see them—the sight of them is singed into my memory forever. I force myself to keep going despite the acidic burn at the back of my throat.

I finally catch the garbled words in my ear between the splashing of water. The women all say the same thing. "Help us. Help us."

"I will."

It's a promise to them, and to myself.

The tunnels go quiet; the ghosts have left me. I am alone once more, but ready.

In the pitch black I crawl down from the mountain of bodies and slosh through the water until I find a wall. It is covered with slime but I don't care. I allow it to guide me through the dark in the direction Étienne and I had come from.

I wonder what room is above me now. If I am going to die below their world of decadence, bound to the tunnels for eternity like so many others.

I trip and my mouth fills with cold liquid as my head dips into the water. I strain my neck to find air, gasping when I break the surface again. "I'm going to find you, Louis. I will find you, and kill you."

I wish I could see. Just enough to see a reflection, to hear the voice—the very same who has haunted me so long—give me a hint of how to free myself from these tunnels. My corset tightens from being wet, and my hair is a wild mess covering my face. I strain to keep my eyes open, even though I can't see in this murky place.

I focus on my senses and intuition. Clinging to my sanity.

I finally find the stairs, and the air changes. I can see again, a glow from candelabras beside this entrance door.

White walls. Candelabras. Doors without gold and paint.

I am in the passageways. The secret corridors where I first kissed Étienne. The boy I love and am willing to risk it all for. The ghost.

Moonlight streams in from a window and I recognize the Hall of Mirrors. I had lost all sense of time in the darkness, but it must be late in the night because the moon shines so bright.

"They won't get away with it! Not anymore!"

Candlelight glows all around the golden statutes on the floor and the chandeliers dangling from the ceiling.

Footsteps creek along the floor behind me. I tremble from head to toe as I listen to the steps move to my side.

Geneviève stands above me. Alexandre and Anne are behind her, holding hands. I want to be happy for them, content with them finding each other in death, but I am too focused on the wounds on all three of their throats.

Blood pours from Geneviève 's neck, splashing all over me. The warmth of it drips down my face while scarlet takes the place of the yellow in my dress, saturating each thread one at a time.

She holds an axe, the base of the handle in one hand and the other wrapped at the base of the blade. "You. It's you, Marie," she whispers.

"Marie!" A man's voice cuts me off. It sounds like Louis from a distance. I lean over to see past Geneviève. It *is* Louis, headed toward me in his bright red jacket. "Marie!" he calls again with urgency.

"You," Geneviève states, as she releases the axe. It smashes down in front of me and Geneviève disappears.

Louis is running my way now. I take hold of the axe and stand up. My head throbs, pounding like a single piano key being banged over and over and over.

It is up to me to end all the death.

I grip the axe with all the strength within my small hands.

TWENTY-EIGHT

My world closes in upon me.

The powders and poisons. The blood and heartbreak. The hall of mirrors spins, my vision blurry with tears.

Versailles. I think of all it took to get here. All that it was supposed to be.

All that it's not.

It all comes to an end with the head of the axe in my hands. The power is finally mine.

Louis continues to call my name, his voice grating in my ears. He's moving fast.

My head is spinning. It's too much. It's all been too much for too long.

I can take no more. I swing the axe.

It slices through the air. "Why?" I yell to Louis. He slows, but my heartbeat does not.

"So many! Geneviève! Anne!" I swipe left and right, again and again.

"Marie," he says softly, "what are you talking about?"

"Don't lie to me! You killed them. You killed your best friend!" I screech with all I have left in me, "Was I next? *Was I?*"

"I did no such thing. I would never—I—people heard you screaming—I—I've been searching for you—" His shoulders shrug, recoiling from me while his face is full of worry. *A guise.*

The axe shakes in my hand, my shoulder aches from swinging it so hard. Louis keeps his distance. "I saw the blue bottles. The violets! You poisoned all those girls!"

"No." He shakes his head, his bulbous nose making me more mad than ever. "Medicine, Marie. Tinctures to try and help heal those dying from disease. Violets to sweeten the mixture. I study the dead, I do not kill them."

No. *No.* That can't be true.

The bottle.

We drank. We float. He killed them. I know it. He can't admit it. Can't risk losing the crown. Losing his head.

"Lies!" I spit, letting the weight of the axe drop to one hand—ready. "What about Geneviève? Anne? Alexandre? Chloé?"

"I don't know whose hand they died by. I've been exhausting the guard to figure it out." He rubs his temples hard.

"Liar." My voice softens as I cry.

Louis takes a small step forward, his hands straight out in front of him.

No.

My eyes pinch closed. I lift the axe high above my shoulder and swing so hard it spins my body.

Glass smashes. Pieces of mirror tinkle against the floor as they rain down around my feet.

My face looks back up at me in every little shard—covered in blood, unraveling hair and wild eyes. I barely recognize her. *Marie Antoinette.*

The voice doesn't rise up from the many reflections of my face scattered across the wooden floor as I expect it to. Instead, memories crash into me, crawling from the depths of my mind like the dead climbing from a grave.

Walking away from Josepha's room after watching her die. I remember burying that reality. Deep down to never face again.

Geneviève.

Bile rises up my throat as I remember the chase. Running through the hedges, the blade I stole flashing bright in the moonlight as I caught up to her. It sliced through her skin so easily.

No. I couldn't have done that. *Never.*

Yet, I know it to be true. The darkness of truth coming to light.

I could feel her abandonment to my core as she told me about her father. I knew the same grief she felt with the loss of her mother, taken by the same illness that took my sister. I hated how she became popular with boys—a feeble attempt to fill the pieces of her heart her parents left hollow.

I had to save her from the hurt of it all. From being tossed to the side by her father, from giving herself to men that only whispered about her between their laughter the next morning.

My fingers lovingly placed the violet over her broken heart.

The mirrors flicker with the candlelight shimmering in the chandelier above me. Louis is frozen beyond the destruction the axe has made. Scared.

I grind my teeth, realizing I had been wrong about him. I was so *sure*. It all made sense.

My eyes fall back to the kaleidoscope of reflections beneath me.

Feeling the handle of the smooth wood in my hands transports me back to Alexandre's room. My palms ached afterward—it was difficult attempting to separate his head from his body, and Anne's stirring put an end to everything. I threw the violet down for him before running off.

I *had* to. Alexandre had to die.

He left a mess. I was drenched in his blood and was forced to throw my dress in the fire and wash myself in my bedside basin in the small hours of the night. It took many wrings of the sponge before the water ran clear again.

I thought ending him would be enough. But it wasn't. Not to help Anne.

Poor Anne. I found her outside the theater boxes. She was so sad about Alexandre. Her eyes were deep red, exhausted from tears. She gave her heart to him so easily. And returned it to him again despite his repeated trampling of it. I had to help her, and stop her from giving her heart to someone new only to be hurt again.

The chair was there. My only option. I didn't mean for it to land so many times on her throat, but I wanted to make sure she was dead. That she would no longer suffer.

I was the one who left violets on all of their chests. Mourning those I had killed.

The pounding in my head is louder than ever as I remember the memory I want to bury deep in the earth. Yet it's there, bright as day. Suddenly, when I look into my eyes in the glass, I see his ocean eyes.

Ocean eyes I knew from his visits to Austria every summer as a child. He loved me even then. How could I not have remembered him the second I saw him in Versailles? He was my everything. But I shrouded him in darkness once it happened. Told myself he never existed. Over and over again.

Until it was true.

Pressure builds in my chest, and I can't breathe.

It was *my* puppy. The girl he cared for was *me*. He wobbled along that fallen tree to save Mops. I can feel the breeze now, the memory suddenly fresh. Josepha died a few days before and he wouldn't allow me to lose something else. When he slipped and hit his head on that rock, he screamed so loud for help.

I waded out to him, leaving Mops on the shore surrounded by blossoming violets. I knew it was my chance to make sure he never experienced loss like I had. If he died, his heart would never ache like mine did when I lost Josepha. I loved him enough to hold his head under the water. I would do anything for him.

But as his body went still, I wanted to take it all back.

I fall to my knees, crying beyond repair. I wish I could take it all back now.

Étienne was where my killings began.

Yet he was here for me in Versailles. Supporting me, even though I ended him.

A love everlasting.

The axe drops from my hands, bouncing off the floor before Louis runs to me and kicks it down the hall of mirrors. A swarm of guards charge toward us, but Louis puts a hand up to them before cocooning me in his embrace. He holds me tighter in his arms, and I wonder why he shows such kindness. But I sink into it, cradled with knees to chest, rocking back and forth like a child.

I was never a child. That was stolen from me. I was bred to be flesh and blood, used to serve in the name of duty.

Is this why I am who I am?

My life is the omen. The voices haunt me, their riddles making me see who I am and all I've done. I've ignored them in order to slip into a shadow of myself and end others.

To save them from the heartache. From the loss and pain I've endured.

I was trying to save them. I was doing it *for* them. I hate what I have become.

But *they* did this.

Those who transformed me from pupa to butterfly, but broke my wings in doing so.

An innocent turned monster.

THE END

EPILOGUE

Louis grows on me.

Grows like ivy crawling up the palace walls. Covered, protected. Eyes always on me, keeping a careful watch on my movements. Not out of lust—our bed sheets still pristine after four years—out of fear that I'll suffer another illness.

That's what he called it. *Illness.*

I remember it all so clearly now as I walk through the Hall of Mirrors alongside Etiquette. The way Louis sat with me on the shiny wooden floor surrounded by shards of reflective glass, memories crashing into me with the force of the most violent waves of the ocean.

Everything has been so quiet since that night. Even now, the half-naked women made of gold lining the hall only hold their candles high, I don't feel their eyes on me. The people of the court no longer chatter in my presence.

I turn my head from Etiquette every few moments to check the mirrors that make up the walls, waiting for a glint of light upon the glass to return the voice. The voice that sounded like my sister. Singing unsettling taunts and tales of doom.

But it never comes. I believe there is no need, now that I've faced the truth it reflected.

A piece of me misses it.

I feel the omens stirring, a heavy churning in my stomach, angry to have been hidden away since that night. My intuition creeps up my spine. They are ready to play.

"Marie. Are you even listening to me?" Etiquette asks.

My eyes meet hers, assuring that I'm paying attention. "Yes, Madame Etiquette, of course."

"I do hate you calling me that." Her eyes narrow, but they are still full of warmth.

"And I hate all the rules." I shrug.

Etiquette clicks her tongue and shakes her head at me, the hint of a smile tugging at her lips. Her silver hair glimmers in the sunlight filling the hall, reminding me of her age. She has seen so much happen in Versailles. Lost so much.

She's opened up to me these past few years. Shared how she took Geneviève under her wing as she does so many of the abandoned girls. How she admired the way I helped the chambermaids, determined to find the killer. She still praises me for it now.

She doesn't know. *Nobody* knows.

"Marie, there will be many more rules now," she says. "More responsibility on you."

I inhale a deep breath and focus on the purple toes of my shoes as they peek out of my matching dress with each step. Their sound echoes up to the ceiling, embellished with a painting of more Gods and Goddesses, lightning striking amongst the clouds they sit in.

"I understand." And I do. I know what is coming, even if I don't want to face it. I think of the last time I felt this overwhelming sense of duty. How it ended with my stealing a blade on my wedding night. Traipsing through the waters where the dead are brought to keep the stench and horror out of sight—a place where Louis never even stepped foot.

Louis. A sharp pain strangles my heart. I was wrong about him. I never really listened to him, or even tried to understand him. His interests were so dark, I was convinced of his guilt. But he was only studying the dead to help save the living. Blue bottles of medicine pushed to lips. Not poison.

And though there have been many more deaths from disease, there have been no more throats slit in the night.

Because it was me. It was *me.* And I have stopped. The crushing truth was enough to end it all, and I am ever present with myself and with others to be sure the moments of black don't return.

I'll never hold a blade again.

"Come, look in the mirror." Etiquette takes hold of my hand and pulls me towards my reflection.

I gaze at myself. My hair piled higher than I can reach, bits of feather and lace jammed into the wavy strands. Fashion has become one of my great distractions, apparent from the lilac dress I wear now, adorned with glittering jewels and crafted from the most expensive silks.

Yet, my eyes are hollow. Dark shadows below my lashes from lack of sleep. Endless nights of holding my secrets to myself. Long days of pasting a smile on my face. The ghosts aren't with me anymore, but I am still haunted. Terrorized by what I have done.

I would sell my soul to take it all back. To bring back the dead.

"Look how far you have come since the day I met you in that tent. You have grown into a beautiful and strong young woman, ready to fulfill the ultimate duty," Etiquette says as her hands graze the top of my shoulders.

I don't feel like I've come that far, and stay quiet, continuing to look at the way the muscles in my jaw tense.

This is the place where I smashed the mirror with the axe. Nobody would ever be able to tell, though. The glass was fully replaced and the remnants of the old were cleaned up. Versailles has smoothed away the imperfections, like nothing ever happened in the first place. As I have had to do—perform until everything appears perfect once more. Secrets festering underneath.

I drink it down most evenings, sharing champagne with my new friends. Friends who are living and not swallowed up by smoke and shadows. I never get too close to them though. I've learned that humans in the palace are more monstrous than the actual ghosts.

I am the most frightening monster of all.

The court was pleased that whoever murdered Geneviève, Alexandre, and Anne stopped. Disappeared. Died of disease. They cared not about an explanation, only that they were gone.

But I'm still here.

Me, and the unseen ghosts.

It took time to put all the pieces together. To understand why Josepha and Geneviève didn't tell me sooner.

Why Geneviève, Anne, and Alexandre stood in this same spot in the Hall of Mirrors and handed me the axe. I had to be led to the answers. Answers that lay deep within me. Answers that I could not truly face. If they told me—I would have simply pushed it all back down, covering it up with another layer of denial.

They must have thought I would stop killing if I faced the truth. End the growing numbers floating below Versailles. In a world with an uncontrollable disease, there is a high enough body count.

It worked. I stopped killing and I stopped seeing them. I thought Josepha would come back to me, console me as she did when I was a child. But I haven't seen her purple ribbon bouncing in the gardens since she convulsed on my bed. I miss her, but hope she truly has moved on from this place.

Women have died over the years, but never from poison. Poor Louis was trying to help. Mixing medicines and studying cadavers in the name of saving those in the future who suffer from disease. I swallow down my guilt often for thinking so poorly of him.

I ache to see Étienne again. I call to him in the night sometimes, even now. I search for him in the halls, cloaked in midnight. He loved me in death. Even when his end was by my hand. Stayed with me as I came to a new country. I can only assume the other spirits took him away from me that horrible night because they knew he would protect me at all costs. A love everlasting.

I will see him again. He is somewhere here. Étienne would never break a promise.

Everlasting. Everlasting.

I will see the ghosts again. The omens will make sure of it. But for now, to Louis and to the court, I no longer cry and shout and flee.

My *illness* cured.

"It won't be long now," Etiquette says as we look at each other in the silent reflection. "Are you ready?"

"I shall stand tall." I lift my chin slightly and she nods with approval.

The king lay on his deathbed. It is but a matter of days until everything changes and I assume my new role.

So little time until I must focus again on all of Paris loving me. Even more so than before.

In a few days, I will be crowned the Queen of France.

I stare at myself in the mirror, sunshine sparkling against it.

"You cut them apart, ripped through their skin, no longer a girl, now fit to be queen."

The first carriage ride to Versailles is fuzzy in my mind now. The vibrancy of Geneviève's red hair faded over time. It's difficult to maintain a firm grasp on those memories from over twenty years ago. Yet, I always tried—attempted to honor those who I—

I—

Always the throat.

Geneviève. Alexandre. Anne.

Now, it is my turn. A tickle traces across the delicate space below my chin—a phantom of the blade destined for my neck.

With wobbling knees, men usher me across the wooden scaffold toward my executioners. The insults are so loud from the sea of people—hundreds—gathered to see me. To see my life come to an end.

The people of France brought their children. Young girls with wide eyes, hopeful for what is to come. Not hopeful for love as I had once been.

No.

They hope for blood.

I focus on the fresh air hitting my face. A sensation I've craved since being within prison walls. But it is tinged with the scent of rot and burning wood, bringing me back to the fate which shakes my bones.

I understand their anger now. How the uprising and revolution came to this. I would do anything to feed my children. Pain fills my belly at the thought of my own. At least one good thing will come from today—I will be reunited with my poor babies.

The ropes are tight around my wrists, slicing through flesh, pulling my arms behind me.

POWDER & POISON

Each step toward the contraption of death is forced, hands angrily pushing into the soft of my back. How did I become the enemy? The villain in their story?

The silver encased in its tall wooden frame glints brightly, causing me to squint.

"Pay for the crimes you didn't commit. Still swallowing down the killing you did."

A thin coating of dirt sits atop my skin and the plain white dress I wear. How I do miss the lush silks and satins that once adorned my body. I stumble on the skirt as I come closer to the guillotine, and step onto the foot of a man in a black mask. The same man who cut off my Louis' head.

"Pardon me, sir. I didn't mean to," I say, only to be thrown down to my knees, pain vibrating up my legs.

The cheers from the crowd grow louder. I peer down into a brown woven basket, and pretend they are screaming how much they love me, and that they are happy to have me here. Like they did when I was at first their dauphine.

I struggle to twist my neck to the side, to face the people who have cast down this sentence. My eyes strain to look across the platform until they find the eyes of a boy laying on his side amongst the dried blood and dust next to me. Gazing back at me with a familiar blue twinkle and a smile that warms my frozen heart.

"I told you I'd find you," he says. A whisper so clear the rest of the world falls silent. "Everlasting."

Étienne's return is all I ever really wanted. Even after all this time. His voice a melody my ears have ached to hear.

About time, I think but don't say aloud. I don't need to speak. It's finally our time now. My smile slowly creeps from cheek to cheek as I look into his ocean eyes.

The screeching sound of metal slices through the air above.

But I don't care. Not anymore.

I am ready for our everlasting to begin.

Acknowledgments

When we take a moment to truly reflect on all those who played a part in our journey, we realize just how supported we are. I am forever grateful to those I thank in the following pages, as well as to anyone who has crossed my path along the way of this wild ride.

I must start with my dad, Glenn Jackson. You may not have read this story—with pencil in hand ready to take every word I write as the most important thing you've ever seen—but I know you're cheering me on from wherever you are in the stars. Thank you for looking over me, my Starman waiting in the sky.

To my mom, Michelle Jackson, thank you for always allowing me to be me. You've been my roots, my safety, and my support in any and all things I choose to endeavour. I am one of the lucky few that has a mom who is also my best friend and sees me through the bright sunny days as well as the storms. Can't wait to celebrate this book with you with a good porch night.

Josh and Nova, thank you for always wanting the best for me. Your unwavering support in me following this journey of writing and having my own creative outlet is an incredible gift. Thank you for helping me through time away at retreats, late writing nights, and long hours at bookstores. Thank you for being my family and loving me as much as I love you. Nova, I hope you too follow your dreams, no matter how big or small they seem—you can do anything, my cute little chicken. Josh, forever plus one…I love our little life.

Amanda Havill Adgate. We did it. My best ghoulfriend, I am so thankful that we somehow found each other and that I tricked you into being my CP. You are so incredibly talented, and I am excited for the world to read your beautiful and heartbreaking stories. My stories wouldn't be what they are without you in my corner. Thank you for reading this book over and over and over again and for spending so many late nights plotting and planning and writing with me. You are so much more than my CP, and we will be together forever through the highs and lows of writing and the chaos that is our lives. I will always be your biggest fan (sorry, Levi).

Jessica Ferguson, J, thank you for 24 years of being my crazy, psychotic, beautiful, brilliant ride or die. Thank you for getting me, for being my creative support, for swapping books with me, and for building my website. And thank you for designing the cover and chapter headings for this book. To have your creativity be a part of my debut novel is so special to me. To the moon. Always.

Cathrine Swift, I am so lucky you came into my life! You are such an amazing, strong, kind soul, and this book would literally not have been possible without you. Thank you for believing in me and my words enough to be my Book Doula. I wish you a lifetime of sweet, sweet Charlie Cox dreams.

Kristin Dwyer, what would I do without you? Nothing. I would die. You saw who I am as a writer and the story I was trying to tell. You gave me the tools I needed to lean into the kissing scenes, and to not fear the romance. You helped me make this book so much better. Beyond that, you saw something in me and took a leap of faith in having me be a part of your Breaking the Story Retreats. You've taught me so much about reading, writing, and life, and you inspire me with your incredible heart day after day. I regret to inform you that you are stuck with me for life now.

Toni—thank you for being you and for supporting me. And of course, thank you for our unhinged conversations, laughs, and Tanner content.

Aurora—you amaze me every day with the beauty of your work and the beauty of your soul. Thank you for the most incredible illustration of Marie and all the incredible designs that made this the debut experience of my dreams. My witchy sister for life.

To those who reminded me of the promise I made to myself of writing a book, at a time that I had lost so much, thank you.

To all the doctors and people who helped me recover after the accident, helping me go from not being able to read anymore, to writing a book, and now publishing a book, I can't thank you enough.

From the bottom of my heart, thank you to my writing community! I am in awe of how people from all around the world have become my family. Alex, Alexa, Belle, Beth, Caitlin, Casey, Chelsea, DeAnna, Desi, Elizabeth, Emily B, Emily V, Eva, Jamye, Jazzi, Joss, Kathleen, Maggie, Marissa Lynn, Marissa F., Nirmaliz, Patricia—I love you. There are so many more people to thank, and I know you know who you are!

Of course, I am so grateful to my little community of those who have taken Channeling Story with me—it has been such an honor to be a part of your writing journey, even in the smallest of ways. I will always be here for you and your writing.

To my beta readers, writers who have taught me about the craft, and authors who have inspired me—thank you, even if I can't name you all.

And to anyone who picked up this book, I am forever grateful. I poured many tears and love into Marie's story over the years, and to share it with readers may just be the most rewarding experience of all.

Finally, thank you to Marie.

About the Author

Julia Jackson is the author of *Powder & Poison*, is featured in various international horror anthologies, and is a member of the Horror Writers Association. After a near-fatal car accident, Julia turned to writing as part of recovery and now crafts chilling stories that strip away the masks women wear, revealing emotional depth and damage. Julia has had more surgeries than Frankenstein, is a creature of the night like Batman, and creates memorable heroes and monsters of her own. Julia teaches mindful writing at Kristin Dwyer's Breaking the Story Retreat, as well as to the online writing community. When Julia is not writing, she works in Corporate Communications and watches an unhealthy amount of ghost hunting shows and horror movies.

PRAISE FOR *POWDER & POISON*

"This story unfolds in the glamorous but corrupt world of Versailles and presents a raw, human view of Marie Antoinette. She's got ghosts after her, murder all around, and she's stuck in a court that expects perfection but gives zero mercy. The air is thick with fear, secrets, and the feeling that disaster is brewing. If you enjoy ghosts, gory bits, and plot twists galore—all wrapped up in a gothic, tragic package—this book delivers in spades."
H. EVEREND, author of Cursed Legacy

"The fantastical horror elements will have you recoiled in disgust one moment... And then leaning right back in the next for more of her delicious mix up of spine-tingling ghost story grounded in the historical foundation we are all familiar with on some level. This debut is spectacular on so many levels and will find it's perfect home on the shelves of readers who adore elements of truth and fact, wrapped up in candy coated 'what if' delectable fiction. Marie was a queen of France, and Julia Jackson is certainly a queen of horror, in my books."
CATHRINE SWIFT, author of Let it Reign

"A haunting and harrowing journey of secrets and lies. POWDER & POISON will leave you holding your breath and clutching your throat in anticipation."
E.A.M. TROFIMENKOFF, author of A Kiss of the Siren's Song

"POWDER & POISON tells the story of Marie Antoinette's introduction to Versailles, a court brimming with mystery, power, and murderous intent. As bodies start to fall, Marie must find the culprit all while deciphering the matters of her own heart. This romance-tinged ghost story will delight and disgust you in equal measure."
FELICITY DEVORIA, author of Mocking Changeling

"Dark and decadent, the ghosts and intrigue that haunt Marie Antoinette's life at court made this novel less BRIDGERTON and more WHERE THE CRAWDADS SING. I really enjoyed this psychological thriller with a twist."
ALEX TILLEY, author of Meshkwadoon